IF ONLY YOU KNEW

MICHELLE ROBINSON

ISBN: 9798364995018

TABE OF CONTENTS

1 SIERRA JOHNSON

Beauty, success and fame. That's how I would describe myself. Others? They would say that I'm rude, bossy and stuck up. But maybe I am? Who are they to judge me for my success or everything I been through to get here? I helped build this company from the ground up. I gave my blood sweat and tears to this damn place. So maybe I am bossy and I deserve to be.

I'm Sierra Johnson the best damn defense attorney in New York City. I take on cases where I get to free the innocent. It's a job that I love to do. We all know the system is messed up. And there are many people in jail or prison for crimes they did not commit. I get cases thrown at me from left to right. But I will only choose the ones that others would seem fit as "difficult". I'll pass smaller cases down to my colleagues.

I've spent hours in this meeting today with the board listening to them speak. As soon as I got out the meeting my assistant/best friend came up to me and started talking to me about her love life. I swear I love Mia but sometimes she just doesn't know when to shut the hell up.

"I swear Mia, will you please just shut up!" I yelled at her. "Not right now ok." She then covered her mouth as she was shocked. I walked the other way and slammed my office door. She then comes into my office and slowly closes the door.

"So, spill." Mia says to me.

"There's nothing to tell." I said to Mia as I continued to type on my computer.

"Bullshit. You don't speak to me that way unless something is going on with you. So, spill it now." Mia yelled out.

"Fine, I had another dream." I said to her with frustration.

"So, because you are having dreams of someone else other than your fiancé, you take it out on me. How exactly is it my fault that this man is rocking your world in your dreams." Mia asked with her arms crossed. "I'm not the cause of that Sierra. Hell, I want to get laid too." She continued to yell at me.

I faced her and giggled.

"That's definitely not funny." Mia replied.

"Would you like to know the details?" I asked her.

"I feel like that's how you should have started this conversation in the first place." She said to me curiously. I laughed And I started to give her the details on my dream.

"It started with him pushing my body up against the wall. He started kissing me from my neck and worked his way down. He slipped two fingers inside of me and I started to go crazy. Once he was done with that, he wrapped my legs around his waist and began to lift me up and down on his dick in slow perfect movements. He had rhythm. He would move me up and down slowly and then picked up the pace. Moved slowly again and picked up the pace. It felt so real Mia. When I woke up, I was wetter than a dip in the pool." I told her.

"Well, that was um, great. You go girl." She said ecstatically and began to cheer. I gave her a very confused look.

"No seriously though. Are you sure you're ready to get married? Maybe you still want other people to pick your raspberries." She said to me and began to dance. I couldn't help but to laugh at her.

"Of course, I'm marrying Brian. We're happy right?" I asked Mia out of curiosity.

"I'm not sure Sierra. I only know what you tell me. I'm your best friend and I just want you to be happy. Whatever you decide I'm for you no matter what." Mia replied to me.

"Thank You Mia." I said to her.

"Sure, but let me get back to the desk. It looks like we are in for a long day today." Mia said.

"Do you want to get some drinks tonight?" I asked Mia.

"How could I ever say no. Maybe I can meet someone tonight to pick my raspberries." She said as we both laughed and she began to walk away. But she did have one thing right. It was definitely going to be a long day.

Once I finally got comfortable and starting working my phone began to vibrate. I looked down and it was a text message from Brian.

"Does my beautiful fiancé have time for me to take her out to lunch today." Brian asked.

"I can't today babe, we are pretty swamped at the firm." I replied to his message.

"Are you ever going to make time for me?" He replied.

"I really don't feel like fighting today, Brian." I texted back to him.

"Fine Sierra." He replied.

I then started typing back in my computer. I swear, Brian is going to be the cause of my gray hair and not this job. I get that he wants to spend time with me as well but sometimes I feel like he can't handle everything that comes with my job. He tries to make every little thing about him. Sometimes I get really tired of it. He runs a company too and I never stress on the things he stresses me about. We had a plan before we decided to get married and now, he's trying to switch it up. Sometimes I think he is jealous of my success.

My work phone then begins to ring.

"Can't I get any damn work done in this place?" I yelled out.

"Go for it, Mia." I said out loud.

"You have a Sean White on the line wanting to speak with you." Mia said.

"No thank you deny the call please." I responded.

"Okay." She responded as if she was confused.

This can't be happening. Was the only thing I could say to myself.

Later on, that day I finally finished up some work and was ready to go home. As I walked in the house Brian was sitting on the couch angry as always. It seems like he's never pleased.

"Hey baby how was your day?" I asked him.

"It was fine. But the only time you want to know about my day is if you already made plans with yours." Brian said with his arms crossed angrily.

"I actually was interesting in knowing. And yes, I'm getting ready to meet Mia for drinks." I responded.

He then got up out of the chair and said, "Well, have a good night." He then presumed to walk off. I got angry. I followed him up into the guest bedroom.

"Can we at least talk about this instead of you stomping off like a child?" I asked him.

"Don't you have something to do?" He asked.

"What has gotten into you Brian? This isn't you." I said to him curious about the man he is becoming.

"You. That's what's gotten into me. You make time for any and everything but me." He yelled at me.

"It's my job Brian, what do you expect?" I asked him. "If you decide to leave me today or tomorrow my job is what I'll still have."

"So, your job is more important. That's what you're saying to me." He asked.

"No that's not what I'm saying. We have our whole life together and once we are married; we'll have nothing but time." I yelled at him.

"I'm not sure marriage is even an option anymore Sierra." He said to me bluntly. I was shocked. I was hurt. And most importantly, I was pissed.

"Because I wasn't able to make lunch today, Brian. Are you kidding me?" I yelled as I pointed my finger at him.

"No because I'm not sure I'm exactly what you want. Tell me Sierra, why have you been jumping out of bed every morning for the past 3 months in sweat?" He asked me. For a moment I was silent. I didn't know what to say without making myself seem guilty of what he's trying to accuse me of.

"Brian it's just nightmares." I yelled.

"I don't buy that for one second. I think your cheating one." He yelled out. I got even more pissed. How could he accuse me of cheating? I'm at work running a firm all damn day. He's able to contact me at all times. No matter what I am doing. No matter where I am.

"Cheating on you? We've been together since college. You were my first and the only man I've ever been with. Why would I cheat?" I yelled angrily at him.

"Maybe that's the problem Sierra. I was your first. You haven't experience anything outside of me." He replied. I got so furious I walked over and slapped his ass.

"You know what Brian go to hell. I didn't need you then and I damn sure don't need you now." I slapped him again and walked out. He had a lot of nerve. All because I couldn't make lunch. I came home with the thought that maybe if it was really important for him to spend time then I would cancel on Mia. But I was definitely getting the hell out of here now.

I took a shower and began to get dress. I wanted to look extra fabulous tonight just to piss Brian off. I was heated. If there was anyone in the world to make you mad. It would always be the man you love. I got in the car and drove to the club to meet Mia.

Once I arrived, Mia met me at the door.

Once we got inside, she asked, " So what do you think?"

"This place is amazing Mia. I need a shot of tequila asap." I said to her and she began to laugh. Once we walked over to the bar I began to dance. I looked at the bartender and yelled out over the music, "I would like a double shot of tequila with a little bit of ice please."

Once I placed my order, I turned to look at Mia and she was looking across the room biting her finger with seduction.

"Who the hell are you looking at?" I asked her.

"Someone who I want to call daddy tonight." She replied and winked.

I turned to the right and jumped as I was startled.

"Denying my calls doesn't exactly boost your reputation now does it Ms. Johnson?" Sean said.

I took a deep breath and sighed. This is not how I expected this night to go.

2 SEAN WHITE

I couldn't believe my eyes. I was doing my best to avoid him. What does he want with me? First, he calls my office and now he's here. Is he stalking me?

"Is there something I can help you with Mr. White?" I asked him. He stared at me with curiosity in his eyes. This man was beautiful. Light brown eyes with a low top fade with waves. Beautiful brown complexion with the perfect amount of hair around his lips. Just the look in his eyes makes me want to melt.

"So, let's see, we got two beautiful stallions standing here right before our eyes." The man standing behind Mr. White said.

"Shut the hell up Law." Mr. White turned to the guy and replied. He then turns back to face me as he continued to stare.

"Can I get an order of sex on legs please." The guy said.

"I should kill you right now for trying to make me laugh." Mr. White said to the guy he called Law. The man began to laugh and turned around and talked to another guy they were with.

"You know, when you denied my calls today you really hurt my feelings." He said to me.

"Unfortunately, Mr. White you would have to go through the same process as everyone else. I can't just drop what I'm working on for you. Send the information over and I'll review it. If I decided to take on your case, someone from my team will reach out to you." I responded to him as professional as I could.

"I'm sorry for wasting your time." He replied. He then turned around and left with his boys.

"Care to tell me what that was all about?" Mia asked.

I rolled my eyes. "What do you want me to say? He wants me to take a case that's impossible to win." I told Mia. "Also, he's the guy I've been (I started speaking gibberish)." I replied to Mia.

"Say what now?" She asked.

"He's the guy I've been dreaming about okay!" I yelled out to her with embarrassment. I then began to breathe deeply. Mia began to stare at me.

"Will you stop it please?" I asked of her. "You're the one who was just drooling over him."

"Actually, I was making flirty eyes at his friend. The one that was making jokes." She said then winked at me.

"I don't think you understand Mia. He's **THE** Sean White. The guy who got in trouble for those shootings at the courthouse." I said to her. The one who constantly stays in trouble for something.

"Well just take a look at his case. Maybe it's worth it." Mia said to me.

"Are you telling me to look at this case because you want to be able to see his friend again?" I asked her with a smirk.

"Yes, and I'll love you forever and a day." She said and we both began to laugh.

"No seriously your one of the best damn lawyers in the city. If anyone can make something out of this case it's you." She encouraged me.

"Yeah, but is he really innocent?" I asked.

"I don't know. And you're not the jury. That's not up to you to decide," She replied.

"You're right, but we'll see. Anyways, I don't want to keep going on with this all night. Let's turn up." I told her.

We than began to drink a few more shots and went to dance on the dance floor for a few. We danced and we drank until we got tired. We then ended up calling it a night. Brian wasn't home when I got back and a part of me was glad. I was getting tired of his shit. After seeing Sean tonight in person, it was much more than I could have handled. He was even finer than ever. I prayed sleeping it off would do me some good.

It was a brand-new day and I was feeling good. I decided to let my hair flow and put on a fitted dress and heels. I was ready to knock out some paperwork. As I got off the elevator and entered my floor, I see Mia laughing and conversating with a man at her desk.

"Mia what the hell are you... Sean what the hell are you doing here." I said as my mind was blown.

"We're on a first name basis now, so at least that's a start." He said to me with a seductive look on his face and Mia began to giggle.

"I told you once we reviewed your case, we would call you if we decide to take it." I told him with my arms crossed. Mia faces him as if she was waiting for him to hit me with a comeback. He stared at me looking at me up and down as if he was trying to study my body. What the hell was he thinking about?

"Man, this is even better than tv." Mia said curiously as she was waiting for a response.

"Shut it, Mia." I said directly. She then laughed.

"**MR. WHITE**!" I yelled out. It was almost as if he snapped back in from a daze.

"My apologies Ms. Johnson you were saying." He said in a sweet and innocent tone as Mia then began to laugh.

"I wasn't saying anything!" I yelled out at him.

"If I hear you out. Will you please stop harassing me?" I asked him. He nods with a yes.

"Follow me please." I instructed him. We then walked in my office and I began to close the door behind me. I instructed him to please have a seat as he then listened to my command.

"So, Mr. White please inform me of your situation." I asked of him.

"Well i was recently being represented by Mr. Green. But he doesn't want anything to do with my case anymore. At least that's what I assume since I can't get in contact with him." Sean said to me.

"Mr. Green is one of the best. Maybe he's afraid or now believes he can't win it, what makes you think I can?" I asked him.

"Ms. Johnson you are correct. Mr. Green is one of the best, but you are the **best**." He replied. I really wish my legs would stop shaking as he spoke. The seduction in his voice was going to cause my panties to become ***wet***.

"Well thank you Mr. White. So, tell me, what exactly is going on?" I asked him.

"Well, I was on trial because those son of a bitches planted drugs on me. They needed to find anyway to arrest me because they can't get anything to stick on me. Next thing you know someone started shooting in the courtroom. Killed the jurors, security, and the judge. Since the shooting Mr. Green doesn't return my calls even though I already paid him. The most important part in all of this, I was one of the victims shot during the shooting." Sean explained.

"Really? Interesting." I couldn't believe what I was hearing. These are part of the details that is being left out about this case. However, there is something that I'm still not understanding.

"Wait a minute, so where the fuck is Greene? He had to be there to represent you. I didn't hear anything about him being found on the scene." I said to him curiously.

"My point Ms. Johnson. Where the fuck is Greene? I was shot and my lawyer is missing and not returning my phone calls." He informed me. "My name is all over the fucking news as if I wasn't a victim in all this. But they aren't speaking on that. I'm not saying that I'm a good guy but... I run my shit a different way. That doesn't mean I don't fucking matter. A motherfucker could never catch me with drugs on me. Tell me Ms. Johnson, do I look like the type of man to be caught slipping?" He said to me directly and as he talked all I could do was admire his features. He was so damn sexy. There was no way God created a man so beautiful. When he asked me that question, I was ready to submit to the sound of his voice. I wanted to say "no daddy" however we all know looks can be deceiving. But I didn't want him to catch me staring so I had to get back into the conversation.

"So, what makes you think I would take the case and be willing to take a chance on something like this?" I asked him directly.

"Well, I didn't know if you would have Ms. Johnson. That's why I was wanting to explain the case to you in person. I will pay you double the amount of course. Money is never an issue." He assured me.

"It's not always about the money Mr. White. But let me go over somethings and I will let you know." Please right down your phone number so I can contact you. Call Green's office and have his assistant forward me everything he has so far and let me review it." I informed him.

"Thank you, Ms. Johnson. I hope you will be in touch." He said as he began to write his number down on a piece of paper. As he began to walk towards the door he turned around.

"Oh and Ms. Johnson?" He stopped and said as he looked me directly in my eyes.

"Yes Mr. White?" I asked him.

"Not even the television can picture the beauty you really are." He said as he then turned around and walked out the door. Shit. I was appalled. Did he notice I was admiring him to? I had to tell Mia.

I began to fill Mia in on what he said to me as he left my office.

"Damn girl, so are you going to take his case?" She asked.

"Of course, I'm going to take it. I just want him to keep sweating a little bit. This case is even deeper than I thought." I said to her and we both began to laugh.

"Just remember, you are getting married. Let's not make this the first case of dreams coming true." Mia said sarcastically. We both laughed and I began to head out. I was on the way to meet my mentor and closest person I ever had as a father, Mr. Harold. He trained me to be the lawyer that I am today. I knew he would have known some information about this case and every piece of information I can get helps.

I arrived at the park where Mr. Harold was waiting for me sitting patiently on the bench.

"Hey Mr. Harold please tell me you have some information for me." I asked him.

"You know I do." He said to me confidently.

"Sean White. Previously on trial for a drug stop. Cops pulled him over claiming they had drugs on him. They are trying to connect him to being a kingpin. The police have been after him for a while now and can't get the charges to stick. That tells me he has people on the inside." Mr. Harold said.

Of course, he wouldn't tell me if he had connections on the inside and apart of didn't want to know. Even though I need to know everything that's the only way I can help. Apart of me is saying run far away from this mess. But my feet just won't move anymore. I know Harold is going to tell me to leave this case where it's at. And this case could either make or break my career.

"Yeah, he told me about that. But I'm not defending him for that. At least not yet." I replied to Harold.

"He came to me saying that while he was on trial for the drug stop, someone came in and shot the judge security and the jury." I replied to him.

"Yeah, I seen it all over the news but what's interesting about it, is while I was pulling up a file on him, I didn't see any documentations on it. Which means they are trying to tie up evidence to pin it on him or they don't have any evidence at all against him." Mr. Harold said.

"But they did come to him about it. that's why he's wanting representation for it. You know what's also interesting about all of this?" I asked him.

"What's that?" He asked curiously.

"He was also shot during the shooting." I informed him and he reacted shocked.

"Are you fucking serious? Something is definitely off now. So why is the story being kept out of the media. Is it a setup to take him down?" Harold asked.

"That's what I'm going to figure out because I didn't hear about it through the media either. I only found out today by him telling me that." I responded to him.

"So, you know what you need to do first right?" He asked me in an attempt to test my knowledge.

"Of course, I learned from the best. Get in contact with the hospital to get hospital records of proof he was shot." I said to him confident in my answer.

"Good girl. That way you will know if he is lying about that information. If he isn't, that's a start to show you he isn't lying to you about anything." Harold said to me.

"Right. Next, we have to discuss Attorney Greene." I said to him.

"Let me guess, Green no longer wants to represent him?" Harold asked.

"Greene is missing." I informed him.

"What the fuck is going on with this case? What do you mean missing?" He asked me confused.

"Greene was there during the shooting as well, but you don't see that in the reports at all. Now he isn't returning Mr. White's phone call. That's why he was seeking me for representation." I informed Harold.

"This case is so fucked up. Greene maybe involved." He said to me.

"Exactly." I told him.

"Well Sierra, if you win the case that will definitely put your name and the company's name on the map." Harold said. "But if you lose, let's just hope danger isn't going to be around every corner. And your reputation isn't ruined."

"Well, I can't say that I haven't thought about the possibilities since he came into my office. I'm just focusing on a win for right now." I said to him with confidence

"Speaking of wins, there is something I would like to discuss with you. Anyone can see that I'm getting old Sierra. And I'm sick. I wasn't actually on vacation. I've been to several doctors trying to get second opinions." Harold told me.

"Mr. Harold what are you saying."

"I have stage 4 pancreatic cancer. I'm dying. And everything I leave behind is going to you." Harold said.

I jumped up shocked. I couldn't believe what I was hearing right now.

"Oh shit Mr. Harold. I can't' It's your legacy." I said to his in an astounding voice.

"It's not up for discussion." He demanded. "And besides, the wife has been doing my head in about this for a while now and I believe she's right. It's time for me to retire and enjoy the days I have left. I fought the fight for as long as I could. At least I'll die knowing I left the company in good hands."

"But Mr. Harold." I began to say.

"No buts Sierra. The paperwork has already been worked out and just needed your signature. The company has been yours for a few weeks now. And now that we had this talk today about Sean White's case, I know that you are ready. And I'm proud of you Sierra." Mr. Harold said. "You keep on dreaming. Don't ever give up on your dream for nobody. Don't let nobody stop you from doing what you love to do. If you know what I mean."

I knew he was directing that towards Brian. It was still a lot to take in. To know the man, I looked at as a mentor, a father, was dying and leaving everything behind to me. I couldn't help but to cry. I had mixed emotions. I was happy my dreams were coming true. But I was sad that my time with him has now become limited.

"I love you Mr. Harold. And I promise your legacy will live on through me. I'm really hurt about all this. Is there anything we can do?" I asked him curiously. I wasn't ready to let him go and if there was anything that we could do to save him, I was willing to do it. I was willing to help.

"I love you too and no. The cancer is already too far gone. I only have about a year left and I will be spending that time with my wife because if I don't, she will kill me before the cancer does." Mr. Harold said and we both began to laugh.

"I won't let you down Mr. Harold. I Promise." I told him even though it hurts I know have work to do. I had a point to prove. I could do this, even if it meant me doing it alone.

"I know you won't" Harold said to me.

We continued to chat for a little while longer before his wife called demanding him to come home. I then went back and told Mia the good news before calling it a day. It was getting late so I decided to go home for the night. To my soon to be husband.

3 THE FIRST MEET

Just watching Brian sleep just does something to me sometimes. He's so handsome. I remember when every girl in school wanted him, but yet he chose me. I know I haven't been fair to him. But I refuse to let any man believe that I need them. Not matter what my feelings are for them. That's what made Brian fall in love with me in the first place. So, what's changed? Just in this moment, I felt like I had to try and make this right.

I climbed on top of him and started to kiss him all over his neck. I know his neck is his spot so that definitely would have woken him up. I continued to plant kisses on him as he then flipped me over. He started to enter his fingers inside me to make sure I was ready. He entered them in and out in a rhythm that made my hips dance with him. I moaned out-loud. He then slid his fingers out and entered himself inside of me. I rolled my head back as I was feeling ecstasy as he moved in motion. I then looked back up at him and all I saw was Sean. What the fuck was really happening? Brian continued to moan my name in pleasure but all I could see was Sean still. I acted as if it was him so I responded his name back. Brian finally climaxed and fell on top of me. Apart of me was glad it was over.

"Baby you are amazing you know that." Brian said to me exhausted.

"So are you." I replied back to him. "If only you knew". I said in my head. As good as the sex may feel, there was just no affection in it for me anymore. Is that why I'm picturing someone else? Whatever, a part of me is just glad that that crisis is now over.

"So, there's something I would like to talk to you about." I told Brian.

"What's up?" He asked.

"Mr. Harold told me today that he has stage 4 pancreatic cancer." I informed him.

"I'm so sorry baby. I know how much he means to you. I can't imagine how you are feeling. He was your mentor." Brian said sadly.

"Yes, I'll get through it but that's not all he told me today. He's leaving everything to me. Including the company." I told Brian and his mouth dropped startled.

"Great, more time we won't be able to spend with each other." Brian said.

"Brian that's not true. Now that I run the company, I can make my own schedule. Of course, I have to be available for important meetings and etc. But my schedule can be a little bit more open. I'd promote someone else to take over my job." I told him in an attempt to try to compromise. I just wanted to try and make him happy for once.

"But you could have made your own schedule before!" Brian yelled.

"Really, so we are about to have this fight again? You know what Brian, good night. I don't have time for this shit." I rolled my eyes and rolled over. It just seemed as if nothing I do is right anymore. I was over it. Is this what its going to be like for the rest of our lives? If so, I didn't want it. I eventually fell asleep hoping he would do the same and not make this more than what it already is.

SOMEWHERE IN NYC

"Shit I got nowhere else to run." The man says as he ran into a dead end.

"See you in hell motherfucker." Sean said as he pulled the trigger shooting multiple times.

His lifeless body dropped down to the ground as blood started to spill out of his wounds.

"Clean this shit up." Sean commanded.

"You got it boss." Law said as he began cleaning up the dead body to remove of any evidence from getting caught.

"That bastard shouldn't have crossed me." Sean said as he continued to walk away.

THE NEXT DAY

SIERRA

I really hope today is a better day than yesterday. Brian will never understand what it took for me to get here. I began to sigh and close my eyes as I let the water hit my face.

"Congratulation's baby. I'm proud of you." I heard a voice say. I opened my eyes to see Sean. He then walked up to me and started to kiss me passionately. As our kiss grew more passionate a loud noise started to go off.

Dammit. This damn alarm clock. These dreams are starting to seem more real. I guess that's my sign to head to the office and give Mr. White a call. Once I was dressed and ready, I headed to my office and gave him a call.

"Ms. Johnson it's great to be hearing from you." He said in a happy voice.

"Hey Mr. White how are you?" I asked him.

"I'm great Ms. Johnson. Have you decided to take my case?" He asked.

"I have. And yes, I have decided to take your case." I told him.

"I'm so glad to hear that Ms. Johnson. So, what happens from here?" He asked.

"Is there any place we can meet up? I'm getting ready to head out of the office and it would be great if we could meet to talk about the case." I asked him.

"If you want to stop by my house that would be cool." He insisted.

SEAN

"I really have to stop thinking with my head" I said to myself. She's, my lawyer. I shouldn't be having these thoughts of her in my bed.

SIERRA

Once he said that all I could think about was not trusting my own self doing that. But I have a job to do and the job must get done.

"Sure, just shoot me the address." I informed him.

"Done." He said and then he hung up the phone. I then grabbed my things to run some errands and then headed to Mr. Whites house.

SEAN

Once Ms. Johnson called to tell me she was taking my case I was glad. Now everything is going the way I planned. Once I disconnected the call I headed over to Law and Emily as they were just standing their asses around talking as if they didn't have work to do.

"My new lawyer is about to come through. So, no funny shit. Now get y'all ass back to work." I demanded.

"Sure boss." Emily replied and she walked away. I swear they act like fucking rookies sometimes.

"Oh, you mean the sexy lawyer from the club with beautiful legs of a stallion?" Law replied. He knew just what to say to piss me off and what can I say he definitely hit a nerve. But he knows me. And he knows that I'm attracted to her.

"I know what you're trying to do so fuck you." I yelled out and he laughed and walked off. There's no way I would let anyone talk about her as if she was just some random. She was my lawyer and they will treat her as such. But then again. If she was just my lawyer, why do I care about what they say about her? All I could do was shake my head. That damn Law. I should kill him. I don't do feelings and I damn sure don't do thoughts unless its ***business***.

SIERRA

As I arrived to Mr. Whites house, I was met by a valet worker. I felt a bit jealous as if he was living a better life than I did. Hell, I was doing things the legal way and he has everything that I don't. I deserve this life. This house was beautiful on the outside. I can't imagine how it was going to look on the inside. I walked up the stairs and rang the doorbell.

An older lady then opened the door and welcomed me inside.

"Ms. Johnson, Mr. White has been expecting you. He will be down shortly. Can I get you anything?" She asked.

"No thank you, Ms.?" I asked her.

"Just call me Sylvia dear. I don't want to feel like an old woman." She said as we both began to giggle.

"Yes mam." I expressed to her respectfully.

"Give me one second to find out if he's ready for you." She said and I nodded. I couldn't believe how beautiful this place was. I know it wasn't right but my feet couldn't stop me from walking. I decided to walk around and check this place out.

I then walked down a hallway and I couldn't believe my eyes. He really has an elevator and stairs inside the hallway. I entered into the elevator and clicked a random floor. Once the door opened there was a club. How big is this damn place? I chose another random floor and it opened up to a bedroom suite. From the looks of it, it seemed as if it would be the master bedroom. So, this is where all the action takes place huh? I thought to myself.

I then laid on the bed and stretched out. Just a for a moment I thought about what life would have been like. I then snapped back into reality and got back in the elevator. I couldn't believe this place had five floors. I clicked another floor and once the door opened, I found two woman and three men standing around a bar having a conversation. Once they all heard the sound of the elevator, they all turned around to see who it was. And there was Mr. White.

"Ms. Johnson, what are you doing down here?" He asked. By this time, I was already caught so there was no reason to lie about it.

"Well, I couldn't help but want to see the rest of your home. It's really beautiful." I informed him.

"I appreciate it. But you can't just go around looking through people's houses. It's an invasion of privacy. Anyway, its fine. But could you please wait for me upstairs. I will be there shortly." He said annoyed. Oh hell no. I think he has me confused with someone else. I have a job to do. He needs me I don't need him. I'm not waiting around for him no longer.

"Listen here, you asked me to come here because I have a job to do. So, either you let me do my job or you can find a job in prison. The choice is yours." I yelled at him.

"Yes mam. I'll be right there." he said seductively. I then turned around and headed back on the elevator as I waited for him to come meet with me.

SEAN

Damn who would have thought her yelling at me would have turned me on. I may have to make her mad more often. She then walked back in the elevator and headed back downstairs. Shit. Here I go again with these thoughts. She's, my lawyer. Why the fuck would I want to make her mad?

"Damn Sean, I never seen you bow to anyone before." Tech said and they all started laughing. He was right but I will never admit that too them.

"Shut your ass up." I said and they still found that funny. I swear I love them with all my hear but they like to take everything as a damn joke. I rolled my eyes and headed downstairs. I refused to keep her waiting any longer. Once I got down to the dining room, I seen her sitting on the couch with her legs crossed. She was so beautiful. I keep having to remind myself that she is my lawyer and she is too good for this life. No matter how much I would love to give it to her. But for some strange reason, my attraction to her won't let me pull away. It was like I had to have her.

"Ms. Johnson, sorry for the wait. I had some business to take care off." I informed her. She then stood up.

"Its fine, just don't have me waiting again." She said directly. I smiled. She was so sexy when she was demanding.

So, here's how this is going to go. I have a few rules so listen carefully. **Rule number one** when we are supposed to meet, be on time. **Rule number two** do not speak to anyone other than myself about the case. If I assign anyone to your case you will be informed and that's when you can speak to someone else about the case. Now listen very closely because this is the most important rule. **Rule number three** <u>DO NOT LIE TO ME</u>. Once you lie to me, it makes it very hard for me to do my job to represent you. It makes my job a lot harder if I don't have all the facts to be able to put together your defense whether your guilty or not. And now that Greene no longer wants to represent you, I will be picking up your previous trial as well. So. I'm going to ask you this one more time. Did you have anything to do with the killings during your trial?" She asked.

She was very straightforward. And for once in my life, I didn't know what to say.

4 LOVING THE DREAM

SEAN

I didn't expect her to ask me that question again. What was I really supposed to say? My mind just began to wonder back on the day it all began. We all met in the meeting room to talk about my upcoming trial.

"Does everyone understand their positions and their role in this plan?" I asked of them. They all began to nod yes. "Good because if any of you fuck this up, I will kill you myself." I told them.

"My trial is in 5 months and we need everything to go as smooth as possible. Tech call Tee and tell him to hurry the fuck up. It doesn't take that long to pick up a package." I then began to breathe back in to reality. I can't tell her the truth. She could never find out.

"Ms. Johnson I can assure you that if there was something that you needed to know I would tell you." I said to her. The less she knows the better. I would hate to have to kill that pretty face of hers. Especially when I want to rub my hands all over her body.

"Great then let's get to work." She responded. We then sat down on the chair and she began to document everything she had so far. Damn she was beautiful. Just watching her work makes my heart pound. I really wish I didn't have to lie to her. But it was for her own good. And I hope maybe one day she would never have to find out the truth. Find out about the monster in me.

SIERRA

I can see him staring at me. I'm trying my hardest not to look up. He's very intimidating but I could never let him know that. So, I decided to break the silence the only way I knew how.

"If you're going to stare you could at least tell me if there is something on my face." I said to him with my arms crossed. He said nothing. The only thing he did was continue to stare at me. He stared for a few minutes before he said anything.

"Would you like something to drink Ms. Johnson?" He asked. What the hell? I was confused.

"Um, sure. A water would be fine." I told him.

"Sit tight, I will go grab you a water" he said to me as he began to get up. Is he out of his rabbit as mind? The way he stares at me, I'm afraid he'll slip something in my drink.

"I don't think so, you can page Sylvia." I informed him.

"You don't trust me Ms. Johnson?" He asked.

"I don't trust anyone." I told him.

"Neither do I." He said directly.

"I don't recall asking you that." I said to him.

SEAN

Man, I love that attitude. She will never know what it does to me. The more she gave it, the more I wanted it. I can tell she was going to make this really difficult. But I have to keep reminding myself, wanting to make her cum was not part of the plan.

"Fine." I said to her.

"Fine." She replied.

"Fine."

"Fine."

"Fine."

"Fine." I was so intrigued that I let her have this round.

"Well Mr. White it's been a pleasure but it's getting late. I should get going." She said then we both stood up.

"Please call me Sean." I said to her.

"I will be in touch Mr. White." She said and headed out the door. I had to breathe. I really needed to get laid. My dick was hard. It was a long day and I was tired. I just wanted to shower and go to sleep. Once I laid in bed I began to doze off. If I would have known I would have had another nightmare, I would have preferred to stay awake.

"Shit I got nowhere to run." Tee said.

"See you in hell motherfucker," I said before I let off several shots.

"Clean this shit up" I told Law.

"Got it boss." Law replied and began to clean up Tee's lifeless body.

He shouldn't have crossed me is the only thing I can keep telling myself. I woke up yelling again. Dammit Tee why did it have to be this way. I went to take a shower again as I woke up in sweat.

This shit gone haunt me forever. I killed one of my closet men because he crossed me. I loved Tee like a brother. But once you cross me you lost me and I will kill anyone who breaks my trust. But Ms. Johnson, hell who am I kidding. If she crossed me, I would have to kill her too but still. She makes a man wonder sometimes. I got out the shower and was ready to start this day.

As I walked in the basement, I see Law, Emily, Renee and Lee standing around doing nothing. What the fuck do they think I pay them for? I already didn't have a good night's sleep so I just decided to snap on them.

"Do I pay you all to just stand around and don't do a motherfucking thing? Get y'all ass back to work. Emily and Renee, check you lines in 10 minutes, I have a job for the two of you." I demanded and walked to the security room. I got into the security room and sent Emily and Renee the information on their next mission. I then watched everyone as they worked. All of a sudden, I received a knock on the door. It was Law.

"You had another dream last night, didn't you?" Law asked. Damn he knew me like a book. It was hard to keep anything from him. Hell, we could even read each other's minds most of the times.

"Is it that obvious?" I asked him.

"Ever since we had to take out Tee you been in a different mood. But you know how it goes. It's always been me you and tech. Tee showed loyalty in the beginning but he was working for the enemy in the end." Law said.

"Speaking of enemies, make sure we have someone on Ms. Johnson at all times." I insisted.

"Ms. Johnson huh? Which head you thinking with boss?" Law asked. We both began to laugh. If there was an award for certified asshole, it would be given to Law.

"Just in case no one tries to kill her for representing me you know?" I informed him.

"Uh huh. I'll get right on that boss. But look I know it's not you killing Tee that's bothering you. It's your insecurities with trust. But remember." Law said before I finished his sentence.

"We all we got." I said out-loud.

"You damn right." Law said then walked out the door. I then continued to watch the cameras before going to help where needed. It was definitely going to be a fucked-up day.

SIERRA

I just woke up as my alarm began to sound off. I can't believe him yesterday. It's like he was playing a game with me or something. Would you like some water? Don't you trust me Ms. Johnson? Why does it matter if I trust him? I'm just his lawyer. I'm here to do a job. But my attraction to him is becoming to be an addiction and I have to draw a line between us. Apart of me hasn't felt butterflies like this in a long time. But I love Brian. At least I think I do. But in reality, the dreams I have of Sean I'm beginning to love more. But I'm marrying Brian. He's my fiancé, not Sean White! I have to draw the line today. I then got out of bed, showered and was ready to start the day.

Once I got to the office, I began to type in the necessary information I needed in regards to this case so far. I don't know why I took this case so far on. He should have brought me this at the beginning. If I'm the best why not come to me earlier, but instead I'm in here working my ass off! I know its petty but I felt as though I had to let him know. So much for drawing the line, right?

"Hey Mr. White. Just letting you know that I really am working my ass off for you and there's something I would like to ask of you?" I texted him.

He responded, "Ms. Johnson, I don't know if you would like me to thank you for doing "your job" but thank you. And sure, ask me whatever you like.

He was a smartass I see. I have the perfect response for him. "My job is to represent people yes. But I also do that by choice don't forget that. And I want to know why didn't you come to me for representation earlier?

He responded," Thank you Ms. Johnson I don't know what I would do without you. And because Mr. Greene has been my lawyer for years.

I responded, "Oh."

"Why are you jealous?" He asked me as he sent me the wink emoji.

"Good bye Mr. White" I sent back to him and then continued to work on his case. I wouldn't dare give him the satisfaction. I received a knock on my door and it was Mia.

"Hey Mia what's up?" I asked her.

"The fax has finally come in from the hospital, and Sean was definitely a patient admitted for a gunshot wound on the day of the shooting." Mia informed me and a sigh of relief came over me.

"Thank you, Mia. Please place that into the documentation folder I have of Mr. White please and thank you." I said to her. Once she put the paperwork into the folder she then came back over to my desk.

"I see you have been stuck in here all day today. You want to get drinks?" She asked.

"Definitely. Let me wrap things up here." I told her. She nodded then left.

We got to a karaoke bar and sat down. We then began to have some drinks.

"So, what's up with you?" Mia asked.

"Well, I was at Mr. Whites house yesterday." I told her and she gave me a surprising look.

"Oh my, spill right now!" She said with excitement.

"We were just working on the case that's all. However, he kept staring at me. I just know that if I don't draw a line between us, I can see myself making a mistake. He isn't the guy for me. Brian is." I expressed to Mia.

"Are you trying to convince me or yourself? Maybe you need to see what else is out there?" Mia said.

"You sound like Brian now! Brian thinks that because he's the only one I ever been with I haven't experienced much." I informed her.

"You want to know what I think?" She asked me.

"Yes." I told her.

"I think you care to much about what Brian thinks. Yes, he's your fiancé. Its reverse psychology. He'll say whatever to take the blame off of himself on whatever is going on between the two of you. He's finding every reason to pick an argument about you working when he should be supporting you. He used to do that. Why the sudden change?" Mia asked me.

"I wonder why everything has changed sometimes as well. Maybe we are growing apart. I don't know." I said to her.

"Well, I can't tell you what to do. But just make sure you do what you think is best for you. I just need to know what to do with my dress" Mia said and we both began to laugh.

"Mia, is it weird to say that I fell in love with the dream and not the reality?" I asked her.

"It's not weird at all. Especially if your dreams are what's keeping you happy." Mia said. We than began talking a little while longer before I was ready to get home. I figured it was time for Brian and I to have a serious heart to heart and figure this all out once and for all. Either we we're going to grow together, or we were going to grow apart. Once I walked in the house, Brian wasn't in the living room as usual and his car was parked out front.

I walked inside of our bedroom and he wasn't' there as well. Where the hell was, he. I then decided to check the guest room. I couldn't understand why he would be there since we didn't have an argument. The guest room door was cracked open and as I continued to walk up to the door, I heard soft moans. As soon as I walked through the door, it was Brian. He was kissing another woman all over her body as she laid there in nothing but her bra and panties.

5 MOVING ON

SIERRA

As I stood there watching them a rush of mixed emotions came over my body. I was furious. I was hurt. And a part of me felt relieved because now I no longer have to feel guilty about the dreams I have been having.

"What the hell is going on here?" I asked furiously. The both hopped up shocked and surprised.

"Brian this is the ultimate betrayal!" I yelled out. I know it's not only his fault but his assistant really? She knew he was engaged. I went off on both of their asses.

"I can't believe the both of you. How long has this been going on?" I asked.

"I'm so sorry Sierra. You weren't supposed to find out this way." Carol said. This bitch had a lot of nerve. I wasn't supposed to find out this way? Really!

"Well tell me Carol, how exactly was I supposed to find out?" I asked her.

"Sierra, Carol and I have been seeing each other for months now." Brian replied sadly. " I was going to tell you but I didn't know how."

"So, you bring her into our home instead? You son of a bitch!" I got pissed. A rage I was once familiar with began to come over my body. I began to see a darkness. I had to snap back. That is a place in my life I didn't want to revisit. I walked up to Carol and punched her in the face. She then started crying. Brian called out my name. I faced him and punched him in the face next. They had a lot of damn nerve.

"Both of you get your shit and get the fuck out of my house NOW!" I yelled. They both walked out. I couldn't believe them. I started tearing shit up in this house. Every memory of him I wanted gone. The way I feel right now. Him leaving was the best thing he could have done before I killed both of them myself. I was so angry. Everyone expected Brian and I to have this “perfect” little life. How the fuck am I supposed to face everyone now? I can’t this shit is embarrassing. What am I to do now? My reputation matters. I now have a company to run.

SEAN

The day is finally almost over. I went back in the security room to make sure everything was closing down smoothly. I then got a knock on the door. It was Law again. I should have known. As he is the only one who is bold enough to harass me all fucking day.

"What's up Law?" I asked him annoyed.

"So, you know how you told me to get someone on Ms. Johnson?" Law said.

"Yeah, what about it?" I asked him curiously.

"Bud just confirmed that Ms. Johnson just walked in on her fiancé with another woman." Law said.

I was shocked. I was angry. Why would anyone want to hurt such a beautiful woman? The thought of her having any tears coming down her eyes makes me want to kill that motherfucker. But she's just my lawyer. I cannot care. I’m not supposed to care. It’s not supposed to be my business.

"So why are you telling me?" I asked Law curiously.

"I just thought you should know boss. I just thought you should know" he said as he laughed and walked out. Fucking asshole.

Damn. As I sat back and thought, this shit was really fucking with me. I had to get the fuck up out of here. I called my driver to have him come pick me up. I had to meet Bud to put a face to this bastard who hurt my girl. Damn, I mean my lawyer. Why would anyone want to cause her so much pain? She's so damn beautiful. I finally had my driver pull over to the spot, and Bud hopped into the backseat.

"You got the picture?" I asked him.

"I got it right here boss." He said as he then took out the photos and began showing me who each person was and some information about their backgrounds.

"Brian, Sierra's college sweetheart. They have been engaged for over a year now. He's been seeing his assistant for some time now. And this is Carol Rodriguez. She has been his assistant ever since he took over the company. Apparently, she has some ties to his family. I tried to pull up some history on his family and there is nothing to pull which means." Bud said before I finished his sentence.

"He's either lying about his identity or has some mob or gang related ties. Thank you. Make sure she doesn't see you and keep a close eye on her for me will you. No matter how long it takes." I demanded him.

"You got it." Bud said before he exited out of the car.

I couldn't believe it. This whole time she was sleeping with a stranger and didn't even know it. Brian huh? Interesting. I started thinking to myself. I will figure out all of your secrets Brian. And I will kill you if you become any kind of enemy of mine. I wish I could kill you now but it would only hurt her more. **If only you knew**. I then had my driver take me back to my place and I instantly started to try and pull up every detail I could about Brian. I was at a dead end so I decided to get some rest for the night. Who the fuck was this guy?

SIERRA

I woke up in tears. I thought that maybe if I could take a shower all of the pain would go away. But Brian hurt me so bad. I never thought we would have ended this way. This is why I don't trust anyone besides Mia. All I can do is cry. And let the water run across my face to match my tears. I was crying so bad I couldn't tell the difference if it was tears or the water. I felt like a fool. But I know it's his loss. Now I can focus on my career. Maybe this was for the best. It's not like he supported my dreams anyways. But they were right when they say, your first love is a different type of hurt. And I won't lie, it hurts BAD! I can't go to work like this. I'm supposed to be the strong one and I needed to get it together. Then it dawned on me. I remember when Harold had to leave out the country on business for the company and no one heard from him until he got back. Maybe that's what I'll send out to everyone. I need this time to heal. I needed this time to remind myself on who I really was.

3 MONTHS LATER

It's been three months and I'm in a way better place than I was before. A part of me needed that break. I was always so swamped with cases that I never took the time to actually just relax. But as bad as I needed it, I really missed Mia. I'm so use to seeing her every day. But I can't lie, the one thing that did stung, was I didn't hear anything from Sean. He didn't even ask anything about his case at all during the whole entire three months. But why do I care? I wasn't working on it anyway. Maybe I just needed the attention from him. Oh well, I decided to shower and get dress and head to the office.

Once I got to office, I stopped by to see Mia.

"Hey Mia, how's it going?" I asked her and she jumped out her seat to give me a hug.

"Thank God, your back" she said ecstatically. "These people aren't shit without you."

I began to laugh. But I knew what she meant. But things are about to change now that I'm in charge.

"I missed you as well. I need you to send out an email to the board to everyone to meet with me in the conference room in an hour and for each one of them to bring their assistants along as well. Once you're done with that, come to my office please." I said to her and continued to walk in my office. She then went to send out the emails and eventually came back into the office.

"How was the trip?" Mia asked me.

"I didn't go on a trip; I took time off because I needed to get myself together." I informed her.

"Wait, you lied to me? Why would you lie to me? I'm your best friend." She yelled.

"I'm sorry Mia. I caught Brian cheating on me." I told her and her mouth dropped as she was shocked.

"Where is he? I'll kill him dead." Mia said angrily.

"It's okay Mia, It's over. I was sad, crying and everything else that was to be expected. That's why I needed the time off. I just wasn't ready to talk about it and with me saying that doesn't mean that it had anything to do with you. I just needed that time to myself. So, I could remember who I am and everything that I worked so hard for. But a part of me feels like a huge weight is lifted off of my shoulder."

"I understand that. And a weight should be lifted off your shoulder. Brian was like a fucking garbage bag." She said as we laughed.

So now what?" Mia asked.

"Right now, I'm just focusing on this case and this meeting we have coming up shortly. I have to focus on that. At the end of the day, I still have a job to do. No matter what is going on in my personal life." I expressed to her.

"Well look on the bright side. Now that you're a free agent, you can do Mr. White as well." Mia said and we both began to laugh.

"Maybe in another lifetime Mia, but not this one. I'm his lawyer." I said to her directly.

"There's this thing called being his boss in and out of the bedroom." Mia said.

"Bye Mia." I said to her than she laughed and walked out of the office. She did have point. I was free now I can do whatever I wanted to do. Yes, I may be moving on quickly. But sometimes hopping you have to hop on the bus to get to the next stop. I guess it wouldn't hurt to give him a ring. I pulled my phone out and began to send him a message.

"Hey Mr. White. Are you available to go over the case today?" I texted and asked him.

"Ms. Johnson, I won't be able to stop by the office, but if you would like to come by you are more than welcome to." He responded.

"Will we always have to meet at your place?" I asked him.

"You could always move in." He responded with a wink. I couldn't believe he was flirting with me. I couldn't help but giggled at his response. But I had to keep it professional.

"Would you like for me to drop you as a client" I asked him sarcastically.

"I apologize Ms. Johnson. See you shortly." He responded.

“See you soon Mr. White." I texted him and then began to head over to conference room. Once I walked in, everyone that was expected to be there was there. It was time to get started.

I'm glad to see everyone and its good to be back. I know this meeting was very unexpected but there are some important things that I would like to discuss with you all. As you all may know, Mr. Harold hasn't been around for a while. And I know there has been a lot of questions and I'm here to answer all that you may have.

“First, Unfortunately Mr. Harold will not be returning.” I said to them as everyone began talking amongst each other before I decided to intervene.

“We all loved Mr. Harold, But over the past year, Mr. Harold has been battling stage 4 pancreatic cancer. He's decided to step down and take whatever time he has left to spend with his wife. So, without further due, I am now owner of the company.” I informed them and they all again began talking amongst each other.

“Does anyone have any questions?” I asked as a couple of them began to raise their hands.

“Is there going to be any major changes?”

“Are you not taking any cases anymore?”

“And how long have you known about this?”

All these questions began to hit me at once and I just began to sigh. I was trying to keep my cool because even though they want an explanation, they aren't owed one. This is just first step of me trying to prove to them that I could do the job and that I would be a good boss.

“Listen, I'll answer everyone's questions one by one. And if some of you have questions and want to ask me privately then that is fine as well. But to start off, nothing is going to change. I believe the process and policies that we had in place for the company was already good. Everyone's schedules will remain the same. The way we assign clients will remain the same and yes, I will still be taking clients as usual. Finally, I've known for months now. That's why I've been away for the past couple of months so I can learn what I need to know to continue to make this place successful.” I said as I lied about the last part. Harold taught me the ins and outs of this company since the beginning. But so, they would not suggest favoritism, I never acted upon what I already knew.

"With me being the new owner of the company, I don't want us to get off on the wrong foot or start this new journey together with lies. So, I will tell you; another reason I have been gone for a few months was because I was dealing with the breakup between Brian and I." I informed them and they all started to talk amongst themselves before some of them asked if I was doing okay.

"I'm great actually. I'm in a much better place than I was before. The bright side to all of this, is that I can now focus on what matters and that's you all, our clients and the company. They all appreciated my honesty in regards to my breakup with Brian and that was the most important thing I wanted to discuss. I didn't need anyone seeing him with someone else and begin to assume an affair was happening. I'm moving on with my life and so should he.

"However, I do want to add one particular benefit to the company handbook. And this is particularly for the assistants of all the lawyers. I know sometimes you all go above and beyond to help us as lawyers even sometimes more than you are trained to do. So, what I want to offer you guys is a chance to go to school to become a lawyer along with job security. You'll still be able to keep your job as an assistant part time while you go to school. This will be an optional benefit. But you will have the opportunity to become full-time here after you graduate. But here's a bonus, for those who do sign up we will give each one of you a practice case, whoever comes up with the best defense, will get their tuition paid for in full." I informed them and all the assistants who wants to participate began to get excited. Some of them stated they wanted to stay where they were.

"I'm glad you all are excited. But if you do not win the competition, do not get discouraged we will still pay thirty-five percent of your tuition for being employed with the company as a benefit and the rest will be on you." I said and they all agreed.

"If there isn't anymore questions as of now, then you all may get back to work and I look forward to this new journey." I informed them and they all left to proceed with their day. I then called Mia to stay behind for a second.

"I have a meeting at Mr. White's house so that's where I'll be. I'm going to take him to turn himself in for a voluntary interrogation just to see what all they have on him so far in this case." I informed her.

"Great. I'll forward all calls to your voicemail and take note of every important call." She said as I nodded and left to head to Mr. White's house.

Once I got to his place Sylvia then answered the door.

"Ms. Johnson, it's great to see you again. I'll let Mr. White know that you are here." She said to me. I was curious to know who she really was so I decided to ask.

"Sylvia I just have to ask, are you related to Mr. White?" I asked her and she giggled.

"No dear, I'm the family butler. This place once belonged to his parents before they died." She responded. I was shocked I didn't know his parents were dead.

"Oh my, I didn't know." I expressed to her.

"I know Sean can be intimidating sometimes. But he's been through a lot. He's not just some. What is it that the press keeps calling him?" She asked.

"A king-pin?" I informed her.

"Yes, that's it. He doesn't have a strong family history. His parents weren't the best role model for him and there's so much more to him than anyone knows. Ever since he was a child, I was always the closet thing he had as a parent. And I'm not making excuses on him doing some of the things that he does. I just pray one day he will be able to get his shit together without having to look over his shoulders." Sylvia said.

"Thank you so much for sharing this with me Sylvia." I relied to her caringly.

"You're welcome. And here's a little secret. Because you are representing him, you won't ever have to worry about a thing. He will always be there for you." Sylvia said.

"Thank you, Sylvia." I replied. She nodded and began to walk off. That was good information to know. I then walked into the city view living he had and waited for him to come.

"Ms. Johnson, it's been a while. How may I help you today?" He asked. I had to admit he was looking sexy as ever. He had on all black looking as if he was about to do something he wasn't supposed to do. His facial hair was trimmed up and the scent of his cologne was to die for. I understand me being away is none of his business, but does he not even wonder why I've been gone?

"Well, there are a few things I would like to discuss with you. Have a seat please." I said to him and he began to sit down.

"So, what's up?" He asked.

"First off, do you have any enemies that you are aware of that would want to ruin you trial?" I asked him.

"Other than myself? Of course, I have enemies Ms. Johnson. But I can't tell you who would set me up if that's what you are asking." He replied. Was this guy kidding? What the hell did he mean other than himself?

"What the hell do you mean other than yourself? Are you trying to tell me some?" I asked.

"No Ms. Johnson. You know how they say we are our own worst enemy. That's what I meant." He replied.

"Ok so it's been a few months since the trial and to make the police think we are cooperating with their investigation; we are going to go head and have them arrest you for interrogation. But they can only hold you up to 96 hours since you are being suspected of a serious crime. But trust me, I'm your lawyer and you **will** be getting back out today." I informed him.

"Ok, let' do it let me just inform my crew right quick and I'll be right back down." He said and then he walked off as I waited for his return.

SEAN

As I headed down to meet the crew in the basement, I couldn't help but to think about how beautiful she looked today. I know she just broke up with her fiancé but I'm going to make her forget about him. All I need is a few days and his ass will be history. As Bud continued to report to me these past few months, I knew everything she was doing. These past couple months also made me realize, that if I didn't want her then I wouldn't care. And if I didn't care, then how she was feeling or doing with her day wouldn't have mattered to me. I had to hear about her tears and everything she was doing these past few months. It fucked with my head! I realized I was ready to share my world with someone else and I can't help but feel it is her. That's if she'll have me. I know she feels it too. But todays the day I'm going to shoot my shot. Fuck Brian! I finally got down to the basement.

"Ok everyone, my lawyer suggest that I go ahead and turn myself in. I will be getting back out so until then Law you're in charge." I informed him.

"Got it boss." Law replied.

"Renee and Emily, I got 2 jobs lined up for you that's going to last a couple days. Make sure y'all look your best. These men are worth over 2 billion a piece." I informed the girls. I know what you're thinking and no they don't sleep with men for money. They are lady assassins and they wine and dine the richest men and rob them. They are very good at what they do. If those men do not comply then they will kill them with no regrets.

"And Tech just be you. No matter what I say you will always do what you want to do." I said and we all began to laugh. It was funny but that motherfucker really didn't give a fuck whether I was in charge or not. He was going to make his own rules and follow his own damn orders. Yeah, he'll listen to me if it's a job he likes to do. But he was my best friend. I trust him with my life. So, I don't stress him because he keeps his self-busy with the warehouse operation controlling what drugs are coming and what drugs are going out. And he makes sure that operation moves smoothly as possible.

I then headed back down to the living room and Ms. Johnson and I got in her car and headed out. As we began to ride down the highway, she started up the conversation this time.

"Are you ready for this?" She asked me.

"Ms. Johnson, I'm ready for whatever and one day you will see that." I responded to her. I had to let her know so she could take that in any meaning necessary.

"Whatever you say" She responded.

"Let's get this over with" I replied to her sarcastically.

"Mr. White would you like to walk? You can always get out." She said as she continued to drive.

I couldn't help but to laugh in the inside. There goes my girl with that fire attitude. The asshole Brian is going to miss what he had and I damn sure am going to make sure of it.

"I apologize Ms. Johnson." I said to her and we rode the rest of the way there. Once we pulled up to the police station it was finally time to turn myself in.

6 WILL YOU GO OUT WITH ME

SIERRA

Once we got to the police station we walked up to the front desk.

"My client Sean White is here to turn himself in for questioning. We would like to get the process as soon as possible. I also ask that my client be released immediately after question for cooperating with the investigation." I said demandingly.

"I can't promise that but let's get started. Mr. White you are under arrest for obstruction of justice and murder. You have the right to an attorney. If you can't afford one, one will be provided to you. Right this way please." Officer Louis said. We then followed him to the interrogation room.

"So Mr. White, I understand you we're in the middle of your trial when the shooting happened?" Officer Louis asked Sean. Sean just sat there unbothered with anything as if he knew I had this. He didn't say a word. And he looked sexy as hell doing so. He was slouched down in the chair with his arms crossed and legs opened. I wanted to hop on top of him, but this wasn't the place.

"Cut the shit. My client doesn't have to answer that. You already know what he was there for and why he was there." I replied defensively.

"Ms. Johnson, I'm just doing my job." Officer Louis said.

"No your job is to ask my client relevant information in regards to the what you are accusing him for. Not to ask him things you already know and what is not relevant to why we are here today." I said to Officer Louis.

"Ok so Mr. White, there is reason to believe that you put this plan in motion to avoid being sentenced." Officer Louis replied.

"And why would my client do that if my client was one of the victims shot during the shooting.? I asked.

"Ms. Johnson, we have new evidence." Officer Louis said. He then began to pull out an evidence bag with a gun in it and slid it over across the table.

"Mr. White, this gun was found on the defenses side taped under the chair where you were sitting." Officer Louis said.

"That's speculation. Anyone could have put that gun there. If my client was shot. Why would he be the shooter? And why would the gun still be taped under the seat and not used?" I asked.

SEAN

Listening to Ms. Johnson grill this man right now during questioning was turning me on in a major way. I can see why then don't play with her in the courtroom and have to have their information lined up. If you are going up against her client, you're going to have to come with some hardcore evidence or no matter way you say won't matter to her. I could kiss her right now. She has beauty and brains and I couldn't help but to have her on my team even more now.

SIERRA

"Ms. Johnson your client was on trial for a drug bust?" Officer Louis said.

"Which is not the reason we are here today. Now if you don't have any real questions for my client about this case then my client should be free to go. It's obvious you don't have anything against him to hold him any further."

"Ms. Johnson, I see you all the time and I never thought you would take a case like this." Officer Louis said.

"I'm sorry am I the one on trial here?" I asked him.

"No." He replied as he blushed.

"Then an explanation on my job description isn't relevant. Now is my client free to go?" I asked him demandingly.

"Yes, he is free to go for now. But we will see each other again." Officer Louis said.

"Let's go Mr. White. And Officer Louis in light of any new evidence shall be brought to me first before my client or I will have your whole departments ass on the line." I said to Officer Louis and began to walk out. Sean then followed behind me. We then got back into the car and I started driving to take Sean home.

SEAN

My thoughts were running wild behind this woman. I would love to make her mine but then again, she's too good for this life. I started to breathe heavily.

"Mr. White, Is there something wrong?" She asked me.

"No mam I just want to thank you for what you did for me back there. You were great." I expressed to her.

"No problem just doing my job" She informed me. We then eventually pulled up to my house and something inside of me just got the courage to ask. I walked up to the driver's side window.

"Mr. White is there something I can help you with?" She asked.

"Would you like to have dinner with me sometimes" I asked her.

"Sean." She said whispered softly. Dammit she sounded so sexy the way she called out my name.

"Ms. Johnson." I replied back seductively.

"My name is Sierra and as for if I would go out with you? I guess you will find out once I let you know." She said and then she drove off. I laughed. I loved playing the hard-to-get games. It's one of my specialties. I headed inside to continue handling my business. Just by here saying that, I knew I had a chance. I just knew she was going to call.

SIERRA

I couldn't believe he just asked me out. Apart of wants to say yes just to fulfill the desires of my dreams. But then a part of me just wants time for myself. I may have been falling out of love with Brian for a while now but what he did still hurts. It was unexpected. So, I headed back to the office to get some advice from Mia.

"Hey is it still a slow day?" I asked her.

"You got that right. How did everything go?" She asked.

"It went great. You know the cops always get in line when I start talking." I said and she giggled.

"As they should. You're the best damn lawyer in New York City." She expressed to me with excitement. And she was right. There hasn't been a case I lost yet. You really have to bring it to the courthouse when you go up against me. I will never take a case that I think I couldn't win.

"So, Mr. White asked me out when I dropped him back off." I told her and she was shocked as her mouth dropped.

"This is great. So, what did you say?" She asked.

"I told him he'll find out once I let him know and then I drove off." I told her and she began to laugh.

"Playing hard to get. You know that turns a man on. Look, I know you just caught Brian cheating but let's be honest. You didn't love him the way you use too. He constantly failed to support your dreams the minute he asked you to be his wife. Plus, you have been dreaming about this guy since forever now. You obviously got the fetish for him the moment you first laid eyes on him on tv." Mia said.

"I know Mia. And I know I've been falling out of love with Brian for a while. And it's not that. I'm scared to open back up to someone else. What if he doesn't support my dreams like Brian did? Besides. If I decide to pursue this, Mr. White would only be the second guy I ever been with. Maybe I should weigh out my options." I informed her.

"Well look on the bright side, he may even be a better lay." She said and I giggled. "Whatever you decide I will support you."

I then decided to pick the phone up and give Mr. White a call. What the fuck was I really doing. He's, my client.

"Hey Mr. White. What's up?" I said to him on the phone as if I was unbothered.

"Sierra, I knew you'd be calling. I can't blame you for not being able to resist my sexiness." He said to me seductively. I rolled my eyes and Mia started laughing.

"Mr. White I could always cancel before I say yes." I expressed to him sarcastically.

"Well, I wouldn't want that. I'll pick you up at eight at your place." He said to me.

"Ok. I'll send you, my address. See you then." I said then disconnected the call.

"Mia I can't believe I'm going on a date as if I wasn't engaged" I yelled out.

"You were engaged months ago. You can't expect not to move on. Stop worrying about what everyone else would think of you." She said to me bluntly and I nodded in agreement because she was right. I had to move on. Brian did it with no hesitation. I deserved too at least be happy too.

"Come on let's go raid this closet of yours." Mia said to me as we then left the office and headed to my place so I could get ready for my date with Sean.

Once I got home, I hopped in the shower. Once I got out the shower, I headed into my room to find that Mia already laid out an outfit for me. I swear she was the bestest friend any girl could have. She laid out an all-black tight fitted sheer dress with some black lace stiletto heels. It was obvious she was trying to get me laid tonight. It was beautiful. I had this dress still in the closet with the tag on it because there was no reason for me to even wear it. But I guess tonight was the night. I got dressed and curled my hair. I put on some black lipstick and eyeliner and I decided to wear some gold jewelry. It was becoming more and more real now and I was beginning to get nervous. I walked downstairs and I peeked around the corner to hear Mia singing to her favorite song as she waited for me. I don't know if she could have felt me coming but she instantly turned around.

"The way that Gucci looks on you amazing. But nothing can compare to when you're naked. Now a backwood and some henny got you faded. You're saying you're the one for me I need to face it." She sang. "Hurry your ass up. I'm becoming a very impatient woman. I know you're hiding over there."

"I don't know about this Mia. I'm getting jitter knees." I said to her.

"Bitch what the hell is jitter knees." She asked.

"You know, when your knees get scared and won't move." I expressed.

"Sierra, I swear if you don't get your ass." She started to say as I began to walk from around the corner. She began to clap.

"Are you happy now?" I said sarcastically.

"Ecstatic. Now let's go. And by the way you look beautiful." She said as she winked.

"Thank you, my dearest best friend. Let's do this" I said and we began to head outside. As we did. Mr. White was already there waiting outside in a limo. I took a breath in and out as my legs began to shake. It was now or never.

"Get your man boo," Mia said to me and I got even more nervous. But I couldn't back out now. So, I then started walking to the limo.

SEAN

I finally made it too Sierra's place. I made sure we arrived early because I didn't want to start this off all wrong. I know it's not right because she is my lawyer but I can't stop myself from being drawn to her. But what the hell is she doing to me? I don't dress like this. It's obvious she has very high standards and I just want to at least try to look like what I think her expectations would be. I watched her as she came out of her house and God, she was so beautiful. I began to swallow spit and I was nervous as hell. I'm not the kind of guy she needed in her life. I would only be bad for her. But is it selfish because I know she would be good for me? I'm not sure in which ways yet. But my heart isn't sure if I need her to make me a better man or to help me beat this case? I guess only time will tell right. But here she was as my driver opened the limo door for her. She looked even better up closely.

"Sierra, you look amazing." I implied to her as she got inside the limo.

"Thank you. You look great yourself." She acknowledged to me. I smirked.

"So where is that we are going?" She asked me in curiosity. But little did she know the way she looks tonight. She could have it all.

"I'll take you to the stars if you'd like." I said and she laughed. But I was serious. If I could give her the damn moon right now I would. She was a sun that was shining bright. Seeing her gorgeous smile that's all I wanted to keep doing.

"Sid, let's go please." I informed my driver as he then started taking us to our destination.

7 THE FIRST DATE

SEAN

We arrived to the restaurant. The View was a spot I found on the internet and the pictures of it was even better in person. We ate dinner and I then led her to the rooftop where they had a beautiful bar on the roof. A band was playing jazz music and the vibe was just right.

"Can we get a seat for two.?" I asked a waitress. She then led us to a table.

"Can I get you both anything to drink." The waitress asked and I pointed to Sierra first.

"Sure, can I get a margarita no salt around the rim please." She informed the waitress.

"And I'll take a double shot of Hennessy." I told her.

"Sure thing. I'll be right back with those." She said and she walked away from the table.

"Wow this place is so beautiful. I been in New York my whole life and I've never visited this place. The view of the city at night time is just wow." Sierra said.

"It is beautiful. But not as beautiful as you." I told her and she began to blush.

"So, tell me, why is it that you're not seeing anyone?" I asked her. She doesn't need to know that I know anything about her personal life. That was going to be one way she would run off and I need her as close to me as possible.

"I was recently engaged. But it's over now and that's all that matters." she said.

"I'm not sure why anyone want to let you go." I said to her smoothly. Brian was a dumbass. But I was determined for him to see what he was missing.

"I'm not sure either. But hey everything happens for a reason, right? What about you. Is there a Mrs. White?" She asked me.

"I don't have time for it. I haven't found anyone worth giving any of my time too. I use to see different women from time to time. But nothing ever serious." I informed her. I wanted to at least be honest about something.

"So, am I interfering in your schedule?" She asked.

"Since the day I saw you at the club, you became one of the best parts of my day." I told her. Smooth right? I needed her next to me. I know it's wrong but something still felt so right.

SIERRA

He was so sweet but dangerous. Maybe if I asked him some questions, I can get a feel on who I'm really dealing with.

"So, what exactly is it that you do?" I asked him.

"Sierra, I think you know what it is that I do. But what I would call myself is a business man. I have an "organization" and have men work for me. That's the best I can give you about that without criminating myself." He informed me.

"Its fine if you don't want to give me full details. That was good enough. I know what you meant. So do you ever plan on getting out of the game?" I asked him curiously. But to be honest, I didn't really care. My only issue is taking me back to a place where I once been.

"Ms. Johnson I'm not in the game. I run it." He said in a demanding voice. He was so sure of his self to the point where it was a turn on. Nothing phased him. I could tell he was a man that really didn't have emotions. His demanding demeanor brings me chills all over my body.

"But yes. Once I'm ready or have a reason to get out of the game. I will." he said.

"So would you ever lie to me?" I had to ask. I'd definitely know more about the man I'm dealing with. And will I have to question his theory about his case. It was wrong because I was here to get to know him, I'm not here for work. But I just had to know.

"Yes, I would. But I'd only lie to you if it was for your best interest." he said. Hell, what can I say, at least he's honest? So, it makes me wonder. Did he really do it? Or didn't he? He was so blunt it was still hard to tell. I guess the only thing I can do is go by what he tells me.

"So, what is it that you're wanting for me since you don't have time to date?" I asked him out of curiosity. You know what they say. Sometimes curiosity can kill the cat.

"Well, if things were to get serious, I want to show you things you never seen before. If you say let's go to moon, I promise you we'll walk it. I may live the life that a lot of people don't agree of but I'm still a man and I take care of mine. I won't hurt anyone if there is no reason too. And to be quite frank, I don't even know what love is. But I'm at a point in my life where I want to learn. This life gets lonely and I'm tired of different women in and out of my bed. So, what is it that you want from me?" He stated and I'm not sure if I should be jealous or not. I hated the thought of him touching other women, when in my dreams his hands were all over me. To know what he feels like in my mind I can't imagine what he'd feel like in my heart. Its terrifying. But for now, I'll get back to the questions at hand.

"I'm not sure yet. I wasn't the one who asked you on a date." I said as we both began to laugh. "Aww so he does laugh I see."

"Not too many people outside of my crew who can make me laugh." He said and he put his serious demeanor back on.

"So do you have any siblings?" I asked him.

"I'm an only child. My parents died when I was thirteen." He expressed to me. I acted as if I was shocked. I didn't want him to know that I already knew from Sylvia.

"I'm sorry to hear that." I informed him.

"Its fine. They weren't the best. They are the reason I am what I am." He said to me.

"You know you don't have to be the way you are." I said to him

"Then teach me Ms. Johnson. I wouldn't mind." he said. Once he did my heart began to melt. It was obvious he has beautiful intentions on the inside. But the pain he's been through brings someone else on the outside. I get it. But is it really worth it? Is he worth it? My life, my career, my time and my heart?

"Do you plan on sleeping with me tonight?" I asked him and he laughed.

"No matter how much I would love too it wasn't my intentions." he said. Dammit. I would of gave in if he tried. I know this isn't the man that he is. He put on a suit and that's not what he does. The fact that he went above and beyond to do what he thought would please me definitely didn't go unnoticed. It makes me wonder if he would change his ways for me? Only time will time.

"You know you don't have to keep calling me Ms. Johnson. We should be on a first name basis by now. We're having drinks and dinner for god's sake." I said and he laughed.

"You really have a sense of humor. I like that in a woman. I haven't had anyone else make me laugh in a while. But I love a woman in control. And depending where you want this to go is all in your control Ms. Johnson." he said. I pulled his face forward and kissed him on the cheeks. He was so sweet. I downed the last bit of margarita and asked the waitress to bring me another.

"I would ask you to dance Ms. Johnson. But I don't know how." He said curiously. And I giggled.

"Its fine. It was the thought that counts and I'm actually good just being here talking to you as we drink."

"So do you have any siblings?" He asked me.

"I don't actually. I was in system for as long as I can remember. I can't remember the age I got there. No one adopted me. I was there until I turned 18. I wanted to make sure I graduated high school. Once I left, I did what I need to do to survive. I got a job to tried to make a living until I saved enough money to get my own place. I met a man named Harold one day and that's when my life began to change. He helped me get into a good college and he molded me into the attorney that I am today. I'm forever grateful to him. I was all I had until him and his wife came along and changed my life." I let Sean know.

"To think a beautiful woman like you went through something like that is breathtaking. But it also explains where your strength comes from. I respect it. And I respect you Ms. Johnson. You deserve everything and more." he said. For someone to be judged so badly through the media this man had the heart of gold. At least to me. It reminded me of the conversation I had with Sylvia.

"You know all this time. I was thinking the company belonged to you. Its Johnson and Johnson. Is that where it came from?" He asked.

"Yes actually. Harold and his wife's last name were Johnson as well. So, the company was called Johnson and Johnson from him and his wife. He met me and that made everything greater. I'm actually in charge of the company now. He just handed everything over to me. So, there's no need to change anything."

"Wow, that's amazing. Congratulations. You definitely deserve that and much more. So, you have no one to share your world with?" He asked.

"Well, I have my best friend, Mia. We been friends since college. She's, my assistant." I informed her.

"Yeah, I remember her. When I came to your office, she was asking me about my crew member" he said and we started laughing.

"Yeah, that sounds like her. She's not shy about what she wants and that's for sure." I said to him.

Sean and I continued to talk and the waitress continued to bring us rounds after rounds until it was getting late. I can't lie I haven't been able to just sit down and talk to someone one in a long time and I loved that fact that he just sat there and listened. He didn't seem to get tired of anything I had to say. He kept wanting to know more and more about me and only me. But it was getting late and I still had to work on cases tomorrow so I figured it was time to go. Even though I didn't want to leave.

"It's getting late Sean and I still have cases to work on. I think I should get going." I informed him.

"Your right. Let's get you home," he said. He then paid for the check and we got back in the limo to take me home.

We've been in the car for 15 minutes now and it's been complete silence. I guess I've been living in the dream for so long their becoming my reality. I mean he is my client. So why would a part of me risk it all for him? It surprised me because at the restaurant or conversations were nonstop and now it's just silence. Maybe I'll be the bigger person and break the ice.

"I really had a good time tonight. I'm assuming your bored now since you haven't said a single word since we got in the car." I confessed.

"Don't ever think for a second that you could be boring company." He said defensively. "I just can't stop looking at how amazing you are. There are no words to describe it. After all you've been through. I do apologize if that's how you felt." this man has a way with words I swear. But I can't let him into my heart. As we pulled up in my yard, I told him I had a great time and I would give him a call. Once I got out the car he got out on the other side.

"Ms. Johnson wait up." He said and I turned around. It was at that moment I should have kept on walking. But yet, my legs began to fail me again. He then pulled me close and kissed me. Did I like it? Yes. But did I feel like I was a game to him? Yes. He's too smooth. And I needed to be careful.

"Wait, what do you think you're doing? I hope you don't think I'm going to fall for your games. Because games aren't something that I have time for." I said to him.

"I can assure you the only game I want to play is laying you down softly and spreading you out so I can feed into my hunger." He said and my mouth dropped wide open.

"By your body language, I can tell you like it slow. So, I'll take my time. However, I want to speed up every other minute so I can hear you scream. Letting your fingers dig deep in my skin while your toes curl. Your neck? Your neck is your favorite spot I can tell. You ever had kisses all over your dripping wet body Ms. Johnson?" He informed me so seductively. And man, why did I have to respond?

"No." I expressed shyly.

"Hmmm. So, in other words. Your last man wasn't doing it right. It's time to fix that. I'll give it to you. Everything your body needs right now. Just tell me what you want." He said as he whispered softly in my ear. His third leg began to rise and he pulled me closer so I could feel it.

"You feel that?" He asked.

"Yes." I said passionately as I then fell for my desires and kissed him. Leading him all the way into my bedroom.

8 HOW DO YOU PLEAD

DAY OF THE TRIAL

"Mr. Walker how do you plead?" The judge asked. **BOOM!** The door of the courtroom gets kicked down. Multiple gunshots are fired. All the jurors were shot including the judge. The masked and armed men then walk up to the defenses table and aim the gun at Attorney Greene.

"No, No, please don't kill me. I'll do anything you want." Greene said. **POW!** Another shot was fired.

"It took you long enough to shoot his ass! Now hurry up and let's get this over with. Aim for my arm. Don't forget to dump green." Sean told Lee.

"Got it boss." Lee said. Another shot was fired.

"I'll call Renee and Emily to let them know that their up. Let's get Greene and get the fuck up out of here." Tech said as he picked up his phone.

"Yeah." Emily said.

"Y'all up go!" Tech told Emily. She then disconnected the call and called Renee.

"Get ready." She informed her.

"On it." Renee said as she then pulled away in the police vehicle. Emily then makes a call on the pay phone.

911 what's your emergency?

"I heard gunshots coming from the courthouse on 33rd street." Emily said.

Ma'am can I get your...

Emily then disconnected the call while the operator was still talking. She then walked into a back alley.

"Everything good back here?" She asked.

"Everything is good on our end." Lee said.

"Yo, where the fuck is Tee?" Tech asked.

"He never showed up." Emily said. The guys were shocked.

"Dammit. Lee, go ahead and finish off our half. Em is going to need a second hand with this." Tech said. Lee nodded and left.

"I got Tee's change of clothes right here." Emily said and she handed Tech the paramedic outfit. Once he changes, they then get in the ambulance and head to the courthouse.

PRESENT DAY

SEAN

As she kissed me and leaded me to her bedroom. I was beginning to become more anxious as ever. I was ready to let her feel all the things those other men failed to do. I laid her down gently on the bed and began to kiss her passionately. I then moved her neck to the side as I began to kiss on her neck. She moaned out. Just as I thought. Her neck was her favorite spot. That is until she finds out that she has other pleasures in store. I then sucked on her neck to leave a mark of me on her. I needed her to remember this night. I needed her to remember me.

I began to run my tongue all down her stomach to her thighs. I kissed her all over her body until I got in between her thighs. I began to pull her panties off with my teeth. I then spread her legs out wider and planted a kiss right above her clit before I put my face in and began slipping my tongue in and out of her to quinch my thirst. She moaned out loudly. I let her water drip all over my face. It felt like a faucet running through me. I lifted my head up and sucked on her nipples as I caressed her breast. I went back down and began to quinch my thirst again. She tasted so good I didn't want to taste anything else.

"Sean don't stop" She cried out. I worked my tongue faster for her pleasure as she continued to scream out. It was making me go crazy. The sounds of her moans were the most beautiful sounds I've heard from any other woman. I then kissed her and she pulled me in aggressively as if she couldn't wait on me any longer. I stopped and looked at her. I needed to remember every ounce of her. She was beautiful and I had to take it all in.

"Are you ready for this? Because once I'm in your mine." I said to her and I meant it. I didn't want anyone else to feel her drip. I didn't want no one else to have her but me.

"Make me yours Sean." She said and I slipped in side of her and she moaned out loudly. It started to drive me wild. I gave it to her slowly and then sped up the pace.

"You feel so good daddy, don't stop" She moaned.

"You feel good too baby girl. Tell me this pussy is mine now." I whispered in her ears.

"It's yours daddy. Take me how you want me." She cried out and I started to go insane. I flipped her over and I slapped her ass and she cried out in pleasure. I began to stroke her in a rhythm causing me to slid in and out of her as she dripped all over me. The sheets on the bed were soaked. She came again. I just wanted to make her cum over and over again but I couldn't go any longer.

"I'm cumin baby girl." I moaned out. I couldn't hold back no longer. I had to bust.

"Yes daddy." She screamed out. I then sped up and then pulled out as I put it all over her ass. I then fell out on the bed as all my energy was gone. She got up and walked over to the other side of the bed and held her hand out.

"You kicking me out already?" I asked her and she giggled.

"No silly. Have you never had a woman wash you off after sex?" She asked and I raised my eyebrow in curiosity. Hell no, I never had a woman do that to me. Hell, this the first time I haven't just left after sex. She was a queen. She wanted to cater to me after sex. I could get use to this. I took her hand and she led me to the shower. Once we were done, we dried off, laid back in bed and I fell asleep with her in my arms.

THE NEXT DAY

SIERRA

I couldn't believe what happened last night. It was everything and more. It was better than I dreamed of. It was amazing. I couldn't believe that he was still here. I haven't slept in or been comfortable with no one like this before. I felt complete. He looked so peaceful as I watched him sleep. He looked as if he hadn't slept so peaceful in forever. I then kissed his cheek in an attempt to wake him up.

"Good morning beautiful." he said as he began to yawn.

"Your morning breathe is horrible." I said and we both began to laugh.

"As if yours smelt like roses." He said then I giggled.

"I'll definitely remember that one Mr. White." I informed him.

"I was daddy a couple of hours ago" he said confidently and winked and I just stared in embarrassment. He then began to laugh.

"I have to get going though. I forgot all about Sid in the car last night." he said.

"Oh shit. So, did I. Why didn't he knock or something? I would have let him sleep on the couch." I said and he laughed.

"It's funny but I'm serious." I told him.

"Its fine. I'm sure he left and came back here first thing in the morning to make me think his ass stayed here all night. He's my driver but he can be full of shit sometimes." He said and we both began to laugh.

"But seriously. I have to go. I'll call you later." He said and I nodded. He then kissed my cheek grabbed his things and left. I laid down staring at the ceiling as if I was under some spell of him. I couldn't get last night off my mind. With me being his lawyer, we're risking everything for this case. The both of us. I snapped out of it and hopped in the shower. I wanted to head to the office and work on the case for a little while. As I got dressed and was ready to head downstairs, I heard the sound of my doorbell. As I opened the door there was a vase of roses with a note attached.

-***There's a thin line between life and death***. -

I dropped the vase instantly. How dare he sleep with me and then send me a death threat. I was pissed. Instead of me driving to the office I headed straight to his place. He was going to feel my rage.

Once I got to his place I banged on the door. And too my surprise he answered the door and not Sylvia. I slapped the hell out of his ass.

"What the hell was that for?" He asked.

"You sleep with me then turn around and threaten my life that's what's going on." I yelled.

"I don't know what you're talking about" he said.

"Ooh really. As if your breathe smelt like roses. that's what you said. You're the only one who ever said anything to me about some damn roses."

"Well, you're wrong. I have no reason to threaten your life Sierra. Calm down and just tell me what's going on." He said demanding.

"You had roses dropped off to my house with a note attached saying there's a thin line between life and death." I yelled at him.

"I told you I didn't know anything about it. I don't know who sent it. All I know is that it wasn't me. But I'll take care of it." He yelled out and then walked off. He had a lot of nerve walking away from me. So, I followed him.

SYLVIA

I heard Sierra and Sean arguing in the living room as I was in the kitchen cleaning up. The way that they were arguing, I was 100% percent sure they slept with each other. I was happy. He needed someone like her by his side. But my only worries are if she can handle someone like him on hers? She'd have a lot to lose being with someone like my Sean. But no matter what I'll be rooting for them because it's obvious they are into each other and that didn't just start when they slept together. So, for now I'll just keep listening and hope that they can find a way to deal with their emotions before it causes everyone trouble in the end.

SIERRA

"How do you mean you'll handle it?" I asked him demanding some answers as I followed him to the kitchen.

"Exactly how it sounds. I'll handle it!" He yelled.

"You're going to tell me what's going on and I want to know what's going on now! Because if anyone finds out about us, I will no longer be able to represent you!" I yelled out.

"Okay fine. I honestly don't know who sent the flowers. But one of my men were supposed to be watching you at all times." he said. I was shocked. He had someone watching me? I felt as if I was about to explode.

"Are you fucking kidding me right now? You had someone watching me the whole time! How many times have you seen me naked?" I asked him as I was pissed and all he could have done was laugh.

"Is that what you're worried about." He said and laughed again as he walked off. I continued to follow him as I was still in rage.

"Don't walk away from me Sean. How many times have you seen me naked?" I asked demanding an answer from him.

"I have way more respect for you than that. No one saw you naked except for me last night. Does that make you feel better?" He asked demandingly. Apart of my nerves began to calm but I still had more questions. It was one thing if I knew about this but I didn't.

"Then how did he watch me?" I asked him curiously.

"He was supposed to be in a parked car. But I will get down to the bottom of this. Trust me." he said.

"Trust you. You want me to trust you as if you didn't have someone watching me without my approval!" I yelled.

"Because of reasons like this! Don't you see that I did it for your best interest. I'm only sorry about the fact of not telling you. Not my protection of you!" He yelled at me. It was sweet and crazy at the same time. He could have at least asked and gave me the chance to say no before going behind my back. That's what has me upset the most.

"Can you at least ask me next time? Can't you see that that's the reason why I'm pissed. You can't just make decisions for me based on what you feel as though is best for me. Give me the chance to say yes or no before going behind my back. And if this is going to go anywhere between us you have to communicate." I expressed to him.

"I'm sorry. And I understand. I'll ask next time. And I'm going to handle it. Until then you will be staying here and Sid will be taking you too and from work." he said. What? This guy was crazy.

"Are you out of your mind? I'm not staying here with you!" I yelled.

"I'm not going to argue with you about this. It's not up for discussion. You're staying here and that's that. I'll be back shortly!" He yelled out and stormed out of the room. He's lucky he's fine when he's angry. This is all just moving too fast. We just had our first date. We just slept together. But move in? I understand he's just trying to keep me safe. But it's a little too much right? What the hell am I going to do now? If anyone finds out that I'm living with my client, my career is over. This is bullshit.

9 THE REASON WHY

SEAN

"Listen, I called just the two of you down here because you are my closet men and the main ones I trust." I said to Law and Tech.

"Tell us what you need." Law said.

"I need for y'all two" I began to say before my phone rang. It was Sierra. I swear she's going to cause me gray hair.

"Yes Sierra."

"Since you're holding me hostage here, can I at least get some clothes to wear?" She asked.

"Already handled. I had Sylvia pick you up somethings. Is there anything else?"

"Sylvia? No offense but I never seen her in anything outside of what she has on." she said.

"I assure you it will be fine. I will be up there in a minute." I said and then disconnected the call.

"She's already doing my head in." I told the boys as the started to laugh.

"So, what I was saying was." I began to say again as my phone began to ring.

"Yes Sierra." I said and the boys started to laugh.

"Don't hang the phone up on me. I don't care what it is that you're doing." she said.

"Okay Sierra, you can be the one who hangs up." I said and then she disconnected the call. The guys started to laugh.

"You slept with her, didn't you?" Tech asked.

"That's not the point." I said and they began to laugh again. That's all those two assholes want to do.

"The point is I need y'all to find Bud and kill him." I commanded them and they were shocked.

"Damn, what happened with Bud?" Tech asked.

"I don't give a damn what he did. I'll blow his fucking brains out just because." Law said as Tech and I laughed at him.

"What?" Law asked.

"You sound like an addict man" I told him.

"Well maybe I am. I'm not ashamed of that." He said and we laughed at him again.

"I hate the both of you." He said and we continued to laugh at him. Now he knows how it feels when they always laugh at me.

"Okay "TECH" here's your reason why. I had our killer Law here assign Bud on Ms. Johnson to make sure nothing happens to her. This morning when she was headed out, she found roses with a threat card attached. If Bud was watching her like I pay his ass to do I wouldn't be dealing with this bullshit that I am going through today." I said and they laughed.

"Nobody told you to sleep with your lawyer. That ones on you man." Tech said.

"Man have you seen Ms. Johnson though? I don't blame that man." Law said and I chuckled. He was right. She was beautiful any man would want her by their side.

"Look she's going to be staying here until everything is settled so, please don't embarrass me." I said and they laughed.

"Why are you ashamed of us?" Tech asked.

"Yeah, and can here friend stay too? You know so we can have a sleepover?" Law said.

"You know what, both of you. Please go to hell." I said and they busted out in laughter. They get on my nerves but I love them too death. I wouldn't know what I would do without them.

"Let's go Tech. I'm pulling the trigger this time too." Law said and Tech and I laughed.

"Fine brother let's do this." Tech said and I nodded and headed back upstairs.

SIERRA

I'm not even going to lie. The clothes Sylvia picked out for me were nice. But Sean is not my boyfriend. Why would she pick these type of bed clothes for me? I chose to wear the robe with the brand-new underwear set. I decided to take a shower and watch a movie. That asshole better have a good excuse for keeping up here all alone all day. I then heard the door shut as he walked in.

"So, is this what you were doing all day?" He asked me.

"Don't you dare come in here and talk to me about what I did all day when you were supposed to be up here hours ago." I expressed angrily to him.

"I have a business to run baby. So, what's up? And if we are going to see where this goes you have to accept that. You have to accept all of it. You're going to have to accept all of me." he said. And he was right. I shouldn't pressure him to give me all his time. I was starting to sound like Brian. If anyone should understand, it's me. And It's not what he does that bothers me. Because honestly, I don't care about that. I just happened to forget we have two different worlds.

"Your right I'm sorry. But honestly, I'm not comfortable staying here. For one I'm your lawyer and two we aren't in a relationship."

"Listen babe, all that you're my lawyer and not being comfortable shit went out the window the moment you let me take them panties off. I told you once I was in it you were going to be mine. So, I don't want to hear about it anymore. We're taking it day by day so let's leave it at that." He said demandingly. Damn.

"But" I said before he cut me off.

"Are you going to complain all night? He asked.

"Well, I didn't." I began to say as he cut me off again.

"Good because your looking good tonight and I sure don't want to go bed without some of your sweet loving." he said. This fool just cut me off twice then have the nerve to ask me for some. He's definitely using the lotion and his hands tonight.

"Sorry baby, but when you're a naughty boy the gates are closed" I said to him as I got off the couch, blew him a kiss and walked off.

"Don't forget I know where you sleep." he said.

"Don't even think about it Sean." I said and he laughed.

MEANWHILE

"Damn, I can't believe we about to take Bud out." Tech said.

"Damn right we are. I'm going to light his ass up too." Law said and Tech began to laugh.

"And when the hell are you going to get a new car man? I can't be seen with your ass in this piece of shit. All this money you got and you rather drive our high school car. You're a fucking weirdo Tech." Law said and they both began to laugh.

"I'm going to push the bitch till the wheels fall off." Tech said and they began to laugh again. The two of them then pulled up to Buds house as they found Buds car parked outside.

"You ready?" Tech asked Law.

"I'm always ready." Law replied. And they began to knock on the door. No one answered. They then busted the door down to find Bud laying on the floor dead with his blood everywhere.

"Damn, somebody got his ass before I did." Law said and Tech laughed.

"You are sick man, should we clean it up?" Tech asked.

"Hell no. We didn't make this mess. Let's get the fuck out of here." Law said and they ran out the door and headed back to the car.

"I wonder who killed him first?" Tech asked.

"I don't know. But with Bud dead and Ms. Johnson getting a death note it may be connected." Law said.

"It's definitely connected. Looks like a war is coming." Tech said.

"Your right about that brother. And I'm ready. It's my favorite part of the job." Law said and they began to laugh. They then headed back to house to update Sean on everything that was going on.

BACK AT THE HOUSE

SEAN

"It doesn't take a rocket scientist to see that you have feelings for your lawyer." Sylvia said to me.

"Well, I'm not going to lie, it just feels different with her you know. I can't even say when it began." I expressed to her.

"But she is right. If anyone finds out about the two of you it's a conflict of interest. Not only for the case but for her as well. She could lose everything behind it." Sylvia said.

"I know mama. So, what should I do?" I asked her.

"Son, no matter how hard you try I keep telling you that you cannot have it all. You need to pick and choose what means the most to you. You need to decide which is more important." Sylvia said.

"That's what you keep telling me. But I want it all. And I wouldn't mind her being by my side when I get it." I told her.

"Well, it looks like you already made your mind up. No matter what I say it won't change a thing." Sylvia said.

"Are you saying no?" I asked her curiously. If there was anyone's opinion that mattered to me, it was hers. Sylvia was always a mother figure to me.

"I'm not saying yes or no because I like her and I think she keeps you on your feet. But right now, you need to figure out what's more important to you. Her representing you or the relationship you want to have with her." Sylvia said as we both then turned around from a bang as the door busted open.

"What the fuck man." I yelled out.

"We couldn't kill Bud." Tech said out of breath.

"And why the fuck not" I yelled at them.

"Because Bud was already dead before we got to him." Law said to me and my mouth dropped. I was shocked. I was completely lost for words.

10 FIX IT

DAY OF THE TRIAL

The police sirens began to go off.

"Just in time." Tech said as him and Emily hopped in the ambulance and headed to the courthouse. Once they got there they pulled in and there were officers there on the scene.

"What do we got?" Emily asked the officer.

"There's a total of 8. 7 dead at the scene and 1 with a gunshot wound to the shoulder. Our shot victim is bleeding pretty bad." The officer said.

"We'll take him." Emily said as she and Tech began to push the stretcher that Sean was in into the ambulance.

"Call the closest hospital please. Tell them they have a gunshot wound victim on the way." Emily commanded as they finished loading the ambulance. They then arrived to the hospital.

"What do we have?" The doctor asked.

"Male victim. Gunshot wound. He's losing a lot of blood." Emily said.

"Nurse prep a surgery room. We need to get him to surgery now." The doctor yelled. They then took Sean to surgery where he was being treated. Law then comes to the hospital as if he was a concerned family member.

"How is he? Is he okay? Please tell me he's going to be, okay?" Law asked as he was panicking.

"Sir calm down, who are you looking for?" The nurse asked.

"My brother Sean White," he informed the nurse.

"Mr. White just got out of surgery. He was shot. So, he may be in pain for a while but she should make a full recovery." Doctor Pierce said.

"Oh thank God. When can I see him?" Law asked.

"I can take you to his room now. Follow me please." the nurse said and then took Law to Sean's room.

"The anesthesia should be wearing off shortly. Is there anything else I can get you before I leave?" The nurse asked.

"Yes your phone number would work please." Law said and the nurse began to giggle.

"I hope your brother feels better sir." The nurse said and then she walked out the door. Sean then leans up in the bed.

"You are one sick bastard you know that." Sean said as they both laughed.

"Man she was fine bro." Law said.

"Did everything go according to plan?" Sean asked.

"Everything went to plan except for Tee didn't show up. We had to pick up his slack." Law said. Sean began to get pissed.

"Are you kidding me. So, who went with Emily?" Sean asked.

"Man Tech and Lee had to split so he could ride with Emily. Everything still went smooth. Lee dumped Greene and Tech went with Em. And of course, Renee made sure she followed behind the ambulance in the police car." Law informed Sean.

"Good you all break down Tees cut between each other. Once I catch him, I'm going to kill his ass personally." Sean said and Law laughed.

"I'll be right there with you." Law said.

PRESENT DAY

SEAN

"What the fuck do you mean Bud was dead when you got there?" I yelled out to them.

"I mean I don't know how else you want us to explain it. He had a bullet in the back of his dead head on his living room floor. He was laying in his own pool of blood." Law said.

"It looks like your guys have somethings to work out. I'll be downstairs." Sylvia said and she walked off.

"With Ms. Johnson finding the note and Bud being dead, it all seems connected." Tech said.

"No shit." I replied and Law laughed.

"Call the rest of the crew and let them know what's up. All of you will be staying here. Nobody will be left alone until we can figure all this shit out. Whoever it is, if they want a war that's what we're going to give them." I yelled out.

"That's what the fuck I'm talking about." Law said and Tech and I started to laugh. I was pissed but he would always make a way to make a joke out of everything.

"How do you think Ms. Johnson is going to feel about this?" Tech asked.

"I forgot all about it. Now I have to go deal with her shit." I replied and they laughed.

"Well we'll leave you too it. Goodnight, Boss" Law said as him and Tech walked off laughing.

THE NIGHT BEFORE LAST

"Drive now" The hitman said with a gun to the back of Buds head.

"You're making a big mistake. You don't know who you're fucking with man." Bud said.

"Shut up and drive before I shoot you now. Go to your place." The hitman said.

"Who are you working for?" Bud asked.

"Make sure to park your car where it can be found." The hit man said dodging his question. As they pulled up to Buds house they then walked inside.

"What is it that you want money?" Bud asked.

"The black crow sends its condolences to your boss." The hit man said as he then shot Bud in the back of the head.

"Its war time." The hitman said as he then left buds house to report back to his boss.

BACK AT THE HOUSE

SEAN

Out of all the places she can sleep in this house she chose to sleep in my bed. She's definitely going to give me some sweet loving tonight. I said to myself as I laughed.

"Ms. Johnson wake up!" I yelled out and she jumped up.

"What the hell is going on?" She asked.

"In my bed huh?" I asked sarcastically.

"I know you didn't wake me up for that shit" She said and I started laughing.

"Do you want me out of the bed Sean?" She asked tiredly.

"Not at all. But just so you know, I like my women in the bed naked. And why the hell do you have all the lights on?" I asked her.

"After everything that's happened today, I wasn't comfortable sleeping in the dark honestly." She said and I began to get undressed and slipped in the bed.

"Is this better?" I asked her.

"It's perfect she said as she climbed on top of me and began to kiss me slowly. I rubbed on her ass as she continued to kiss me. She started kissing me all over my chest as she then put my cock in her mouth. I moaned out the way she licked her tongue around me then swallowed me whole. As she continued to jerk and suck, I played with that pussy and she moaned out. She came back up and she sat down on me and her juices flowed down all over me. She rode my dick like a professional horseback rider.

"Shit baby girl," I moaned out and she continued to ride me slowly. I then grabbed her waist and began to boss her up and down on my dick so she can feel me in her stomach. She began yelling my name out.

"I'm about to come." I said to her as I then slapped her ass.

"Cum daddy" She cried out as she began riding my dick even faster. My leg began to shake as I was cumin. She then put her mouth on it and sucked it up. She was an undercover freak and Brian didn't even know. She then went to bathroom and cleaned herself up. I was worn out. She takes all the energy out a man. I dozed off. I didn't remember anything else.

THE NEXT DAY

SIERRA

"Wake up!" I yelled out and Sean jumped up. I had to get him back from what he did to me last night.

"Good morning beautiful," he said. But deep down inside I knew something was up. I could just feel it. I didn't say anything about its last night but now I want answers.

"So what's up?" I asked.

"What do you mean?" He said.

"Well I know you didn't just come in here last night just because so just go ahead and tell me what's going on."

"One of my men was killed. The same one that was supposed to be looking out for you." He said and my mind was blown.

"Are you fucking with me right now? So, I'm in danger because of you?" I asked him frustrated.

"I wish I could say no babe, but that's how its looking." he said. I was pissed. No matter how hard I tried not to think about it but this was my life now too. And I had to face the reality. If I was going to make something out of us, I had to accept everything for what it was.

"You're going to fix this and you're going to fix this now. I don't give a damn how you do it or what it is that you have to do." I said as I pointed at him with anger.

"Are you telling me this as my lawyer or my girlfriend?" He asked. Shit. And there it was. The question I have yet to talk to myself about. There was no doubt I feel more for him than I did for Brian when we first met. It took me months to feel what I feel for Sean now. Is this the life that I was truly destined to live? Even though I was running from it? I have to sort this shit out. But as of right now my heart and mind is telling me to see where this will take me.

"Both. But only because I'm in this shit of a mess now as well. But as your lawyer, don't do anything where it could fuck up my damn case. But as your girlfriend, you make sure to bring your ass back home." I said to him.

"Yes mam, so are you moving in?" He asked and wink at me.

"Don't press your damn luck with me right now" I yelled at him.

"Fine. Some of my crew will be staying here as well while we figure this shit out." He said.

"It's your house, you don't have to tell me. Besides. I was going to get Mia anyway. I can't let nothing happen to her." I told him.

"But I thought this was my house?" He asked. He was right but, in my mind, this was also mine while I was going to stay here. I just didn't want him to know that.

"I'm going to get breakfast." I told him as I then walked out of bed and headed downstairs.

"Good morning, Sylvia." I expressed to her.

"Good morning. I see you liked the clothes that I picked out." She said.

"I sure did. I was hoping maybe you and I could talk after breakfast.?" I asked her.

"Definitely dear. Breakfast will be ready shortly." She said.

"Well hot damn baby. Can I get your number, rub a piece of leg or something?" I heard a guy said and then I turned around to face them. And the other guy laughed.

"Good morning Ms. Johnson." Law said and the other guy's mouth dropped.

"Yes Ms. Johnson is right. Tech please don't make me shoot you in the fuckin face." Sean said as he walked in. And both guys began to laugh.

"My bad brother I didn't know this was Ms. Johnson. But goddamn brother you hit the jackpot." The guy said. I then began to clear my throat. They were talking about me in their guy code as if I wasn't right here.

"I mean I am standing right here." I said to all of them.

"Go put some damn clothes on." Sean yelled out and I laughed.

"I didn't know they were going to be here this early. But of course." I said and then I walked off to get dress.

SYLVIA

"Damn man I never seen you act like this over no woman. You falling for your lawyer already?" Tech said as him and Law laughed. I know exactly what they were trying to do. They wanted a reaction out of him. and I can't lie everything that was going on in this kitchen so far has been funny.

"Go to hell." Sean yelled out and the boys laughed.

"Good morning, Sylvia." Law said.

"Good morning boys." I said as all three of them walked in the living room. This house was about to be a damn mess. I can tell already.

SEAN

As I went to the living room, I heard the rest of the crew in there and it was time we all brainstormed and talk about our next moves. As I was getting ready to speak, I saw everyone looking behind me. It was Sierra. In this crop top romper with some shades on with her curly hair hanging down and sandals to match.

"Where the hell do you think you're going?" I asked as jealousy began to hit me. I refused for anyone else to be looking at my girl.

"I'm going to get Mia, is that okay with you, boss?" She asked and everyone began to laugh. She was a smartass. But that was one of the things that I loved about her. Plus, that smart mouth just turns me on.

"Fine Sid will take you." I told her then I turned back around to the crew.

"Sean White don't you dare turn your back on me!" She yelled out.

"I'm sorry baby, but I'm trying to handle business right now." I informed her.

"Sure you are." She said in a sassy voice and walked out the door.

"I love her already." Emily said and everyone laughed.

"You know what, all of you can go to hell meetings over." I said and they laughed. All they wanted to do was play. I swear I needed a damn drink and a cigarette.

SIERRA

I got in the car and Sid drove me to the office. I was trying to think of the best way I can tell Mia about what was going on. I also needed to grab some things in order for me to be able to work inside the mansion.

"Good morning, Mia. Please send out a mandatory temporary office closure notice to everyone. Inform them to take everything they need to work from home and that everyone will continue to be paid as regularly. Shut down the computers afterwards please. We will be closing for a while." I informed her.

"Why is everything okay?" She asked with curiosity.

"I'll explain everything in the car. I need you to ride with me. I'm going to grab some things out of my office and you should do the same." I informed her and she nodded. Once I got all my stuff, I then met Mia in the limo.

"Okay so what's going on and who's damn limo is this?" She asked.

"Sid drive please." I told him.

"Who in the hell is Sid?" She asked.

"Mr. Whites driver." I told her.

"His driver? What the hell is going on." She asked as if she was getting irritated.

"Well first off after my date with Mr. White we slept together." I began to tell her as she stopped me right there.

"Yesss. So, tell me. Was he a good lay?" Mia asked.

"It was mind blowing. So mind-blowing I might be in love with him or maybe it's the "D"." I told her and she began to laugh.

"Oh your serious?" She asked.

"As a heart attack." I informed her.

"Listen you won't be the first to fall after a good lay and you won't be the last. But the both of you had connection before the sex. Don't stress yourself. Hell, I want good sex like that too." She said and we both laughed.

"Ok so now what?" She asked.

"He left that morning I was on the way to the office and there were roses on the porch." I said and she then interrupted me.

"He is such a damn romantic." She said.

"The roses had a death card attached." I told her.

"That son of a bitch. If he even thinks" She said as I interrupted her.

"Mia please just shut the hell up and listen. He had someone watching me this whole time. The guy he had watching me is dead. And now I may be in danger. WE may be in danger." I said to her and for the first time she just sat there quietly. Not even a sound was made.

11 HE'S FALLING FOR YOU

FOUR MONTHS AGO

SEAN

"Anything on Tee yet?" I asked Tech.

"Negative. But word on the street is that Tee has been working with the Black Crow's crew," he told me and I was shocked. I did not expect that one coming at all.

"Are you fucking kidding me right now? He knows the history between us." I yelled out.

"Tell me about it and for him to know that your parents were willing to let the leader of the Black Crow kill you instead of themselves is what makes it even more fucked up." Tech replied.

"I don't give a fuck where you see his ass at. Find him. Get any location on him and I'm going to kill his ass right there!" I demanded.

"We're on it. I'll double up on men and have them searching around the clock. We'll find him." Tech said as I nodded and he left. I'm going to get Tee's ass and once I do his ass is mine.

PRESENT DAY

SIERRA

"We're in danger?" Mia asked.

"Yes." I informed her.

"Well, who is after us? Because they don't know I can get crazy too!" She said and I laughed.

"Well, I'm not sure if you are in danger, but I was not willing to take any chances. You are my best friend. I'll be damned if something happens to you."

"And I love you for that. So where are we supposed to be staying? Mia asked.

"We'll be staying at Mr. White's house." I told her and she raised her eyebrows surprised.

"Wow, you got laid and now your moving in. You definitely fell in love with the D." She said and we both laughed.

"I'm not moving in. Its only temporary for our protection." I informed her directly.

"If you say so." She said and we finally arrived back at the house.

"This place is beautiful." Mia said.

"This is just the beginning" I told her as Sean began to walk up behind me.

"Hello Mia, it's great to finally have a formal greeting." he said.

"Likewise, Mr. White." She expressed.

"Call me Sean we're family now" he said and I rolled my eyes.

"If you don't mind, I'm going to show Mia to one of the guest rooms." I said to him.

"How do you know where the guest rooms are?" He asked me.

"Because I done searched your whole house boo." I said to him with a wink and he laughed and then started to stare at me. I looked back until I finally decided to break the silence.

"Are you going to stare at me all day?" I asked him curious.

"I am actually. You look really nice today. Are you going to have an attitude all day?" He asked and Mia began to laugh.

"Don't you have work to do? You know like trying to save our life?" I replied to him sarcastically.

"Give me a kiss and I'll leave you alone." He demanded. He sounded so sexy. I walked up to him and gave him a kiss.

"Are you happy now?" I asked him.

"Ecstatic." He said and he walked away and Mia giggled. I turned to face her.

"What the hell are you laughing at?" I asked her.

"Because my girl is in love" she said to me.

"I'm not, but is he loveable? Yes." I informed her bluntly.

"Look at my girl growing up." she said. And I giggled.

"Is his sexy friend here?" She asked and I rolled my eyes and laughed.

"Yes, he's here." I told her.

"Fuck the room take me to him instead." She said and I busted out in laughter.

"Okay let's go." I told her and we headed towards the backyard where they were hanging out.

"So, as you all know everyone will be staying here until we can figure out who is behind the attacks. No one will leave here unless someone is with them at all times." Sean said.

"Will Ms. Johnson be with you at all times?" Law asked and everyone laughed.

"Yeah, what's going on between the two of you boss?" Emily asked.

"Why the fuck is my love life so important to y'all?" He yelled and they laughed and so did Mia.

"Shhh, Mia, I want to keep listening before we interrupt." I whispered to her.

"I mean we all know you're getting laid now. You've been in a much better mood." Emily said and they started laughing.

"Laugh all y'all want. Y'all think everything is a fucking joke." he said to them as he chuckled.

"So, is she your lady or what?" Renee asked.

"Yes, she's, my lady. Damn y'all are fucking nosey and sickening." He said while the guys laughed and the girls clapped. I smiled and Mia elbowed me.

"Finally, someone around here to keep your ass in check." Renee said.

"Speaking of which? What's up with the friend man?" Law asked and they all began to laugh.

"Do you need something to drink man?" Sean asked.

"No why?" Law asked.

"Cause you sound thirsty." Tech said and they all laughed.

"Here's our que Mia, let's go." I told her and she followed behind me.

"Hey everyone" I said as I waved and walked over to Sean.

"Hey Sierra." Emily and Renee said.

"Hey Ms. Johnson." Tech and Law said.

"Just Sierra guys. I assume we should all be on a first name basis since we all are going to be seeing a lot of each other." I informed them nicely.

"Sure." they said.

"Speaking of which. This is my best friend, Mia. She's going to be staying here as well. I thought it was only right I introduced her to everyone." I expressed.

"Damn baby is this your meeting or mine?" Sean asked and everyone began to laugh.

"Shut the hell up Sean." I said as they continued to laugh and he just rolled his eyes.

"Hey Mia." Law said and everyone laughed.

"Fuck y'all I'm out of here." Law said then he walked off and we all began to laugh.

"Whys he leaving?" Mia asked.

"Because he was just asking about you." Emily said.

"She literally asked me about him too." I said.

"Second floor first door on the right is where you will find him." Sean said and Mia nodded. As she went to find Law. The rest of us just sat around and talked. I got to know Renee and Emily more and I love them. They made me feel comfortable. Being with them out here and just talking and getting to know everyone made me feel at home.

A COUPLE MONTHS LATER

It's been a couple months since Mia and I moved into the mansion and I can't lie, I loved it here. All of us became closer than ever. Christmas was today and I was more than excited. Sean was still sleeping but I decided to wake him up with a bunch of kisses.

"Wake up babe, it's Christmas," I said as I then began to kiss him all over his body.

"Well ho ho ho," he said as he was getting turned it.

I giggled. I then began to taste all of him in my mouth. I began to suck him while I continued to rotate my hand around his dick. I loved to hear him moan out. It always made me wetter. I then released him as I got off the bed.

"Woman where the hell do you think you're going?" he sighed out and I laughed.

"Shhh," I said to him as I pulled out a bag with his Christmas gift.

"I know damn well you're not about to give me a Christmas gift right now." He yelled out to me and I laughed.

"Shut the hell up Sean before you ruin the gift," I said to him.

"Yes ma'am," he said as I then instructed him to close his eyes. I then pulled out the bag a blind fold and placed it over his eyes.

"Woman what do you have planned? I know you see my dick jumping." He said and I laughed. I then pulled the handcuffs out the bag. I crawled up on top of him and grabbed each of his wrists and handcuffed him to the headboard. Once I was done with that I then but on my naughty Miss Santa outfit. I then took the blindfold off of his face so he can get a view of what I had on.

"As turned on as I am, you have me handcuffed basically so I can't touch you with that outfit on?" he asked me and I giggled.

"You've been very naughty Sean White. Why should I let you touch me?" I asked him as I then put my mouth on his dick and sucked him the way he liked it.

He moaned out, "Fuck, baby girl I need to touch you. I need to feel you."

"But why?" I asked him as I sucked on his spot again to have him moan out.

"Baby girl you know I don't express myself," he whispered out.

"Ok, if you say so," I replied and nibbled on his spot again.

"Ok, baby girl. You're the only one I want. I have to touch you. I need to rip that outfit off you." He said to me seductively. As good as that sounded it wasn't good enough.

"Mm mm, I don't know. You've been a really bad boy. Are you going to behave if I let you go?" I asked as I sucked on him again.

"Whatever you want baby girl," he said to me as he I them crawled on top of him. I was unlocking the cuffs as he started licking my breasts. Once he was released, he quickly flipped me over.

"Oh, baby girl, you don't even know what you started." He whispered in my ear before he started kissing me. He then placed each hand on one of my breasts before ripping off my Miss Santa dress. He then licked and kissed me all over before he got in between my legs. Once he was there, he then began swirling his tongue all around my clit and he fingered me in and out as I was yelling out in pleasure. He then used his tongue instead of his fingers to tongue fuck me as he made sure his tongue made its way up and down so my clit could still have pleasure. I was in heaven. He came up with wetness all over his face. I was ready. He was ready as he entered me and I screamed out.

"You gone be a good girl for daddy?" he asked me as he continued to stroke me slowly before speeding up the pace.

"Yessss daddy." I cried out as I was cumin all over him.

"You thought you could play with daddy huh," he asked as he then rubbed his hands through my hair as he continued to stroke. He then pulled out of me as he put his fingers in me to put my wetness all over his fingers. He then stuck his fingers in my mouth so I could taste me as he followed sucking it off his own fingers.

"Mmm mm mm, you deserve to know how you taste." He said as he then entered me again as I moaned out and he flipped us over so I could be on top. I can't even lie; I think this was the best sex we ever had with each other. It felt different. It felt like a whole new connection. I wonder if he felt it to?

I looked in his eyes as I continued to ride him slowly. He grabbed my face as he then pulled me in to kiss me passionately as I continued to ride. I began to feel him getting harder as he was inside me. That's when I knew he was ready to cum. I then sped up on him as he grabbed my back and he pulled me close to him as he came. This was the first time he ever came inside of me. I didn't know what to think. I laid on top of him silently.

"You ok," he asked me.

"I'm good babe. You?" I responded.

"As long as you're good, I'm great," he said as we then eventually showered up and headed downstairs. Everyone gathered around and played cards and drank the day away as Sylvia prepared us a nice Christmas dinner. It definitely was a night to remember.

NEW YEARS EVE

It was the evening of New Year's Eve and I was I was bored as ever. Sean has been with the guys all day working and we normally don't work on cases as this is a paid holiday for the company.

I was so bored, I decided to go upstairs to see what Mia was doing. Since we been here, I know we haven't been able to spend as much time together as we use to. So, I then knocked on her door.

"Hey can I come in?" I asked.

"Sure come in." Mia said.

"So, how is everything with Mr. White?" She asked me.

"It's been good, but a part of me is still afraid that if anyone finds out about us then I will no longer be able to represent him. But yet here we both are, both willing to take the chance."

"So, I've been meaning to ask you. Are you okay with what he does?" She asked.

"I already know what you're about to say Mia. And yes, I'm okay. I'm doing okay." I expressed to her already knowing what she was implying to.

"I just have to ask because I know about you and I know something like that is okay for me. It's different for you. But it's always up to you if this is the kind of life that you want. Not every dealer is bad though." Mia said.

"I don't care what he does. I have my own job that separates me from that and my past. He did state that if he had a reason to get out, he would." I informed her.

"And you want to be that reason?" She asked.

"You got that right." I told her and we giggled.

"So, how's everything with Law?" I asked her.

"We're good actually. Whether we are together or no I'm not sure about. But I like him a lot and I hope we can put a title on it." She expressed to me.

"Have you tried telling him that?" I asked in a curious voice.

"I've been afraid to. I'm scared he's going to give me the answer that I don't want." She explained to me.

"Well, if that is the case at least you would know. And to be honest, I highly doubt that would be his answer. Hell, y'all sleep in the same damn bed every night and spend every damn second together that y'all do have available." I told her and then there was a knock on the door.

"Come in." Mia said and it was Sean.

"Hey is everything okay in here?" Sean asked.

"Yeah, we're good. What's up?" I asked.

"I was wondering if you wanted to go on a private dinner date tonight?" He asked.

"I'd love that." I expressed to him as I blushed.

"Can you be ready in thirty?" He asked.

"Yeah sure." I told him and he started to breathe heavily.

"Why are you breathing so hard?" I asked him.

"**If Only You Knew**." He said as he then walked out the door.

"Awww, I think he's falling for you Sierra." Mia said.

"I think I am to I just don't want to be the first one to say it because we just started dating." I informed Mia.

"Ever heard of love at first sight? Or Sometimes people feel instantly connected to someone. There's nothing wrong with that. Don't look at him differently even if he is. These guys never gave another woman the time and affection that they give to us." Mia said.

"Why would I look at him different? Especially when I feel the same way?" I asked Mia.

"Good because I like him way more than Brian." She said and we both laughed. But here I got the perfect dress for you to wear." Mia said as she went through the things Sylvia picked up for her. "Here go try this on." She said as she handed me the dress and I went in her bathroom to take a quick shower. It was a silk lace criss cross top dress that showed part of my stomach. It was beautiful. I had the perfect heels to match. Once I was done, I put the dress on and walked out so she could see it.

"You look beautiful. " Mia said.

"Good because I'm going to rock his world tonight." I said and she laughed.

"Good now get going before it gets too late." She said and I nodded and walked out the door and headed to Sean's room. I was ready. More ready than I have ever been before.

12 THE PRIVATE DINNER

SEAN

As I waited for Sierra, I couldn't help but to pace back in forth. Why am I tripping? It's not like I haven't took her on a date before. I have to toughen up. I've never felt this way before. The thought of her just makes my heart sink. I started to breathe heavily. As soon as I turned around there she was. Goddamn she was beautiful.

"Damn girl I just want to snatch that dress of your ass right now." I told her and she giggled.

"So where are we going?" She asked.

"Straight to the bed if you'd like" I told her as I winked and she laughed.

"So I was thinking maybe we can take a walk down near the water. Grab something from the carts out there and sit around by the water. Something different. I figured we don't need anything fancy." I expressed to her gently.

"That actually sounds perfect. Let's go." She said as I then leaded her out the door. Once we got to River Park we stopped at a hotdog and nachos stand to grab something to eat. I then found a bench and led her over so we could sit and eat.

"Its beautiful out here tonight. The wind is just right. I really love this." She said.

"I wanted to try something different. I didn't want everything to be about money. Emily said sometimes it's just the simple things." I informed her.

"And she's right. I would have been happy with a picnic." She said.

"I'll have to keep that in mind. So, what do you think about everyone so far? And have you been comfortable these past months?" I asked her because I needed her to feel like this place was her home. I'm to use to her being there now and I don't want her to be anywhere else.

"I love everyone here. They all have their own personalities and its perfect. Everyone gets along, there's no bullshit and most importantly everyone respects each other's privacy. Mia and I get along with the girls good. The guys always make us laugh every chance they get. It feels like a family. What more could I ask for?" She said as she giggled. I think now is the time I'm going to ask her to

"Sierra, I've been thinking. I really enjoy your company and we have gotten so close and I'm use to you being here. When all this is over, I don't want you to leave. Will you stay with me?" I asked. I don't know if it was because I loved her company or I just love **her**. Whatever it was I couldn't get enough of it. Maybe that's the strange feelings I'm getting.

"You don't think you'll grow tired of me?" She asked me.

"I don't think that's possible. Since you've been here, you've been one of the best parts of my day," I told her.

"Yeah, I'll stay with you," she said and I began to smile before I kissed her.

"I see you are working on expressing your feelings," she said to me and I laughed. It was true. I don't do feelings, but for her I'll always change the simple things.

"For you baby girl, I'll do the best I can." I informed her.

"You want to know something?" she asked me and I was curious.

"What's that baby girl?" I asked her.

"We heard Law and everyone else making fun of you that day I went to pick Mia up to come to the house with me. It was funny. I can see why Mia is interested in him. Those are the type of guys Mia likes. She loves the bad boy type. Funny with a loveable personality." She informed me.

"What about you? Do you like the bad boy type?" I asked her curiously.

"I won't lie because this is the first time, I'll be dating one. Besides my ex-fiancé, you're the only other man I've ever been with." She informed me. My heart began to beat really fast. That told me a lot about her and I can't lie I felt like the luckiest man on Earth. I already realized that she had not experienced much but with me only being the second man in her life explained to me why she never had some of things I've done with her sexually. I was the second guy for her and she would be the first woman that I've been in a relationship with. I really hope I don't fuck this up because I want this to work with her. I want her to be the first woman to belong to me and only me. I think I'm falling for her but I don't know what this feeling is that's inside of me. And she's so honest about her life and her past. She was just amazing.

"I won't hurt you Sierra." I expressed to her.

"I hope not. I'm not sure if I can take another heartbreak. Especially since I like you." She said.

"You like me?" I asked. And she giggled.

"Yeah, you alright." She said and I laughed.

"Just alright huh?" I said seductively.

"Yeah, but the funny thing is, is that this is exactly all I ever wanted. Someone to talk to. Someone who actually cares about my day you know?" She said.

"I wish I could. But I've never gave other woman this much attention. I'm learning as I go. If it weren't for Emily, I'm not sure where we would be tonight." I told her and she laughed.

"Well keep doing what you're doing. I'd never want to trade it for nothing." She said and I began to kiss her. I don't think I could ever get enough of her lips. That feeling with her lips on mine was everything. She was everything. She pulled me in and began to lift up my shirt.

"Damn baby girl you want it right here?" I asked her.

"Take me anywhere Sean." She whispered in my ear and she started kissing on my neck. I then started to look around because I'll be damned if another man watches my girl. I spotted a bathroom stall and pulled her towards it with me. I walked in the bathroom and looked around to make sure no one else was in there. I grabbed my girl and pulled her into a stall. I began to kiss her all over neck as she began to moan out. She then unbuckled my pants and went down to swallow me whole.

"Shit baby" I moaned out as I grabbed the back of her hair to help guide me in and out of her mouth. She then swirled her tongue around my tip and swallowed me whole. I moaned out again.

"Fuck." I moaned. As I then grabbed her and lifted her up against the stall door. I slid her panties to the side and entered her and she moaned out. I started to bounce her up and down on my dick as she leaked everywhere on it. Shit. I didn't even bring an extra pair of pants. I stopped for a moment and kicked the pants out the way and started bouncing her on me.

"Yes daddy." She moaned and I bounced her faster. I then sat down on the toilet seat and let her ride me. You could hear her wetness dripping in the toilet.

"It's mine Daddy, this my dick." She moaned out.

"It's all yours baby. Ride that shit." I moaned back and she began to speed up. I was about to cum.

"I'm cumin baby girl fuck." I said to her as I grabbed her hair and pulled her head back as she continued to fuck me.

"Cum daddy. I'm cumin too." she said. She started to ride me slow then sped up again and I was cumin. I pulled her up off of me and she then lifted her leg so her foot can be on the wall as she played with herself. Fuck. I kept jerking my shit as I continued to watch her play with herself. She kept moaning out. All of a sudden, the door opened in the bathroom and she stopped.

"Boss you in here?" Sid asked.

"Yeah man. Get the fuck out of here." I yelled at him and he laughed.

"I just wanted to make sure everything was straight. I'll be in the car." He said and then he left. I then got up and slid my fingers inside her so I can feel her juices pour. I had to get back in it. Even if it was just for a minute. I spun her around and had her touch the back of the toilet and she began to arch her back. I slid back in it as she moaned out.

"Scream my name baby." I said as I then smacked her ass.

"Sean." She screamed out.

"Who's Sean?" I asked.

"He's, my daddy." She said.

"Who's pussy is this?" I moaned out.

"Yours." She said and I began to pump harder. This shit was making me crazy. I grabbed her hair as I pulled her head back and kissed her as I continued to pump from the back. I was damn near ready to come again. Her pussy was so wet and tight. I couldn't never get enough of it. Eventually she grinded with me and I was coming as I pulled out and I aimed it in the toilet to get out whatever nut was left. We then began to clean ourselves off and headed to the pier to take a look before we left to go home and shower.

"Man the breeze from the water is beautiful. I really had a good time even the food was great." She said.

"I just have to ask. Have you been happy since we started this?" I asked her because I didn't want anything else. Fuck the case. All I needed was her.

"The happiest I've been in a long time." She said as she smiled.

"I feel the same way. Before I met you, nothing in my life felt right. Until now. You know I don't care if you can't represent me in order to be with me. I can find another lawyer. I don't think I could ever find another you." I said to her and she began to blush.

"Aww come here." She said and I came closer to her and she pulled me in with a kiss. I had to steady myself because if we became aggressive like we normally do she would of fell backwards in to the pier. As we continued to kiss, a gunshot let off and she became slump in my arms.

"Noooo," I screamed out. As I called Sid immediately so we could rush her to a hospital. Someone shot my girl and I had refused to lose her.

13 WHAT HAPPENED

MONTHS AGO

SEAN

It was a slow day so I decided to watch the security cameras to make sure everyone was doing what the fuck they were supposed to be doing. As I was watching I got a knock on the door and it was Law.

"What's up Law?" I asked.

"I got a location on Tee." He said.

"Where at?" I asked.

"Hustling in an alleyway." Law said.

"Good. Tell Sid bring the car around I'm going to kill his ass now." I demanded him. I already met Ms. Johnson to see if she'll take my case. Now all I have to do is kill this motherfucker who thought he could cross me. But because I still love Tee, I'm going to just shoot him. I'm not going to do him the way I would do someone else.

"You don't have to tell me twice." Law said as he then called Sid to bring the car upfront. Law and I then got in the car and we drove to where Tee was. As we got out the car, Tee spotted up in an attempt to run. But the idiot ended up running towards the alleyway with a dead in.

"See you in hell motherfucker" I said as I shot him multiple times.

"Clean this shit up." I demanded Law.

"Got it boss." Law said as he then began to clean up Tee's lifeless body. That bastard shouldn't have crossed me. I then went back in the limo as I waited for Law to come back and we headed back to the house. I trusted

Tee with my life but once you cross me you lost me and your life is how you'll pay for it.

PRESENT DAY

SIERRA

I keep going in and out and all I see is bright lights. Where the fuck was I?" I kept saying to myself.

"Come on. Move it move it. We need to her to surgery now." A man said.

"Doctor she's beginning to bleed out. Faster people lets go." A woman said. And I was out of it again. All I saw was black. Was I dead?

SEAN

As we rushed Sierra to the hospital, I couldn't stop panicking. I couldn't believe this happened. Once we got to the hospital, I carried her over my shoulder.

"Somebody help she's been shot." I yelled out and a nurse came as she paged a doctor. She then helped me lay her on a gurney as they rolled her down the hallways. I refused to let her hand go so I ran with them.

"Come on move it move. We need to get her to surgery now." The doctor said.

"Doctor she's starting to bleed out. Faster people lets go." The nurse said. Once she did tears became to roll down my face. I can't lose her. We were only just beginning.

"Sir you can't go any further than here. You have to wait in the waiting room as we try to do surgery." She said and I punched the wall. I started to go crazy.

"This is my girlfriend you're talking about. How the fuck can you tell me I can't go back there." I yelled out.

"Sir calm down." The doctor said to me.

"Don't you fucking tell me to calm down" I said as they started to grab me. And sat me down and explained to me the situation. I then sat down and waited for them to tell me about the surgery.

"How did everything go doc?" I asked.

"We were able to remove the bullet. But there's a chance she will or will not wake up." The doctor said and I started to hyperventilate. Next thing you know all I could see was black.

LAW

I was laying her with Mia as we were watching the news and I can't help but to realize how much I have grown to care for her. She was the realest and more. When I was getting ready to come in the room earlier, I heard her tell Sierra she didn't know what we were. And I admit I'm not good with my words and I thought she was already my girlfriend. But it's true, we never talked about it and I didn't ask. I assumed I didn't need to. But, instead of me interrupting their conversation, I left and decided to address it later. I assume the time should be now while I got her here in my arms.

"Mia?" I called out her name.

"Yes babe." She responded.

"I've been thinking. We sleep together. We make love. We do everything a couple does. And I want to make things official with you if that's what you want from me as well."

"Is this your way of asking me to be your girlfriend Law," she said as she giggled.

"You know I'm not good with words love," I said as I giggled back.

"Of course, I would love to be your girlfriend. It's about damn time you asked me." She said as we both laughed. I said to her. Next thing you know, we saw a breaking news report about a shooting that took place where Sierra and Sean went. My immediate reaction was to call and no one answered the phone. Not even Sid.

"Mia somethings not right. We should go to the hospital no one was answering the phone." I said and she immediately got up. That's the type of woman I like. Ask questions later. We then headed to the hospital and Mia began crying in the car. All I could do was grab her hand. There was nothing I could really say because my heart was hurting on the inside as well. Even if I didn't show it. As we got to the hospital I immediately ran up to a nurse and doctor.

"What the hell happened? Who was shot?" I asked.

"Who is the name of the patient you are looking for and your relation?" The nurse asked.

"I'm looking for Sean White. I'm his brother and this is Mia Jenkins. She's the sister of Sierra Johnson.

"I'm so sorry but we did everything we could. Mrs. Johnson was shot in the head." The doctor said and Mia ran off crying.

"Hey wait" The nurse said as she began to run after Mia.

"And my brother doc?" I asked.

"I wasn't done Ms. Ms. Johnson isn't dead as of now." The doctor said.

"Then what state is she in?" I asked.

"Ms. Johnson got lucky. We were able to remove the bullet but the bullet was 1 inch away from her skull. We won't know the exact state she in until she wakes up. But that's only if she does wake up. There's still a chance of brain damage. Her chances of suffering a brain bleed are still very high. We got all the bleeders as of now but possible rebleeds can always happen." The doctor said.

"And she's in ICU?" I asked him.

"Yes. But we had to sedate your brother. He went insane when we started to tell him about Ms. Johnson's condition. It was like he blacked out. I'll take you to his room." The doctor said as he began to lead me to Sean's room. I'm going to kill whoever did this. This is going to kill my brother if Ms. Johnson dies. Sean then begins to wake up.

"Man we have to stop meeting like this." I said and we laughed. I know right now isn't the time but I thought maybe I'd try to lighten the mood.

"Fuck you. I need to find Sierra now." He said as he then hopped out of the bed.

"Slow down man before they have to sedate you again." I told him.

"Law what the fuck is going on man. You're trying to stop me from something," he said. And he was right. He already knew because we've known each other forever and there's nothing we could hide from each other.

"She's in ICU and she can't have any visitors." I told him and he was shocked. He was hurt. He was sad. He began to walk back and forth.

"This is fucking crazy! I can't believe this bullshit." He said.

"It gets worse than that Sean have a seat." I said.

"I'll stand" He yelled.

"The doctors say they won't know what state she's in until she wakes up. That's if she wakes up. She could have brain damage. There's a possibility that if she does wake up, she'll be a vegetable." I told him and he stood their quietly. I already knew what that meant. He was angry. And when the doctor said he blacked out. He did. I had to stop him from doing it right now in this moment.

"Sean listen to me." I said and he snapped back.

"Tell them assholes to discharge me now. I want to find out who is behind this today! Find out if any of our men had their ears in the streets." He demanded.

"Yes sir." I told him and I left to go check on Mia and I began to handle business.

SEAN

As Law told me about Sierra's state my heart broke. My baby girl can't die. We got so much more ahead of us. If I knew that bullet was coming, I would have taken it. I walked out of that room to find the doctors to discharge me. I had to find the motherfucker that did this. I called Tech and Law and told them to meet me at the tracks.

"Thank you all for meeting me here." I told them.

"Man you don't have to say anything. We're going to take care of it." Tech said and I smiled. We had a brotherhood that no one could break. Law and Tech were blood brothers. They were twins but they always treated me as if I was their blood brother too. We were friends since I was 7. We were always all we had.

"Thank you. I just can't believe she may die because of me."

"Don't beat yourself up man. But I've been thinking." Law said.

"About what?" I asked him annoyed as if he was about to say some bullshit.

"It's funny because all of this started once the two of you started getting close." Law said.

"What's your point?" I asked him.

"The point is, what if it's her that they are after and not you." Tech said.

"I don't give a fuck who they are after. They tried to kill my girlfriend." I yelled out.

"We understand that. But think about it. We haven't had this much heat until now." Law said.

"If they are after her, then why kill Bud?" I asked him interestedly.

"Yeah you got a point there." Tech said.

"We'll keep our eyes and ears to the streets to find out who is behind this but as of right now no one is talking." Law said.

"And that's what's making it harder" I said as I turned my back to them piss.

"Anyways you should get back to the hospital. We'll hold it down from here." Law said as I nodded and went back to the hospital. I pulled a chair up next to her and held her hand as I fell asleep. There was no way I could leave her side. Not now and not ever.

14 MY DECISION

SEAN

Days went by and Sierra has yet to wake up. Mia and I continued to rotate around the clock. She would be there during the day and I was there at night. Most the time I was there 24/7 and no one could stop me. If I left it was to shower and change and I was always right back. No one is talking. Not even a piece of information is being said on the streets about what happened. But I had to be strong for her. I know my baby girl can do this. Even if she is in diapers, I would take care of her.

1 WEEK LATER

SEAN

"What do you mean we have no leads still. Try harder." I told Law and I then hung up the phone. There was no way no one knows anything about what happened. By this time, I didn't give a fuck if they started killing motherfuckers. I needed some damn answers and that's what I meant!

2 WEEKS LATER

MIA

"So, what now?" I asked the nurse and she was checking Sierra's vitals.

"Well the good thing is that her brain activity is beginning to pick up slowly which is normal. But will it go back to normal? That's where the waiting game begins. But we will continue to monitor and draw her blood to continue to watch for any signs of infection." The nurse said.

"Thank you nurse." She nodded and then left the room.

"Come on baby girl you got this." I said to Sierra and then I kissed her cheek. I missed her. I refused for our friendship to end right here. I wasn't ready to let her go. I refused.

5 WEEKS LATER

SEAN

It's been 5 weeks and baby girl still hasn't woken up. Both Mia and I were here today as the nurse said she had some good news. That's the best thing a man could here. These past 5 weeks have been hell and I missed my girl!

"Well we do have some good news." The nurse said.

"We scanned her brain activity this morning and her brain activity is back in full function." The nurse continued on and Mia got excited. I couldn't help but smile. I knew my girl was strong. She was a survivor.

"So now we are just waiting for her to wake up." I asked.

"Yes and of course when she wakes up, we will need to test her brain functions. Also, we ran her blood today." The nurse said.

"And?" I asked

"Her blood suggested that her hormone levels are high. Ms. Johnson is pregnant." The nurse said and both Mia and I were shocked.

"Pregnant? How far along?" I asked. As my heart began to race.

"Test confirmed she's about 4 weeks pregnant. I take it as though you're the baby's father." She asked me.

"Yes, I'm the father." I said and the nurse nodded.

"Well since she is pregnant, how has she been eating? Is the baby getting what it needs?" Mia asked.

"We feed her through a tube once a day. Don't worry the baby is getting full nutrients." The nurse said. "And because she's on IVs she definitely getting all the fluids that she needs."

"Do you think she will come back from this nurse?" I asked.

"In my professional opinion. It's hard to tell. But as in my personal opinion I'd say yes. We get patients a lot with gunshot wounds to the head and they don't survive out of surgery. She made it 5 weeks with no rebleeds in the brain and now she has her normal brain activity back. She's blessed sir." The nurse said.

"Thank you, nurse." I expressed to her gratefully.

"No problem." She said as she then walked out of the room and I turned and faced my girl and began to rub her stomach.

"Come on baby. I need to you come back from this. We got a baby on the way that's going to need their momma." I said to her hoping that she could hear me.

"OMG! Sean I'm so excited. I can't believe I'm going to be a Godmother." Mia said. I got up and turned to face Mia.

"You? I'm about to be a father. I never saw myself as someone's dad and now the day has come. I love her Mia." I said.

"I know you do. And I don't doubt that for a second. Especially seeing as you never left her side through all this. And now she's got a part of you inside of her. I can't wait I'm so excited." Mia said as she started jumping around in excitement and I began to laugh. But deep down I was excited too.

“Can I tell you something?” Mia said to me.

“Sure, anything.” I said to Mia.

“Law and I are together now and I’ve been dying to tell her. I know she likes the thought of Law and I but has she ever like said anything to you about it?” Mia asked me.

“Naw, she never said anything to me about it but I’m sure she’ll be fine with it.” I reassured her and she nodded.

7 WEEKS LATER

"What the hell is everyone doing? I need men around the clock getting me some damn answers!" I yelled and then disconnected the call. They were working my fucking nerves.

"Hey," a voice said. I turned around and it was my baby girl sitting up in the bed. I was shocked.

"Sean what's going on? Why am I in the hospital?" She asked me.

"You don't remember babe?" I asked her.

"No I don’t what’s going on?" She asked. I knew it wasn't right but I had to lie to her. I needed her to be at her best health for the baby and not stress or panic about what happened.

"We were out to dinner. And out of nowhere you fell over and hit your head. You were in a coma for quite some time." I had to make up something. Telling her the truth will devastate her.

"How long have I been in a coma?" She asked.

"7 weeks." I informed her.

"Wow. Okay. Don't you think you should go and get the nurse now." She said.

"You right. Let me go and get her." I said and I left to get and get the nurse. As bad as this may be, but I needed that nurse and the doctor not to tell her what happened. No matter the cost.

SIERRA

As I listened to Sean telling me the story about why I was in the hospital I knew he was lying I could feel it. I just didn't have any proof. But the nurse will tell me what happened she has too. Something is not right I can just feel it.

Sean then came back in the room.

"So what happened?" I asked.

"The nurse said she'll be right in here." He said and I stared at him.

"What?" He said.

"I know you're not telling me the truth." I informed him.

"And why would you think I'd be lying to you?" He questioned. Before I could answer the nurse came in. Good. now I can get some damn answers.

"Ms. Johnson, how are you feeling?" The nurse asked.

"I'll be alright once I know what happened to me." I said to her.

"You hit your head really hard. We discovered you had a small brain tumor. We got all the tumor. You had a concussion from you hitting your head so that's what had you out for so long." She explained to me. Wow I had cancer? I couldn't believe it.

"Are you sure you got all of the tumor?" I questioned her.

"Positive. Other than that, I do have some other news for you." She said.

"And what's that?" I asked interestedly.

"We kept running some blood test while you were in a coma and the blood test confirms that you are pregnant." The nurse said and my mouth dropped. I just knew it. Fucking Christmas. Merry Christmas and a Happy Fucking New Year to me.

"Well since we drew blood that confirmed your pregnancy 2 weeks ago you would now be 6 weeks along." The nurse said. But why didn't he tell me?

"Sean why didn't you tell me that I was pregnant." I asked of him.

"I wanted to babe but you were already not believing shit that was coming out of my mouth." He said to me. He was right. But did he want the baby?

"And you are okay with the pregnancy?" I asked him.

"I mean yeah I have no choice but to be. It's my kid. 9 months will be here quick." He said.

"But what if I don't want the baby?" I said to him and he got pissed.

"Okay well it seems you both have a lot to talk about. So, Ms. Johnson we will continue to monitor you tonight and run some more tests on you in the morning. If all is well, we will discharge you within the next few days." The nurse said and I nodded. As soon as she walked out the room, I knew we were going to argue.

"What do you mean what if you don't want the baby?" He asked me.

"Just as it sounds. I just started my career, Sean. I couldn't get pregnant for years and now that my career is kicking off, I'm not ready." I explained to him.

"I think you hit your head a little too goddamn hard. You are not aborting my child. If you don't want the baby, you can have the baby and give the baby too me." He yelled out and then left. He was definitely angry. I've never seen him this mad. But it was my decision at the end of the day.

15 THE MYSTERY MAN

SEAN

I was so pissed I stormed out of the hospital and headed back home. I couldn't even think straight. Maybe if I talk to Mia, she could get her to reconsider. I know I may live the life that makes me not look like I could be a father, but damn. I would love to at least try.

Once I got to the house, I went up to Laws room. I hear the damn music playing. These motherfuckers in there making love while my girl is in the hospital. I don't give a damn I'm going in. Someone needed to fix this shit!

"Law, I know you're in there I can hear the damn music playing. I'm coming in!" I yelled. And I walked in to see Law butt ass naked on top of Mia. They popped up in shock.

"Really you guys are fucking sick." I said as I then rolled my eyes. "Hurry the fuck up man Sierra woke up." Once I said that Mia hopped up! I turned around quickly.

"Wait you just going to leave me stuck?" Law asked Mia. And she giggled.

"Mia, I need you to have a conversation with Sierra. She's talking about aborting the baby." I said.

"What?" Mia yelled out.

"Baby? What the fuck am I missing?" Law said.

"Shut up Law." Mia said.

"I'll talk to her Sean. Don't worry." Mia said.

"Thank you. I doubt she wants anymore visitors tonight so you too can finish whatever the hell it was y'all were doing I'm going to get some rest." I said.

"Cool." Mia said. And I went to my room. I can't believe she would even consider not keeping the baby. I mean I get that we weren't together that long and she's my lawyer but damn. I would drop her as my lawyer if it meant I can have all of her. If she can't except my baby then it's going to be hard for me to except her. Our lives would never be the same.

THE NEXT DAY

SIERRA

"So how am I looking Doc?" I asked him.

"Everything seems great. Your exam is perfect. Your scans are clear. I don't see any reason on why we have to keep you." Doctor Pierce said.

"And my memory?" I asked him curiously. Something just felt wrong. I could feel it deep down inside of me.

"Your neurological exam was perfect so you have memory. Sometimes when we face **trauma**, we make ourselves forget. It will come back eventually. I'll have nurse Amy grab your discharge papers." He said as he then walked out of the room.

"Hey can I say something to you?" Nurse Amy asked.

"Well I'm sure you're going to tell me anyways so go ahead." I snapped. I know its rude but there's something about her that I just didn't trust.

"Your baby's father was here day and night since the day he brought you here. Him and your sister rotated but most of the time it was him, here by your side. The day he found out you were with child he never left this place. He had her bring him clothes and he showered here." The nurse said.

"So what are you saying?" I asked her irritated.

"What I'm saying is, women like me would love a man like that in our corner. Don't push him away." She said as she then turned around and walk out the room. But little did she know, I would kill any woman who tried it. If only she knew. I pulled out my phone to call Sid. It was time for me to get out of this place.

"Sid can you come pick me up please. I'm ready. And don't tell anyone not even Sean." I told him. He agreed and was on the way to pick me up. I know I'll have to face him about the baby once I get there so all I can do now is think about a game plan because I still didn't know what I wanted to do.

SEAN

When I got up this morning I still couldn't stop thinking about Sierra. As bad as I wanted to go back to the hospital, I still couldn't face her. It was hard. But what was even harder was looking the woman I love in the face while she tells me she's not going to keep my child. Mia gave me her word she was going to talk to her and I haven't seen her or Law yet today. So, I went up to their room to find their ass still sleeping butt ass naked.

"Wake y'all asses up!" I yelled out. Sierra must be forgot that I pay Sid. He's going to tell me his every move at all times. But I'll play her little game. I'll act as if I didn't know she was coming.

"Sierra is on her way home. And she doesn't know about the two of you yet. Also, Mia I need to ask you one more favor." I said.

"What's up?" She asked.

"Sierra knows about the pregnancy but she doesn't know she was shot. She thinks she hit her head from falling out from a brain tumor."

"And you want me to keep the story that way?" She asked.

"If you could please. That would be great. Look, I don't want to force her to have a baby but at the same time if she aborts my child, I could never look at her the same." I voiced to her.

"Listen I hate to break up y'all bonding moment but I'm hanging out here." Law said and Mia and I laughed.

"I'm sorry man." I said and I left as the doorbell rang. I went downstairs to answer the door. I knew it was her. My heart began to drop. I then opened the door.

"Hey you." She said and I just turned and walked away from her. I couldn't even look at her. This was going to be harder than I thought. I just walked outside to the garden.

"Real mature Sean. Real mature." She yelled out as I could feel her following me and I just sat down at a bench outside.

"Speak your mind." She demanded.

"No matter what I say your mind is made up. Can I just have some space please." I asked of her.

"Just tell me why do you want this?" She asked.

"Why don't you is the real question? I'm not the kind of guy who would make a kid and not take care of them. And I definitely am not the kind of guy who would make a kid and ask anyone to abort them." I informed her.

"And if we keep the baby, we'll be in this together?" She asked.

"More like till the day one of us dies. I don't know what else to say." I told her as I then began to stand up and she walked up closer to me.

"You promise?" She asked.

"I promise." I told her. She then walked up and kissed me. I couldn't have been happier in my life. My baby is having our baby. Next thing you know I hear the door bust open and Sierra and I both turned around.

"Tech what the fuck? You break the fucking door you're going to pay for that shit!" I yelled out.

"I know who was behind the attacks." Tech said. And my ears began to listen.

SOMEWHERE IN NYC

"So, what do you have for me?" The mysterious man asked.

"I just got word that she survived the shot sir. And she's pregnant" The hitman said.

"Pregnant? Interesting. Before I call anymore shots I need to find out about the baby." The mystery man replied.

"Of course sir. And he paid Amy 2 million dollars to keep her mouth shut." The hitman said.

"Does Amy know that it was us that shot her?" The mystery man asked.

"No sir. She just came home saying that a guy paid her 2 million dollars just to tell his pregnant girlfriend that she didn't get shot in the head." The hitman said. And Brian then shows his face.

"Interesting. Let's just keep watching for right now. Let's not make any more moves until I find out if the baby is mine first. I need to know how far along she is," Brian said.

"Yes sir. Anything else you need for me to do?" The hitman asked Brian.

"Not right now. Take today off." I'll send you a plan shortly." Brian told the hitman and the hitman left as Brian is left in his thoughts.

16 THIS KEEPS HAPPENING

SEAN

When Tech said he found out who was behind the attacks was the best thing I could hear besides my girl voice when she woke up.

"Baby go head in the house. I'm coming we to discuss business." I told her.

"I deserve to know who sent me a death threat." She demanded.

"I'll let you know once there is something to know." I demanded her.

"I'm not going anywhere. Tech talk. " She demanded and I just rolled my eyes because this was clearly not going to go anywhere.

"Fine. Tech go ahead." I commanded him.

"You know how we had smoke with the black crow's crew for a long time now." Tech said.

"Yeah what about it." I asked him.

"Think about it. Gonzales." He said.

"Tech stop beating around the fucking bush." I yelled.

"Brian Gonzales." Tech said and Sierra gasped.

"As in my ex-fiancé Brian?" She asked.

"Yes, I did some research though. I went through everything in Buds car. And Bud did take a video of the two of you. It was clear that he thought he saw something but wasn't sure. Look at this." Tech said as he then pulled out the video for us to see.

"Ms. Johnson wait up." Sean says as he then kisses her and you can see Brian hiding behind a bush.

"The video shows him behind the bushes. I had Carla work her magic and Brian Gonzales was a match." Tech said.

"I don't understand. Brian would never. I've been to his company multiple times It doesn't look like anything out of the ordinary." She said to Tech.

"It's a cover up Sierra. You been inside but you never seen what actually goes on there. Now it gets better. Louis Gonzales." Tech said.

"Yeah, he's been the head of the black crow for about 20 years now." I said informative.

"That's Brian's dad!" Sierra yelled out.

"He died just a few days ago. Which means." Tech began to say before I interrupted him.

"That Brian has been in training for a long time now to take over. And now that Louis is dead. Brian is the leader and has all the power." I said dramatically.

"Exactly." Tech said.

"But why would Brian want to kill me?" Sierra asked.

"He didn't at first. That day he was in the bushes, he was just there watching you. And once he seen you came back with Sean, that's when the threats began. The pictures that Bud took of Brian and Carol that day Sierra caught him cheating is what really helped identify him." Tech said and Sierra gasped. Shit. She never knew about that part. It was about to be hell.

"Hold up what pictures?" She asked me.

"Why did you have to bring that up?" I asked Tech.

"Okay so not only was I watching you around that time, I already knew you caught Brian cheating on you. " I told her and she got pissed.

"But yet you left out that little detail. Is that the only reason you asked me out Sean? Be honest with me for once." She said sadly. How could she even think that?

"No. That's not the only reason I asked you out. I wanted you the day I seen you in the club. Why do you always insist on doubting my feelings for you." I reassured her.

"For reasons like this. This is just too much for me right now. I'm out of here." She said as she ran away crying.

"Where the hell do you think you're going." I yelled out to her and then rolled my eyes.

"Great I just dug myself out a hole with her and now I'm back in the dog house." I told Tech and he laughed.

"Well she wanted to be here for this conversation and that's not your fault. She will be okay. She's been through a lot and emotional right now." Tech said.

"And pregnant." I told Tech and his mouth dropped.

"Now that's funny." He said and I began to stare at him.

"Oh, you're serious. So, what now?" He asked.

"I don't know Tech. But I swear I can't take this shit for another 8 months." I said and he laughed.

SIERRA

I ran to the front of the house crying. I couldn't believe Brian would try to kill me. I can't believe all this is happening. Everything is just happening so fast. At this point I didn't know who I could trust. I just wanted to get away from everyone. And boy why did I speak up so fast. Next thing you know I felt someone come up behind me and grabbed me as they put their hand over my mouth.

"Don't you make a sound. You scream and I'll kill you!" The man said and I nodded.

"What do you want from me?" I tried to say as he had a tight grip over my mouth.

"Let's go Princess. You're coming with me." He said and he grabbed me and threw me in the trunk of his car. I couldn't believe this was happening. Now I'm being kidnapped.

BRIAN

As I sat there and thought about everything my hitman was telling me I couldn't help but to wonder. How far along was she? Was the baby mine? We did sleep together and I let off all in her before we broke up. I know I did her wrong but she still gave me the best fucking sex a man could have. She used to get so wet it makes my dick hard just thinking about it. I know it's wrong to think about since I'm married now. Carol and I got married a few days before my father died. It was time for me to take over and I needed a wife by myside since she was carrying my child. If I would have known Sierra would be into this life it would have been her that I would have married. Not Carol. I use to complain about the time she didn't spend only because I needed something to complain about. I couldn't let her know what I was doing. I needed to complain so she would never see what I had to do behind closed doors. You never miss a good thing till the water runs dry and I missed her. Even after she put me out, I watched her. And I watched him put his hands all over her. My father's biggest rival putting his fucking hands all over my fiancée and she let him. To say that she wasn't cheating on me she moved on pretty fast and that's what pissed me off. To see that she moved on with the man my father hated most made her a target. I would have never tried to kill her if she didn't start seeing him. It was a disgrace. But I know the type of effect that she has on a man and in that moment, I knew, she would be his weakness. She would be the target on killing him. If killing her is the way to get to him then so be it. No matter how much it hurts but I will finish my father's work. I will make him proud in the afterlife. But I needed answers. I had to kidnap her. If I had to kill her after I got my answers then so be. I pulled out my phone to call my hitman back up.

"Yes boss." He answered.

"Listen change of plans. I know I told you to take the rest of the day off but I need one more thing from you before you do." I informed him.

"Sure what is it?" He asked.

"Kidnap her. Bring her to me in the basement. Make sure you don't leave a trace." I demanded him.

"Got it. I'll do it now." My hitman said as he then disconnected the call. I went to the basement as I waited for him to bring me her patiently.

MIA

"You don't have to be afraid" Law said to me.

"Afraid of what you?" I asked shyly.

"Yes. Are you scared of me?" He asked.

"How can be afraid of a man as fine as you?" I asked him. I could never be afraid of him. I wanted to be like him. Deep down inside I loved my job as Sierra's assistant but I always knew I was a bad girl at heart.

"If you think I'm gorgeous I must be the luckiest man on earth by having the most beautiful woman in front of me." He said and I began to blush.

"You really think I'm beautiful?" I asked him as I blushed.

"Yes. And never let anyone tell you any different. " He said and I smiled.

"Can I ask you something?" I asked him.

"Sure babe. Anything?" He said to me. It was now or never.

"What is it that Emily and Renee do?" I asked curiously.

"They have rich men take them on dates and they finesse them for their money why?" He asked. Okay here goes nothing I said to myself.

"Because I don't want to go back to the office. I want to be a part of the team." I told him.

"You want to be a part of the team?" He asked.

"Yeah I mean. I want to do what you do." I explained to him.

"Well, I don't go on dates with men." He said and we both began to laugh.

"Well what do you do?" I asked him.

"I'm the hitman for us. I'm a killer. I don't hesitate to kill if I'm told to do so. I do my job so well that's how I got the nickname Law. I always break them." He said and it turned me on. I loved everything about it. It excited me.

"Well I want it. Can you teach me?" I asked him softly.

"Teach you what?" He asked.

"To kill. I want to be part of this team so that means I need to know how to protect myself and the team." I explained.

"I don't think I like the idea of my girl going on dates with other men." He said and I giggled.

"So is that a, yes?" I asked of him before I attempted to get excited.

"I'll have to talk to Sean about it but no promises okay." He said.

"Thanks babe." I said and I kissed him on the cheek. Speaking of the devil Sean then walks through the door.

"Has either of you seen Sierra?" He asked.

"No, we haven't we didn't know she was here already." I told him and he began to panic.

"Shit I got to go." He said and he ran out of the room and I looked at Law.

"What the hell was that about?" I asked interestedly.

"I'm not sure but somethings going on. I know him like a book. Come on let's go." Law said as we then ran out the room and followed Sean to the security room.

SEAN

Shit. I know it's bad to always think the worse with all this shit going on. But it was exactly what I feared.

"What the hell is going on?" Law asked.

"Look up there." I told Law as him and Mia watched as a man kidnapped Sierra and threw her in their trunk.

"How the fuck does this keep happening." Law yelled out.

"She got upset and said she was out of here but I thought she was going to our room." I tried to explain to them.

"We don't even know who took her." Law said.

"Actually, we do. While you and Mia were up there getting your freak on Tech found out who was behind all this." I said.

"Well aren't you going to say something.?" Law asked.

"It was Brian." I said and Mia gasped.

"The cheating asshole she was dating?" Law yelled out and I rolled my eyes.

"Wait how did you know about Brian cheating?" Mia asked.

"That story is for another time Mia. Right now, we have to find her." I uttered to them.

"Brian bet not let me get my hands on him. I'm going to kill that asshole." Mia said.

"I think I'm in love." Law said and we laughed.

"Listen we all want to lay his ass out right about now. But right now, I'm more concerned about her safety." I confided in them.

"I couldn't agree more." Mia said.

"So we not at war with the black crow anymore?" Law asked me.

"Ahh so here's the thing my brother. Brian is the new leader of the black crow." I said and Law was shocked.

"Well what the fuck happened to Louis?" Law said.

"Louis is Brian's dad. That bastard kicked the bucket a few days ago." I informed law.

"Well my God." Law said and we busted out in laughter.

"What the hell is so funny?" Law asked.

"You man. You're a funny guy." I explained to Law is I continued to chuckle.

"So what now? There's no telling where Brian has her or if he's going to harm her." Mia said.

"See this is the thing. Nobody knew about her being in the hospital except for us. Either we have another snake or someone in the hospital is talking." I said to them.

"Well I can tell you it wasn't none of us. We all got drunk last night till we passed out. And no one talked to Lee since he left to take care of his mother. Lee doesn't know shit about what's going on right now. And we didn't want to tell him because then we all know he wouldn't hesitate to leave his mother and that would be selfish of us." Law explained.

"Your right and maybe" I started to say before I remembered the conversation I had with the nurse at the hospital.

"I need you to not tell her about what happened." I said to the nurse.

"2 million dollars if you tell her that she hit her head from passing out from a brain tumor." I asked of the nurse.

"And what about the pregnancy?" The nurse asked.

"She can know that part." I said to her.

"Ok. I'll have to get the doctors on point but I'll do it." The nurse said as she walked away. It's crazy what people would do for money sometimes.

"Hello! Earth to Sean." Law yelled out and I snapped back in from my thoughts.

"Oh shit! The damn nurse!" I yelled out. I began to get an instant rage all over me. A lot of motherfuckers was about to feel my pain.

17 AMY THE NURSE

SEAN

"What nurse?" Law asked.

"The same nurse who's number you were trying to get when I was shot. Her name was Amy, right?" I asked him interested in his answer.

"Yeah, at least that's what she told me." Law said and Mia laughed.

"I paid her 2 million dollars to not tell Sierra about what happened to her." I informed them.

"2 million dollars? Are you off your fucking meds?" Law yelled out.

"We'll talk about that another time. But now I recognize her face. Little Amy." I said to Law.

"Jr's little sister Amy? The black crow's top hitman?" Law asked.

"No shit." I said sarcastically.

"Well, I'll be damned." Law said.

"Honestly I don't give a fuck whose sister she is. I'm going to find her and beat her ass." Mia said as she then walked out of the security room.

"I tell you what. If she is any kind of killer like me, I'm going to marry her ass." Law said and I busted out in laughter.

"Let's go man. You are sick." I told Law and we went behind Mia and headed to the hospital.

SIERRA

I began to open my eyes. I fell asleep in that damn trunk. Knowing that I'm pregnant all the signs are starting to come. Where the hell was I?

"Well hello love?" I heard Brian say.

"You have some damn nerve, Brian." I said to him angrily.

"How's my kid? Is the baby mine or your client?" He asked.

"Fuck you, Brian. Are you fucking psychotic? This is not your kid and you know that. Besides, you can play these games all the hell you want but once he finds me, he's going to kill you." I warned him.

"How about I kill you first. And once I get a hold of his ass kill him next." Brian said. I refused to keep arguing with this asshole.

"Brian why are you doing this? This isn't you?" I said and he began to laugh.

"You see you don't know me you knew what I allowed you to know. You don't know shit about your little boyfriend either but yet you still opened your legs for him." Brian said and I got pissed.

"Fuck you." I yelled out.

"Poor Sierra you think your boyfriend is a fucking saint? How stupid can you be? He was the best assassin in the streets before Law came about. And now I'm trained to be the best. And do you know what else?" Brian said.

"Well, I'm sure you're going to tell me anyways Brian." I replied to him unbothered.

"Your little boyfriend killed his own parents. What makes you think he wouldn't hesitate to kill you too." Brian said and I was shocked. Sean killed his parents? There was no way in hell.

"You'll tell me anything to make me hate him. I'll never believe anything you say. Are you going to kill me? If so hurry up. I'm tired of listening to you. Save me from my misery." I explained to him.

"I see your sense of humor still hasn't changed." Brian said.

"I would love for you to change the subject." I expressed.

"I'm married now." He said to me. What the fuck? Is he trying to make me jealous? I honestly don't give a fuck.

"Honestly Brian. I don't care" I explained to him drained.

"Still with the hard girl act huh? That explains how you got him." Brian said.

"How's Carol? " I asked him.

"Oh, you mean my wife? She's pregnant with my kid, waiting on the new about you being dead." Brian said. But that made me think. How did he know I was pregnant?

"How did you know I was pregnant?"

"I honestly thought you were dead when you took that bullet to the head." Brian said. What?

"What the fuck are you talking about?"- I yelled out.

"Your boyfriend paid the nurse 2 million dollars to keep her mouth shut about what really happened to you. Now I don't know if that was just sweet or just straight stupidity." Brian said.

"You're a liar." I screamed out to him.

"Come on baby, you can't be that stupid. Your one of the healthiest women I know. Amy had to give the doctor half of her cut to even get the doctor on board." He informed me.

"And why should I believe you?" I asked him.

"Because why would I tell you all of this if I'm still going to kill you anyway." He replied.

"Well can you hurry up and pull the trigger please because this is getting boring." I told Brian even though I knew he wasn't lying. I just didn't think Sean would hurt me this deep. I just refuse to let Brian see it.

"Not so fast love. I'm not going to kill you just yet. The fun is just beginning." he said.

"Did you ever love me, Brian? That's all I really want to know." I asked him curiously.

"I did. But you were too good for this life at least I thought. Until you started dealing with him. If I would have known I would have married you. I never would have cheated." He informed me.

"Okay so you loved me. But yet you're not going to kill me yet. Make it make sense Brian. What is it that you want from me?" I asked him dramatically.

"Sleep with me Sierra. Just one last time. For old times' sake." He asked me. What the fuck? Was he off his fucking meds or something? Did his mother drop him on the head as a child? Because there was no way in hell, I was sleeping with him.

SEAN

As we got to the hospital I was pissed. I wanted to kill every fuckin person that stood in my way but right now wasn't the time. I had to bring her back home. But these motherfuckers are about to bring out a beast in me that I laid to rest. Before there was the black crow's hitman there was **me**. I still am and will always be the best killer in these streets. I taught Law everything he knows and Louis knows that. So that would explain why Brian was in training for so long. They were trying to prepare him for me. But they may think Brian is ready but **he is not**. And now that my child is involved all I see is red. I'm even better than I was before and they don't even know it. **Never forget the beast in me**. And my beast is what everyone should be afraid of. Even Sierra. We spotted Doctor Pierce and we all ran over to him.

"Excuse me sir." Mia said as he then turned around.

"How can I help you?" He asked.

"We're looking for Nurse Amy." Mia said and the Doctor began to laugh and then stared at Mia.

"Is there something fucking funny doc? And don't stare at my woman." Law yelled.

"I'm sorry I didn't know you guys were serious." He said to us.

"We've never been more serious in our lives." Mia said. I was doing my best to remain calm.

"Mam' I have no way of calling or paging Amy because Amy is dead." Doctor Pierce said and we all were shocked. What the fuck? There's some deep shit going on here and I planned on getting down to the bottom of it.

"What the fuck happened to Amy?" Law asked.

"We're not sure. She was shot and killed. She was already dead-on arrival." He informed us.

"Where was she shot at?" Mia asked.

"Apparently her brother found her body with a gunshot wound to the chest." Doctor Pierce said and Law and I exchanged looks. He killed her. She must have found out the truth and that son of a bitch killed her. Shit. Now we were back at another dead end.

"Wow we didn't know. Thank you for your time, Doctor." Mia said and we turned around and left the hospital. We then got back in the car and headed back to the house.

"I can't believe this shit. He killed his sister. My only guess is she must be figured out something or threatened to tell something and he had to shut her up." I said out loud.

"Wait how do you assume it was him that killed her?" Mia asked us.

"Well, it wasn't us. He's a fukin hitman of course he did it. And he just found her dead body. There was no way they would find him as a suspect." Law said.

"Good point. Law call everyone and have them meet us at the loft. I need all products shut down temporarily. We need to brainstorm how to find Sierra and we need to prepare for war." I instructed him.

"Got it." Law said and began calling everyone.

We then pulled up in the loft. Everyone was ready to listen as they seen me walked through those doors.

18 THE ESCAPE

SIERRA

"Are you out of your damn mind Brian. Your mother must have dropped you on your fucking head as a child. First off your married and I'm pregnant with another man's baby!" I yelled at him.

"Don't act like we didn't have an awesome sex life Sierra." He said.

"You are one sick person you know that!" I told him and he began to laugh.

"So, I've been told." He said and I stood up.

"There is no way in hell I'm sleeping with you!" I yelled as I pointed at him and he began to walk closer to me.

"I have to admit. Carol's great but you baby will always be number one." He said and he began to kiss me. How is it that this man can try and kill me and yet, he wants to sleep with me? But he's right. We did have an awesome sex life. But he wasn't Sean and he could never be Sean. And he couldn't fuck me like Sean could have either.

It was time I used my brain and not the hate in my heart for him so I could get the hell out of her. Brian was always weak for me and he always went to sleep after sex with me. So, I was going to make this the perfect time to escape. So, I sucked it up. I exhaled. I had a plan and it was time to put this shit in motion. So, I let him lay me down and have his way with me so he can hurry up and finish.

SEAN

After my meeting with everyone, we shut down movement temporarily until I can get everything back under control. I began to pace back and forth as I was left in my thoughts. Where the fuck could she be?

"Damn man you still in here pacing back and forth?" Tech said and I turned around.

"She's carrying my child Tech. Of course. I'm bugging the fuck out here." I yelled and I began to pace back and forth again.

"Ok I need you to stop for one second and breathe." He said and I began to breathe in and out.

"Listen I know she is carrying your child. But we need you to get your shit together so we can all figure this shit out. You the head for a reason." Tech said.

"Your right man. But damn, can you believe he killed little Amy." I asked him still in shock.

"Unfortunately sometimes that's just how things be. In this life we live, family or not if you become a too much of a threat you have to die. You know that." Tech said.

"Yeah but I killed my parents for other reasons." I expressed to him.

"Does Sierra know that you killed your parents?" Tech asked.

"No she doesn't need to know that either." I said demandingly.

"Well let's hope Brian doesn't tell her. But let's go everyone is waiting for you at the warehouse so you can tell us where you want these products to go for the time being." Tech said as we then headed down to the basement.

"Mia what are you doing here?" I asked her.

"I'm joining the crew. Law recruited me." She said.

"Are you out of your fucking mind. Sierra would kill me if something happens to you." I yelled out.

"Chill out bro. She was made for this life. I'll never recruit her for our work. I recruited her with Renee and Emily." Law said.

"So, you will send your girlfriend to seduce men for money?" I asked him dramatically.

"No disrespect Sean but I am a grown ass woman and I agreed. Everything is fine. Once we get Sierra back, I will tell her myself." Mia said.

"Damn right you are because I'm not going down for this." I said and they all began to laugh.

"You all are idiots. Is Renee still sick?"- I asked curiously.

"Yeah, she is. But she's trying to wait it out for Sierra to come home before she goes to the doctor." Tech said.

"Emily, you and Mia go take Renee to the doctor to get check. We will handle bringing her home." I instructed them.

"But she's my best friend I have to be there." Mia said.

"You work for me now remember. I'm the boss. You follow my rules. There will be no special treatment. Now go." I demanded and they walked off to take Renee to the hospital.

"Okay y'all let's get to work." I told them as we went to handle business.

SIERRA

As always. Brian goes straight to sleep. He's such a fucking idiot. Now it was time for me to get the hell out of here. I bent down slowly to grab the keys out of his pocket. I took them and found my way out the fucking door. I just ran for my life. I didn't care who was looking. Fuck those clothes. All I know is once I get to Sean's house I will be out of here. I had enough bullshit for one lifetime. So, I kept running until I found where I was and made it to Sean's house. I know I lost 20 pounds with all this running. I busted in to find the house quiet.

"I'm back is anyone here?" I yelled out. The house sure was quiet. I wonder where everyone was. I went to the kitchen to find Sylvia dead on the floor laying in her own pool of blood and I began to scream.

"Oh my God. Oh my God." I began to panic. I turned around to find the phone on the counter. Shit. The phone lines were cut. I ran up to Sean's room I through on a shirt and leggings and grabbed the gun he kept in his room. Now I can protect myself. As I ran towards the front door I was stopped by a voice.

"Not so fast sweetheart." The man said and I then turned around and pointed the gun.

"Stay back" I yelled out.

"You don't have it in you too shoot me. If I can kill my own sister, you wouldn't stand a chance." He said.

"What the fuck does your sister have to do with me?" I asked furiously.

"Oh sweetheart you don't know. Well, let me tell you. My sister was the one your boyfriend paid the 2 million dollars too." He said.

"So why the fuck would you kill her. She played her fucking part." I yelled out.

"Well let me tell you what happened." He said to be as he began explaining.

HITMAN

As I was going through my things to get ready to handle my next job, I hear my bedroom door slam.

"Don't slam my fucking door. What the fuck do you want Amy." I asked her.

"I just figured out that the lady whose boyfriend paid me the 2 million dollars was shot by you!" Amy yelled out.

"Yeah so. And you got a free 2 million dollars because of it." I said to her.

"The hell if I do. I don't want any parts of it. I'm giving him his money back." She said.

"You wouldn't." I yelled out.

"Try me." She demanded.

"What the hell do you want Amy?" I asked her as I began to get irritated.

"I'm sorry big brother I love you but enough is enough. I have to turn you in. I don't want this on my conscience anymore." She said and I pulled out my gun and shot her in the chest.

"I love you too Amy. But you're violating the code. And that I made a vow too. No matter how much it hurts." I said to my sisters' lifeless body as I then kissed her on the forehead.

SIERRA

"So, you killed your sister for wanting to do the right thing?" I said to him irate.

"I killed my sister for wanting to be a fucking snitch." He said.

"You're a fucking coward" I said and I got pissed even more. I then began to go back to that dark place.

"Maybe but." He began to say before I shot him in the head.

"That's for Amy." I said as I then kicked his lifeless body. Fucking bastard. The first thing he did wrong was underestimate me. I'm carrying a child who I now have to protect with my life and I'll kill anyone who is a threat. But I can't take this shit anymore. I'm getting away from all of these motherfuckers. My life has been hell since I took this case. First, I'll check this assholes pocket to see if he has a phone. Once I found the phone, I dialed Sean's number. I needed to give him a piece of my mind before I leave all this shit behind.

SEAN

"Boss our men checked all their spots that we know of and no one was there. They must have switched shit up. We don't know where they would have her." Tech began to say as I was getting a call from a number I didn't recognize. But something told me I should answer.

"Who is this?" I answered.

"It's me Sierra." She said.

"Oh gosh baby is you okay? Where are you?" I asked her shockingly.

"I'm outside of your home. I got away from Brian. But fuck that. When I got here no one was here. I found Sylvia dead in the kitchen. I killed the hitman who was hiding in the house." She said to be as she was talking fast. My heart began to hurt. Sylvia was dead. But I was also in shocked to find out that she killed a hitman. What the fuck?

"Listen stay right where you are we are on the way." I demanded her.

"See that's why I'm calling you. I'm leaving you. All of this shit is stressing me the fuck out. And you killed your parents. Are you fucking kidding me? I know if you killed your own parents then I don't stand a fucking chance." She yelled.

"Baby I can explain please just wait on me." I expressed to her.

"Explain what exactly? That my child's father is a fucking murderer. And I was fine with that until I found out that you killed your parents. And you paid that fuckin nurse 2 million dollars to lie to me about being shot who happens to be dead now." She said to me. I'm going to fucking kill that fucker, Brian. He told her everything.

"Baby listen to me. I was going to tell you. I just got caught up with everything that was going on. Plus, with Mia and Law trying to keep me all together." I began to say before she cut me off.

"What does Mia and Law have to do with this. This is between you and me." She yelled.

"Well they are in a relationship now." I informed her.

"Ok. So now what? She's a part of your crew too?" She asked.

"Yes but I did not agree to that. She joined through Law." I yelled out.

"I really can't deal with this shit right now. I'm out of here." She said.

"Baby please don't go. I love you." I told her as I then started to breathe heavily. " I know you feel the same for me too."

"If Only You Knew." She said and she then disconnected the call.

"She's leaving me. And she said she found Sylvia dead. Let's go." I said to Law and Tech and we ran up out of there to head to the mansion.

SIERRA

Once I hung up the phone on Sean. I called a taxi to pick me up to take me to the airport. I didn't know where I was going. All I knew was that I was taking the first flight out of here. Once I got to the airport, I ditched the phone by throwing it in the trash and went to the desk to look at the flights. The first flight was to Miami. Fuck it. That's where I'm going.

"Is there any seats left for the Miami flight?" I asked the lady at the desk.

"Yes mam if you are going to board, we have to get you through quickly as the flight will take off within the next 30 minutes." The clerk said.

"Fine. I don't have anything but my purse. Here's my license and card. I don't care how much the seat is. Just get me the fuck out of here." I yelled out dramatically.

"Yes mam." The clerk said as she eventually finished up the process and gave me my ticket. I got on the plane just in time as they were calling for last call for all boarders. The plane began to take off and I was gone. Leaving everything behind me.

SEAN

As I stood here and watched the only woman I ever knew as mother getting cleaned up by my two best friends, broke the fuck out of me. I never thought I would be looking at Sylvia dead in her own pool of blood. She raised me. She protected me every time she could from my fucked-up ass parents. The thing about all this, is I know I'm supposed to cry. Deal with my grief, at least that's what normal people do. But right now, all I want to do is kill somebody. That's all I ever wanted to do since the first time I caught my first body. To lose the two most important women in my life the same day is killing me. I have to bury the women I loved as my mother and now I have to find my baby's mother. Life was a bitch and she definitely fucked me.

19 THE UNEXPECTED

SIERRA

It's already been 3 months since I last seen Sean and Mia. I can't lie and say that I don't miss them because I do. Sean eventually stopped calling me every day. He called for 2 months straight all day every day. I had nothing to say but a part of me felt as though it was for the best. I have to give a better life for my child. I decided to keep the baby because it wasn't fair to the baby if I got an abortion all because of the life that his father lives. My baby deserved a chance. I got my name changed so no one could contact me. I know how good Sean's team was so I hoped this works to prevent him from finding me. I'm sitting here at the doctor's office as I'm waiting on my monthly check up.

"So Ms. Reid, Labs came back and everything looks perfect." The doctor said.

"That's great. So, what is the pain that I'm having?" I asked her.

"It's called Braxton Hicks. They are minor contractions your body will continue to get as your body is preparing for delivery. If the pain intensifies and start coming 1 to 3 minutes apart then we are in trouble. Do you want to know the sex of the baby?" Doctor Molly asked.

"Yes. Can you tell me?" I asked her.

"Sure, lay back for me and I'll give you a quick ultrasound. As always, it's going to feel cold on your stomach." She said and I giggled. This was one of my favorite parts. Being able to hear my baby's heartbeat and seeing a picture of the baby. I'm so amazed at the way they grow inside of you.

"So here is your baby's head. Here's the hands and feet. And here in the middle you have a baby boy. Congratulations." She said and my mouth dropped. I was having a son. All I could think about was Sean. I knew he would have been jumping for joy. But I'm doing what's best for my son.

"Thank you. I'm so excited. Now I know what to buy." I said and she laughed.

"Yes, well that's the perks of not waiting till birth. Pregnancy can be very stressful at this point in time. Your 5 months now. Everything matters. So, continue to eat healthy, drink plenty of water, take your vitamins, and practice your breathing for delivery." Doctor Molly informed me.

"Perfect. Thank you so much Molly." I voiced to her.

"Your welcome. Last thing. Because this is your first child and you're getting further along in your pregnancy I want to start seeing you every two weeks. Do you have any questions for me?" She asked.

"No thank you Dr. Molly you have been great." I stated to her.

"Good I'll leave you too it and I'll see you in two weeks." She said and she then walked out of the room. I began to breathe in and out. I checked out of the doctor's office and headed home. I really hope I'm doing the right thing. I looked down as my phone began to ring. Surprisingly it was Sean. I pressed ignored. Maybe one day I will answer. But it won't be today. I was tired so I was going to take a nap.

SEAN

It's been 3 months since Sierra left me and she still has yet to answer my calls. I stopped calling for a while hoping that maybe if I stopped pushing and gave her the time, she would eventually call me. Or maybe if I tried to call again, she would answer. I decided to push my luck and tried calling her again. She still didn't answer. Fuck. I'm trying to understand her. I really am but I don't know how much more I could take. As I threw the phone Mia walked up to me.

"You're still calling her, aren't you?" She asked. I began to breathe out heavily.

"I can't help it, Mia. I don't know if she is okay. I don't know if she had an abortion or if she's pregnant is she doing okay. I don't know anything." I informed me.

"I'm pretty sure she is okay. You have to give Sierra time. She will come around eventually." Mia said.

"I hope so Mia. I still love her. But I'm not sure how much longer I can keep trying. I don't want to walk away but it feels like she's giving me no other choice." I told her.

"Listen I get it. Just continue to be strong." Mia said as she put her hand on my shoulder and walked away. I was getting frustrated. Maybe if I just knew if she was having the baby everything would be okay. At least so I thought.

SIERRA

After I woke up from my nap, I decided to do a little work in the yard. It's getting harder and harder for me to bend down so I'm trying my best to do what I can while I can still bend somewhat.

"Hey Beautiful." The voice said as I turned around. It was Marc my next-door neighbor. I can't lie he was fine as wine. If I was going to move on, I had to start somewhere, right?

"Hey Marc" I said as I began to blush.

"You know you should not be bending down the way that you are. I told you if you ever needed help with the yard to call me. I don't mind doing it for you. A pregnant woman's body is beautiful and precious. You should be getting your feet rubbed or soaked in a hot tub." He said.

"Marc you're so sweet. I really try not to ask that much of you. I don't want to seem like a burden." I explained to him.

"Beautiful that is something that you could never be. So, I'm going to take over here and I want you to go and kick up those beautiful feet. By the way, I still really think you should take me up on that offer and let me take you out on a date." He said to me in a convincing tone. I have to admit I've been turning him down for months because all I could think about was Sean. But I have to move on. I have to live my life without him.

"How's 7?" I asked him.

"I don't think a man could be any happier than right now." He said.

"Later Marc." I waved as I then walked went in the house to rest before it was time for me to get ready.

SEAN

I can't eat. I can't sleep. I can't even think without knowing that she is okay. Why can't she just pick up the phone and tell me that she is, okay? I even had a balcony built outside of my window just so I could go out there and think. To attempt to keep my sanity. But I don't know how much more I could take. As I then continued to get lost in my thoughts, I received a text from Law.

"Sean you need to get your ass down here quick." He texted.

"What's going on? This better be important." I replied to him.

"Its Renee. She's been shot!" He replied and I immediately dropped my phone. What the fuck? I then headed downstairs.

"Dammit Mia and Emily what the fuck happened?" Law yelled.

"We don't know!" Mia yelled out as she began to cry.

"We were out scouting some guys and next thing you know there were gunshots. We pulled out our piece but we couldn't spot a shooter on sight. It had to been a hitman." Emily said and I just continued to listen as my eyes couldn't believe what they were seeing. I never thought that one of my girls would get hurt. That's why I don't have them do the business we do on the dangerous end.

"Shit Renee, I need you to stay with me." Law said as he then tried to put pressure on her wound. Rage then began to come over me as I knew what that meant.

"Emily and Mia go and go back out there and see what you can find out. Take Tech with you. Keep your phone on you at all times. If anyone even looks suspect shoot their ass on sight you hear me." I yelled and they nodded and ran off to get Tech.

"It's been long enough it's time to bring Lee home." I told Law.

"Yes, go ahead and call him." Law said as I then picked up my phone to call him.

"Shit, he's not even answering the damn phone." I yelled and I walked off to go smoke. I didn't know what else to do.

LAW

As I sat here and tried to stop Renee from bleeding out tears ran over my eyes. We're family and it's like losing Sylvia all over again.

"Law." Renee sighed.

"Shh Shh, now. We'll talk later when you're all healed." I told her.

"You and I both know that this wound is to damaging to fix. Now shut up and listen to me" She said.

"Ok." I said.

"I'm pregnant. And tell your brother I'm sorry. I didn't have enough time to tell him. He would have made a great father." She said.

"Are you fucking kidding me right now. I'm going to be an uncle." I yelled out.

"No, you were. But I know my time here is almost up. I want him to be able to love again. I don't want him to grieve me forever. Make sure that he loves again Law. He's going to need you when I go. I love you guys." She said as she then sighed out.

"Renee no wait." I said as I then seen she was unconscious. Fuck. I can't let her die. I hope there's still time. I have to fix this wound now and quickly. I have to do this the right way. I have to get my niece or nephew to live. They have to see the light of day. I have to fix this. And for the first time in forever, I started crying. I can't lose her. She was my sister.

SIERRA

It was time to go as Marc then knocked on my door to pick me up. We headed to a restaurant as he already had a table booked for the two of us.

"My my my, I just have to say it again. You look really beautiful tonight. Every man should feel on cloud nine just by having you in front of him." He said.

"Thank you Marc you look great yourself." I informed him.

"So tell me Sierra now that we finally get to have some time together. Do you plan on getting back together with your baby's father? I'm not trying to pry but I just want to know how far I need to take it before I let my heart get involved." He said to me. He was bold but I could respect it.

"Unfortunately, my child's father isn't the best role model to have a child around." I replied to him confidently.

"Do you still love him?" He asked and all I could do was sigh.

"Of course I do. I fell in love with him even when I shouldn't have. We had a special connection that drew us together. Regardless of how many lies he told me." I said to Marc.

"I would love to know what happened with you two. So, I won't make the same mistake." He said to me boldly. As good as it sounded, I could never turn my back on Sean. I could never tell his secrets to anyone it was nobody's business but ours.

"He broke my heart and that's all there is too it. I'd rather not talk about it. What you can do is never lie to me." I stated to him demandingly.

"It must have really been hard for you. You're not alone Sierra. I want to be there for you. I want to be there when you're mad. I want to be there when you're sad. I want to be the shoulder that you cry on. I want to hold your hand while you push that beautiful baby out. Rub your feet, massage you in a hot tub. Make love to you every night. Trust me Sierra. We are all not the same." He said trying to convince me. I heard him but I didn't hear him. So, I tried to change the subject and we just talked for the rest of the night. There was nothing but laughs, smiles and no judgement. But who am I kidding, Marc maybe as fine as wine but he could never be Sean? How is it that I'm on a date and still have to talk about him? Still have to think about him. I hope any man realizes that making me have to talk about him is not going to make me get over him. Maybe I never will. Once we finished up dinner, we left so he could take me home. Mama was tired.

SEAN

After I went to try and clear my head, I went back in to try and check on things with Renee. Once I got there, I no longer saw Renee on the floor.

"Law where's Renee, how is she?" I asked and he just began to cry.

"This can't be fucking happening I walked away with finally a tear in my eye. I couldn't believe it. Renee was dead. And I couldn't help but to feel that this was all my fault. I shouldn't have had them out there looking for men when we were getting ready for war. This shit was fucked up man. But all I could do now is call her brother Marc and let him know about the death of his sister.

SIERRA

"I had a really great time tonight, Marc. Thank you." I said to him as I was going through my bag to search for my keys.

"Anytime babe. Let's do this again real soon." He said as he got closer to me as if he wanted a kiss but my phone buzzed and it was a text from Sean.

"Please call me. Renee died." It read and my mouth dropped.

"Sorry Marc I gotta go." I yelled out and I rushed in my house and laid in my bed. My mind was blown. But as of tonight, I was going to rest. What happened to her? This is so unexpected. But I had to call him. It was only right.

20 THE SERVICE

SEAN

I texted Sierra to let her know what was going on. And still there was no response. She could have at least sent her condolences. It's not right. I'm still a person. I'm still human. If she thinks I'm a monster now, what would she think of me when she finds out how dark I could really get. Only the mind could wonder but right now I have to call Marc. I was glad he answered the phone.

"Sean, my man. It's been a while. How have you been?" Marc said.

"It has been a while. Unfortunately, I'm sorry to be calling under these circumstances." I expressed to him.

"What's going on? You sound sad." Marc said.

"Renee died Marc." I informed him sadly.

"Wait a minute, is this some kind of sick joke? I haven't spoken to you in over three years and you call to tell me that my sister is fucking dead? When I got out of prison you were supposed to watch out for her. This is all your fault." He yelled out as then hung up the phone. Dammit Renee. My phone then began to ring. It was Sierra. My heart began to drop.

"I'm glad you called." I said as soon as I picked up the phone. "Sierra are you there?"

"What happened to Renee?" She asked. Damn. So, fuck me still huh?

"She was shot. She lost too much blood." I explained.

"I'm sorry to hear about that." She said and she began to breathe heavily.

"We're going to be having a small ceremony for her and you're more than welcome to come." I said to her and the phone began to get quiet again. We both began to breathe heavy. I finally decided to break the silence.

"Sierra, listen I think we should" I began to say and she then cut me off.

"I have to go" She said.

"Wait don't go." I said and she disconnected the call. I then threw my phone. This was too much emotions in one night. I needed to attempt to get some rest.

SIERRA

I shouldn't be crying. What is wrong with me? I don't know if I'm crying because Renee died or because this is the first time, I heard his voice since I stopped answering his calls. The pain in his voice made my heart skipped a beat. First Sylvia then I left and now Renee is dead. His pain made me feel as if he needed me the same way I think I need him deep down inside. And here I am crying. And to think he didn't even attempt to call me back after I hung up this time.

Did he finally move on? Was another woman kissing him? Tongue dancing with him. Sleeping next to him in my bed? Screaming his name while he made love to her all night. Does he massage her body? Caress her body the way he did mine when we made love? Does he love her more than he loved me? Is she cool with his brothers? Did Mia and the girls love her?

Wait a minute. Renee died. But here I am. Crying out for him. Maybe if I could just get one more kiss. Once more touch. One more time to make love. Maybe I will go the service to say my goodbyes and attempt to try and get my man back. Maybe I just might. Maybe.

3 DAYS LATER

SIERRA

As I boarded the plane to make my way back to New York City my heart kept dropping. Today's the day I get to see his face for the first time since everything happened. Should I be worried? No. But am I? Yes. Deep down since I heard the sound of his voice all of my feelings for him came back to life. I want him. I needed him. I should of gave him a chance to explain. Despite everything I know there has to be some kind of explanation. My heart keeps saying take him back your souls are connected. But my mind is telling me this is a mistake. This is how it's supposed to be.

Attention all passengers. We will be landing in New York City in 15 minutes.

I began to breathe. It was almost time to face him. "I do not miss him". I kept saying to myself the whole 15 minutes until the plane finally landed. I got in the car and headed to the service. I made sure to pick a spot that stayed out of the way because I didn't yet want to be seen by anyone.

"We want to thank everyone who came today to say their farewells to Renee McBride. But as requested by Renee before she died there will be no viewing of the body. She did not want anyone to see her this way." Law spoke. Tech then walked up to the casket crying. He was heartbroken. Was him and Renee seeing each other? Law then kissed the casket as he then went to catch up to Tech to give him comfort. I then watched Mia as she came up crying. Deep down I knew they would bond even closer. Tears began to roll down my eyes as I'm watching on all the things I missed. The bonds that could have been made with me if I was still here. Next there was Emily.

"What am I going to do without my best friend?" Emily cried out as she then passed out. Tech and Law ran to her to pick her up. It was heartbreaking. I can't imagine what it would have been like for me to lose Mia. Sean finally walked up to the casket.

"I'm going to kill that son of a bitch who did this to you. They will pay. Even if I have to kill every motherfucker in this city. I love you, Renee." He said as he then kissed the casket and I watched him as he walked out. I cried as I listened to him. It broke my heart. I needed to see him today. I grabbed my things as I then started to head to the door.

"I let you down sis. I'm sorry." a voice said that sounded so familiar. I turned back to look and it was Marc. Sister? What the fuck Marc?

"I should of came back for you. I'm so sorry Renee." Marc said as he then ran off crying. I couldn't believe it. But as of right now I had bigger fish to fry. I headed to the mansion. It was now or never. Once I got to the mansion, I rang the doorbell and Mia answered the door.

"Sierra!" She yelled in excitement and hugged me.

"I've missed you so much. And the baby bump. Oh my God we have so much catching up to do" Mia said.

"Yes, we do. But first I need to talk to Sean." I informed her.

"I can understand that. He's probably out there on the balcony." Mia said.

"Balcony?" I asked confused.

"Yeah he had a balcony built on his floor after you left. He goes out there to think. He was heartbroken when you left and so was I. But I know you. That's why I eventually stopped calling. I've seen you shut down before but this one was a little different. I didn't know what else to do except stop calling." Mia said.

"That's exactly what I wanted. I couldn't face everything that was going on at the time. I needed space. But right now, I just want to give Emily and hug and talk to Sean." I told her as she nodded and walked me over to where Tech, Emily and Law were standing.

"Hey guys I'm so sorry for y'all loss. As I told them and I hugged Law and Tech. I walked over to Emily and I wrapped her tight.

"I'm here if you ever need me." I told her and she nodded.

"Tell me y'all see the baby bump" Mia said.

"I see it but no disrespect I can't be happy right now. My best friend is dead and I don't think I'll ever be the same. I'll definitely talk to you later Sierra." She said as she then left out the living room with tears in her eyes.

"Tech you have to say something. You haven't spoken a single word since this happened." Law said and Tech remained silent.

"Okay so how about this little brother. I know you were in love with Renee. I've seen the way the two of you use to look at each. You and Renee kept it a secret so Sean wouldn't find out. I always knew. I never said anything. Tech, Sean may be my right-hand man but you're my little brother. You don't ever have to keep anything from me. Your secrets are always safe with me. We're going to catch the son of a bitch responsible for this and put their ass on a platter. That's my promise to you little brother." Law said as he then walked off. I turned to look at Tech as tears rolled down his eyes. I hugged him as I then went to Sean's floor and found the balcony. As I was walking up, I could hear him talking.

"Listen I feel as bad as is. I don't need you coming out here blaming me for shit." Sean said.

"As you should. You we're supposed to be protecting her." Marc said.

"What the fuck did you want me to do? You act like I knew this was going to happen." Sean yelled out.

"That's not the damn point." Marc yelled.

"No I'm going to tell you what the point is. The point is that you feel guilty and want to blame all this shit on me. I was a better brother to Renee that you ever were. You only called and spoke to Renee twice since you got out and that was three years ago. Who the fuck goes three years without talking to their only sister? Now get the fuck out of my house! The only thing keeping you alive right now is the fact that you are Renee's brother."

Sean yelled.

"You're going to pay for this Sean." Marc said.

"Yeah? Well, make me pay for it now while you're still here. You know I'll have your fucking head floating in the damn ocean. You know the beast in me. Just say the word and I'll bring him out" Sean warned Marc and Marc just stomped off. I slid behind the door so he couldn't see.

"Send your best men! Bitch ass motherfucker." Sean yelled out behind Marc as he then left without saying another word. I then started to walk towards him as he then looked back out over the balcony.

"I got enough shit going on and he thinks he can threaten me. I'm the man. I run New York. Anybody want my crown will have to kill me first" He yelled out.

"I mean why not. I got nothing else to lose anyway." He said as he softens up.

"I mean your obviously losing your mind. But hey, I'm not here to judge." I said and he then turned around shocked.

21 FACE TO FACE

SEAN

When I heard Sierra's voice, I was shocked. I didn't think she would have come. And to see her baby bump. She kept the baby. My heart began to melt. She looked so beautiful. She was glowing. I couldn't get the words to come out.

"I apologize if I startled you in anyway." She said.

"Wow Sierra. Pregnancy really suits you. You look beautiful." I expressed to her with gratitude.

"Thank you Sean, I'm" She began to say as I cut her off.

"5 months along I know." I informed her.

"How did you know?" She asked.

"Sierra, you are carrying my child. I was the first to know you were pregnant. I wasn't sure if you kept the baby or not but still in my mind, I counted every fucking day. Every month. Dreaming I was at every doctor's appointment." I said to her.

"I know this isn't the right time but I really think we should talk." She said.

"Yeah we should." I replied shortly.

"You have to know that you hurt me really bad. I told you too always be honest with me." She said as she began to cry and I could feel the pain in her heart.

"Sierra don't cry. Stress isn't good for the baby. I know I fucked up and I know I hurt you and I apologize for that. But does that justify you running away and not let me know what was going on with my child? Not knowing if you were dead or alive. If there was or was not going to be a baby. Yeah, that shit hurt too. I was hurt to. And I'm no longer going to try and keep you. I just want to be there for my child that's all I ask." I said to her.

"I don't know Sean. I don't want our child around that life." She said and I got pissed. These were the fucking games I did not have time for. Not right now!

"What the fuck do you mean? You knew the life I had before we did all this." I yelled and then I began to think about it. I had to get her to see things in my view.

"Listen I didn't mean to hurt you in any possible way. If I would have told you the things that you knew now, what would it really have changed? I asked her. I was curious about her answer.

SIERRA

Somehow what he just said actually made sense. Would it had change anything? Maybe I wouldn't have been carrying this beautiful bundle of joy inside of me. He knows I hate lies I told him that the day we first sat down. At least I would have known then before I caught feelings. Maybe we would have still had a chance with the truth. Maybe it's time I hear him out.

"Tell me, if I ask you questions will you be honest with me now?" I asked him.

"What would you like to know?" He said.

"Did you kill your parents?" I asked him.

"I did Sierra. My mother and father use to torture me. My mother and father use to run the city and Bryans family was always their enemy. They offered Brian's family to kill me to settle the score between them. But before them they tried to start training me at an early age to be a part of this. But I was a child. I had my own dreams. I didn't ask for none of this shit. I wanted to be a doctor as a kid. As so I thought. Those bastards would tie me up and throw me in a basement and I wouldn't eat for days." He said.

"But I thought Sylvia raised you?" I asked curiously.

"She did. When she used to ask my parents about my whereabouts, they use to tell her I was at a friend's house while I would be in a basement starving to fucking death. Until one day she happened to walk in the basement looking for supplies and there she found me. I hadn't eaten for three days. No food. No water." He explained to me.

"Oh my God Sean, you don't have to tell me any" I began to say and he cut me off.

"No it's about time I talk about this. Sylvia went crazy. She untied me immediately. My parents were gone on a business trip that day and I told her everything. She made sure I ate. Bathe. She was furious. I never seen her that mad in my life still till this day. She always knew they treated me bad but she never expected them to do that to me and leave me for dead. The day she confronted them about it they threatened to kill her if she called the cops and if she even thought about quitting, they threatened to kill her. From that day forward I was planning a way out. There whole point in trying to kill me was because I didn't want to be what they wanted me to be.

So, I let them believe I was going to take over. I let them train me. Let them believe I wanted nothing more than to take over the family business. But what they didn't realize is that they were creating a monster. I originally planned to kill them and then just live my life as a doctor. But that day I killed them it felt so good. I released years of anger while stabbing them. Sylvia walked in and pulled me off of them. But she already knew it was bound to happen. She knew I was tired. So, we both go rid of their bodies.

People were curious of course about what happened. Rumors went around about me killing my parents. But word to mouth could never get you behind bars. As long as there was no evidence there was no case. From that day forward I vowed to never let another son a bitch hurt me or cross me. But instead, I didn't become a doctor. I became a killer. I loved the way killing a man made me felt. I was young and dumb. But a part of me changed as the years went on. All I had was Sylvia, Tech and Law. We were all we had since Tech and Laws mother was a prostitute. We always depended on each other to survive. And we promised to always ride together or die together." He said.

"What happened to your parents' body?" I asked him out of curiosity. Even though his story was very fucked up. I'm starting to feel like I fucked up. I should of gave him a chance to explain.

"Hungry gators ate them. So that sums up everything about my parents." He said.

"Do you regret anything about your family?" I asked him.

"If you mean do I regret killing my parents. No. It's the life they chose for me and them." He spoke so bluntly.

"Did you already know about Brian?" I asked.

"I didn't. But the day I saw those pictures I thought he looked like someone but I didn't put it together." He responded to me.

"We're you only trying to be with me because I was a liability?" I asked him.

"Why would I do that? I told you if I ever lied to you, it was for your best interest. I fell for you way earlier than I should have." He yelled.

"So would you ever try to kill me if it was necessary?" I asked him. And I can't lie. I wasn't sure if my heart was even ready for the answer.

"I was afraid this question would come up. Honestly at the beginning yes. But that was before I fell in love with you and you are carrying my child. That's a gift I'd never take away from either of us." He said and I couldn't say anything. Honest was what I wanted and I got it. It was up to me now whether I wanted to deal with it or let everything go.

"Did you find out who killed Renee yet?" I asked.

"No and when I do, I will kill again." He said angrily. Demanding.

"I think those were the main questions that I had." I said to him.

"Yeah, well it was time for you to know the truth. You deserved it." He expressed to me.

CURRENTLY SOMEWHERE IN NYC

"How long would you say he's been down?" Officer Louis asked.

"The blood is fresh. I want to say no more than a couple hours." Detective Lisa said as they continue to inspect the crime scene and take pictures.

"I've seen this outfit before that the victim has on. I just can't seem to put my finger on it." Detective Lisa informed Officer Louis as she continues to take pictures and write in her notepad.

"I haven't seen this outfit before so if you could figure out where you seen it from that would be great." Officer Louis said to the Detective.

"I tell you what, whatever is going on in this city I'm about to put an end to it. And I have a very good feeling Sean White is behind this body we just found." Detective Lisa said confidently.

SEAN

"So, what now?" She asked.

"I don't expect for you to process all of this in one night. But you should know. I know I hurt you. But in the end, you hurt me too when you left. I didn't know if you were alive or dead. Whether there was a baby or not." I expressed to her again.

"So what are you saying?" She asked.

"I'm saying come back home. I forgive you no matter what. I just want to be there for my child." I informed her.

"I have to ask. Was their anyone else besides me?" She asked me. How could she even think that? She doesn't know the half of the shit I went through when she left.

"Anyone else. Sierra I can't breathe without you. I can't sleep without you. Dinner wasn't the same without you. The other side of the pillow was lonely without you. You are the one for me. Was their anyone besides me while you were gone?" I asked her as my heart began to beat faster.

"I actually went on 1 date. It was with my neighbor." She told me so honestly.

"Is it over?" I asked her.

"Yes it's over. It never began, it was only one date." She said as she then walked up to me and kissed me. I've been waiting on this moment. As she continued to kiss me, I began to hear footsteps.

"You know what Sean" Marc yelled out and both Sierra and I turned around and Marc reacted in shocked. He wasn't surprised to see me. He was surprised to see Sierra. And I want to know the fuck why. I was going to get some answers about this shit.

22 DEVELOPING STORY

SIERRA

"Sierra, what the hell are you doing here with him?" Marc yelled out.

"Why the hell does it matter to you? And how the fuck do the two of you know each other?" Sean asked furiously.

"How's that any different than what I just said." Marc yelled.

"Keep talking and I'm going to put a bullet through your shit right now." Sean said.

"I'd like to see you try it. You wouldn't dare shoot me in front of her." Marc yelled out.

"Wanna bet?" Sean said so demandingly as he lit up his cigarette and blew the smoke in Marc's face. I can't lie it was so sexy. But I had to stop it.

"Okay that's enough." I yelled and I turned to face Sean.

"He's the neighbor I told you I had a date with." I explained to him and boy why did I do that. His whole body shifted gears. He was ready for something that I knew was just going to be bad for Marc.

"Oh yeah?" He said as he then took another puff of the cigarette and blew the smoke in Marc's face.

"Ima really put a bullet in his shit now. And I'm assuming you both talked about what exactly?" Sean asked and then he moved me to the side and then pulled his gun out. He was in rage and I could see it all over his face.

"Calm down. She didn't tell me anything about you except that you broke her heart and she didn't want to talk about it. Seems like you finally know how to pick a loyal bitch." Marc said and I knew right then and there it was going to be trouble.

SEAN

You know it was one thing for him to come in my house and blame me for Renee's death. But not only did he take my baby mama on a date he has the nerve to disrespect her right in front of me at that. He was a bold motherfucker and I was about to kill him. I moved Sierra to the side and pulled out my gun.

"Go to hell Marc." I said and I pulled the trigger. One shot to the head. I then put my gun back in place.

"Tech come clean this shit up." I yelled out and Sierra ran away quietly. Shit. I done fucked up again. But he called my bluff and I don't play that shit.

"I'm sorry babe. It was in the heat of the moment." I said and Law came running towards me.

"What the fuck Sean? What happened to Marc?" Law said.

"I killed his ass that's what happened. Besides I called Tech. Not you." I yelled out.

"Tech and Emily aren't holding up well Sean. Tech hasn't spoken to anyone in days and I'm his blood brother." Law said. I'm not going to lie, I heard him. But dammit I needed to vent. This dirty ass motherfucker really tried to call my bluff.

"That son of bitch thinks he can show up to my house and try to blame me for Renee's death and he wasn't even half a brother to her. Then he went on a date with my baby mama. I'm not having none of that shit." I yelled out and Law began to laugh.

"And here I thought I was the crazy one since you slowed down." Law said as he continued to laugh.

"Clean this shit up will ya. I'm going to check on Tech and then Sierra." I told Law as he nodded and began cleaning up Marcs dead body. Fuck him.

AT THE POLICE STATION

"So, here's where we're at. It wasn't hard to get the victim's identity because the victim has been in our system before." Detective Lisa said.

"Well, who was it detective?" Officer Louis asked.

"Lee Phillips." Detective Lisa said and Office Louis mouth drops.

"Do you know this could cause." Officer Louis began to say before the detective cut him off.

"A war on the streets. Yes, I know. On the bright side we also caught a break in another case." Detective Lisa said.

"And what's that?" Officer Louis asked.

"Lee Phillips was wearing the same disguise as the persons of interest in the case with Sean White on trial when they killed the judge and jurors." The detective said.

"So that means?" The officer asked.

"That this whole thing was a set up. I'm going to crack this case once and for all. And I will not stop until Sean White is behind bars for the rest of his pathetic life." Detective Lisa said.

"To be honest, that doesn't necessarily mean that. These streets change every day. And how do we know this Lee Phillips was even in Sean White's crew. We've never seen any of his people." Officer Louis said to Detective Lisa.

"Are you taking his side Officer Louis?" Detective Lisa asked.

"I'm on the side of the justice system. We all know he has Sierra Johnson as his attorney. If our story isn't straight, she's going to eat our ass alive in that courtroom." Officer Louis replied. "All I'm saying is don't let your obsession with Sean White fuck up this case. That's my opinion."

"So, what are you suggesting?" The detective asked.

"I'm not suggesting anything you are the detective on the case. I can only give you an opinion. And everyone here knows I'm fucking good at my job. So, I can only advise that you take a good look through all of this because Sean White and his gang are not the only ones in these streets. They all deal with things everyday that no one in the justice department knows about." Officer Louis said.

"I'll take it into consideration. Oh, and before I forget Lee Phillips is the son of the main Pathologist of the lab all of our autopsy reports come from. I can't imagine how she's feeling." Detective Lisa stated.

"Yeah, me either." Officer Louis said as he then walked away from Detective Lisa and headed back to his office.

SEAN

I checked everywhere for Tech. But there was only one place left that he could be. The camera room. Once I walked in, I saw him. I couldn't help but hurt for him.

"Till death do us part my love." He whispered out.

"Tech we need to talk." I said and he then continued to say nothing.

"Will you say something please. I'm your best friend. We're all going through the same thing." I said trying to relate to him.

"And that's where you're wrong." Tech said as he then turned to face me.

"I was in love with her. We been together for a few years now. We hid it from you because we always knew how you felt about relationships within the family. That day I hit on Sierra was just a cover up. I'm so mad I just want to kill every motherfucker that comes in my sight. But I can't because I don't know who did it. And making more enemies would be stupid. She was supposed to be my wife, Sean. I planned on asking her to marry me this weekend. She thought we were just planning to tell everyone about our relationship but I had other plans while doing so." Tech said as he then began to cry. I went up to him and hugged him.

"We'll get through this together T. We will get the son of a bitch who did this trust me." I told him and he still cried. I know I can't take away his pain but I want to at least try to make him laugh.

"I guess its bad timing to tell you that I killed Marc." I said to him dramatically.

"We just put Renee in the ground and you killed Marc. What the fuck happened?" He yelled.

"That son of a bitch came up here talking shit. I warned him multiple times. He kept going on and on trying to blame me for Renee's death like he was any type of brother to her. I told him get the fuck out and he threaten me. Telling me I was gone pay for everything. And then that son of a bitch goes out on a date with Sierra." I yelled and Tech began to laugh.

"I was just going to whoop his ass with my fucking pistol but then he calls Sierra a bitch. So, he got a bullet to his fucking brain." I said and Tech laughed again.

"Damn, Marc should have known it was coming. He knows the last person he wants to take it there with is you. People forget about the shit we use to put these motherfuckers through. You were the worse. Oh well shit happens." Tech said and then he began to get sad again.

"We'll get through this. Don't shut us out. We need each other more now than ever." I said and he nodded.

"So, pregnancy really suits Sierra. She looks really beautiful." Tech said.

"Tell me about it. I want to put another one in there." I said and Tech busted out in laughter.

"But now I have to deal with the fact that I shot Marc in front of her. So that's more bullshit I have to deal with I should go and check on her." I said and Tech giggled.

"But before I go, I should tell you." I said to him.

"What?" Tech asked.

"Do you know why I always use to pair you and Renee together?" I asked him in a curious tone.

"No why did you?" Tech asked.

"I know each and every one of you like the back of my fucking hand. I always knew about you and Renee Tech. I just never said anything and I was waiting for you guys to tell me. But one thing is for sure. I love you Tech and I'm always here for you no matter the situation. You never have to hide anything from me no matter what it is." I said to him and I then walked out the door to go deal with Sierra.

SIERRA

Never in my life did I even think I would witness Sean killing someone in front of me. I know I killed that hitman but damn to see someone else get shot in the head and watch their blood splatter. I know Sean blacked out and I get it. The gunshot sounds are still ringing in my ears as I was standing right next to his hand. I'm not going to say that Marc didn't provoke the situation because he did. And I know Sean may never change but is this the life I want for our child? Hell, I even tried to get a law degree so I could no longer have to deal with my past shit. Will we always have to face the fact that we're in danger? Constantly looking over our shoulders. I pray there is a better way.

"Sierra I" Sean began to say as breaking news then came on the television.

"Good evening, everyone I'm Julie with Channel 32 news. We are live with breaking news. Police and investigators have identified the body of a man found in an alley way. George tell us what information you were able to gather from the crime scene." Julie said.

"Thank you, Julie. We are live outside of the police department and so far from what we know is that officers received a phone call of sounds of gunshots in the area. Once officers arrived, they found a man in a mask dead from a gunshot wound to the head. We have no suspects at this time. Officers have identified the victim as Lee Phillips. This is a developing story. Investigators has ruled his death as a homicide. Back over to you Julie." George said.

"Thank you, George. We will have more on this investigation as this story continues." Julie said and I then turned the television off and faced Sean. He then yelled out. I knew things were about to get bad.

23 ANYTHING FOR YOU

SIERRA

"How the fuck does this keep happening? Someone is out here killing my people off" Sean yelled out. I then stood up out the bed.

"First of all don't come in here pointing no damn fingers towards me. I'm not the one who shot his ass." I yelled back. And I can't lie that was low. "I'm sorry that came out wrong."

"Its fine I know what you meant. I just wish I knew who was behind all of this. I'm not even sure if this is even Brian anymore. Things with them have been quiet since you were gone. I honestly don't know how much more people I can take dying around me. " Sean said.

"Have you ever thought about who could be behind this?" I asked him.

"Baby if I knew I would tell you." He responded.

"And you sure you don't think its Brian? I mean he did kidnap me last time. He wasn't too fond of our relationship. Plus, he knew I was pregnant. Maybe he stopped so he wouldn't look suspicious when things start happening again." I attempted to explain to him.

"It's possible. But if he is, I swear I'll find him personally and kill him. There's no way in hell I'm letting anyone kill him but me. I will die to protect you and our baby. You have to know that. Both of you are my family now." He said and a silence rolled over us. I don't know if it was because we needed to clear up the elephant in the room or if we both just didn't know what else to say. So, I decided to tell him how I really felt.

"Listen I don't want you to think that I hate you because of what happened. I was just more shocked than anything. I know you would do anything to protect me and Marc crossed the line he knew would have pissed you off. Can I maybe just get a little heads-up next time?" I said and he laughed.

"Anything for you baby." He said.

"I would like to ask you something if that's okay." I asked in attempt.

"Anything." He said.

"Don't you think it's weird that you haven't seen Lee in so long and now all of a sudden he's dead. What if he's involved somehow? Are you sure you can trust him? Something about this just doesn't seem right." I told him and he began to think.

"I'm not sure but if he is the truth will always come out." He said.

"Speaking of truth, I never exactly told you how I got away from Brian that night." I said to him.

"No, you didn't, so how did you?" He asked.

"I had to sleep with him. I didn't want to. But I knew if I did, he would fall asleep afterwards and I could get the key and leave. He could never know my body the way you do." I told him and he got angry at first before he softens up.

"I wish those were not the circumstances but it is in the past now. And deep down I know you only did it because you were trying to escape. And trust me I'll always make sure no one will ever know your body the way I do." Sean said.

"I just didn't want us to go back into all this with a bunch of lies." I explained.

"Your right baby. So, truth for truth.?" He said.

"What is it?" I asked curious on what else he could be hiding.

"I was the mastermind behind the shootings in the courthouse. I didn't know how much I could have trusted you at the time. I always wanted to tell you I just didn't know how. You're the best lawyer in the city and I figured that maybe if I didn't tell you then you would of took my case." He tried to explain to me. I was so angry with him I could kill him myself. Maybe it's the hormones talking because deep down inside I already knew. I just didn't have proof.

"I should kill you right now!" I yelled out.

"For what?" He said.

"Because if you go down for this our child is going to grow up without a father." I yelled.

"Baby that won't happen." He said.

"How can you be so sure." I said and I started yelling and then I began punching him in the chest.

"I should fucking kill you right now! How could you be so damn stupid?" I yelled and he pulled me in close to him.

"What are you doing?" I asked shyly.

"Will you calm down. I already told you that nothing is going to happen to you and our baby. I will protect you by any means necessary. Do you understand me" He said demandingly.

"Yes" I replied softly.

"Yes what?" He asked.

"Sir." I said submissive.

"Good girl." He said as he rubbed his fingers over my neck.

"You have to say you would protect me and our son by any means necessary." I informed him.

"What?" He asked.

"The baby is a boy." I said and he then pressed him lips into mine. Damn. He knew how to shut me up. If it's going to be like this, I need to misbehave all the time. I missed his touch. I missed his kiss. I missed his lips. I missed **HIM** and tonight I planned on showing him that. I pushed him down on the bed as I bit the bottom of his shirt to help lift it over his head. I put my hand in his pants so I could feel his dick. I missed it. I unbuckled his pants as I pulled them down on the floor. I whipped him out as I put all of him in my mouth. He moaned out. I began spitting on it as I rotated my hands jacking him while I sucked. I could feel his legs jerking.

"Still." I demanded.

"Shit I don't know how you expect me to do that baby. Fuck." He said as I continued to suck it. I started giving it some speed.

"Shit." He said as he grabbed me and placed me on the bed. He used his teeth to pull my panties off as his breath gave me the chills. He kissed me as he used his hands to take off my bra. He then kissed me all over my neck as he began sucking on my breast. Lord this was feeling so good. I missed everything about this. He then put his head between my thighs as he began to eat me as if I was a meal that he missed. I moaned out in pleasure.

"This mine baby. Tell me you won't give nobody my pussy again" He said.

"I won't daddy." I moaned out and he began licking me all over my clit and I came.

"Yes baby, come for daddy one more time." He said as placed a finger in me moving in and out as he continued to give my clit pleasure. He sped his fingers up as he continued to lick. It was crazy because he knew my body, he knew what spots to hit to make me come over and over again if he wanted to. I came again and the bed was soaked.

"Shit baby." He said as he then looked at me.

"Will any of this hurt the baby?" He asked. And I was at aww. He was so concerned. But I wish he would have asked before we got this far.

"Boy if you don't bring your ass here." I said as I grabbed him by his neck and pulled him into me for a kiss. He then entered himself inside of me and I moaned out loudly.

"Fuck I miss this." He said as he then started to make love to me slow so he could feel all of my juices pour.

"Me too daddy." I moaned as he then started to speed up. This was feeling so good I could never get enough of this. I was all for him and he was all for me. We were connected mind, body and soul and there was no way he was going to get rid of me now. I love him and I can't see my life with no one else. I could feel his dick growing inside of me even more and I could feel it in my stomach. I knew he was about to come because that's the only time he starts to speed up even more.

"Right there Sean." I yelled out.

"I'm coming baby. Shit." He said as he then filled me up as he started to move slowly. He then laid next to me.

"Fuck baby, I could never get enough of you. Promise you'll never leave me again." He said.

"Will you be honest with me from this day forward?" I asked as I was out of breath.

"I promise. No more secrets no more lies. We will never keep anything from each other. No matter how much it hurts." He confided in me. I then kissed him.

"Then I promise." I said as he then started kissing me passionately again and we were ready for another round. Afterwards we ended up falling asleep in each other's arms.

THE NEXT DAY

SEAN

It was a new day and I was feeling so good to have my girl back into my arms but there was shit that needed to be done. So, I then washed my ass got dress and decided to meet Law and Tech in the garden.

"As we all know Emily is not ready to take action against anything. She may never come back from this. But we are going to stand by her no matter how long it takes. Is that clear?" I said and Law and Tech nodded.

"So now what?" Law asked.

"Now we start killing some motherfuckers." a voice said as I then turned around to find it was Sierra. My mouth dropped.

24 I HAVE A PLAN

SEAN

I was shocked to hear her response. I don't know what's gotten into her but I was loving this side of her. I don't know if it was the pregnancy hormones or what? But if it was, I was going to get her pregnant after every delivery.

"Baby what the fuck?" I said in a shocked voice and she continued to walk over to us.

"Y'all are going to find the people who did this and you're going to put an end to all this bullshit. We have a baby coming and we can't afford all this other shit. Oh, and Sean? As of today, I'm no longer your attorney." She said as she winked at me and she walked back in the house.

"Damn you must of blew her back out last night Sean." Law said and Tech and I laughed.

"Mind your damn business. But I swear if this is the new her, I'm going to marry her ass I swear." I said and they laughed.

"I wasn't expecting that one either but let's not forget she did kill the hitman." Tech said.

"Yo you right. I forgot about that shit. She had a clean headshot kill. Sean, I think she is a lowkey killer too. Because there's no way in hell, she had a good shot like that. That was not a rookie shot. Now she telling us we have to kill these motherfuckers. The girl is a psycho just like you." Law said and we began to laugh.

"Maybe, and just by the way she was talking last night she has the mentality for it. She was thinking about shit that I haven't even thought of yet." I informed them.

"Like what?" Tech asked.

"Like why now all of a sudden Lee pops up dead and no one has been able to get in touch with him for a while. Sierra thinks Lee is a snake. She also has a feeling that Brian is still behind the attacks. She thinks he wanted us to believe he calmed down after she left that way when shit did pop off, we wouldn't suspect him." I told them.

"Wait a minute. Lee is dead? What the fuck!" Law yelled out.

"Yeah it was breaking news last night. They found his body in the alley way with the disguise of the trial shooting." I told them.

"Why the fuck would he still have that shit. He was supposed to burn it like the rest of us!" Tech said furiously.

"I guess it's becoming clearer on why Sierra had a feeling he was a snake because why the fuck would he still be holding on to those clothes. And she had no clue about the clothes part. He better be glad he's fucking dead because if I would have got a hold of him, I was going to cut his fucking head off." I said and they began to laugh.

"What the fuck yo. I think you get off on shit like that. I remember the first time you did that shit and had us mail the head to their crew. I know I'm a killer but goddamn Sean you are a **monster**. I love shooting and you love making and watching motherfuckers bleed." Law said and Tech began to laugh.

"It's my damn prerogative." I said and they both laughed.

"So what are you going to do now that Sierra is no longer representing you?" Tech asked.

"Well I'm kind of glad about that. Now I don't have to worry about anyone finding out about us." I explained to them.

"I wouldn't be so sure about that." Tech said.

"Why you say that?" I asked.

"Because even though she's no longer representing you her reputation may get ruined because of her just being with you." Tech said.

"I didn't even think about that. Fuck. I just want to give my girl the world. I don't want to keep hiding how much I love her." I expressed.

"I understand that but it's too dangerous right now." Tech said.

"Your right. But how are you holding up today?" I asked him in a concerning voice.

"I have my moments when I can't stop thinking about her but I have to get use to the fact that she's gone." Tech said and I looked at Law while he rubbed his arms being weird.

"The fuck is wrong with you?" I asked him. He was acting weird.

"Nothing I just can't believe Renee is gone. We'll get through this though." Law said.

"Yeah. We will." Tech said.

"Listen man we have to finally replace someone in Sylvias spot. We have to eat dammit!" Law said and we laughed.

"Well then hire someone. I thought about it but shit just been too weird. And now that we suspect Lee was a snake, I know longer want any contact with anyone except the both of you, Mia, Emily and Sierra and my son. It seems as if these people try to get in good with our circle to know our ins and outs to fuck us over. No more. It's just us now till the end." I clarified to them.

"Your son?" Tech and Law said together.

"Yeah she told me last night that the baby was a boy." I told them.

"Well I'll be damned." Law said and we laughed.

"So you going to let him take over?" Law asked.

"I'm not sure yet. I haven't fully thought that threw. Apart of me wants him to be able to keep this shit going but then I also want a better life for him. I guess we'll have to cross that bridge when we get there." I said.

"I can't believe there is going to be a little Sean running around here." Tech said.

"Me either. But he's coming in 4 months so I'll be adding on to the mansion again."

"Maybe I'll get Mia pregnant. We'll keep a squad going." Law said and we laughed. As we continued to talk and laugh at one another I thought about a plan. But before I put it in motion, I want to run it past Sierra. I need to know if it would work.

SIERRA

As I left the boys outside, I know Sean wasn't expecting that but I meant every word that I said. They had to put an end to all this shit. I was having a child that I didn't need to be in danger over a war. But as of right now, all I wanted to do was find Mia to catch up. I really missed her. Once I got to their room door I knocked and she answered the door.

"Hey girl what's up?" Mia said.

"I came to talk for a little is that okay?" I asked her.

"Sure come in." She said as she opened their room door to let me in.

"So how's everything? I hear you are in Sean's crew." I informed her.

"Listen Sierra that's not on him. I wanted to do that on my own so I got Law to recruit me. And I love what I do. And I don't want to lose our friendship over a choice I made for me." She said.

"I would never stop being friends with you Mia. I just wanted to make sure you were okay and if you were sure this is what you wanted." I said to reassure her.

"Yeah. I love what I do and I make three times as much as I was as an assistant." She said.

"Hey I paid you good money." I said and she giggled.

"You did but now I'm making so much more. I'm okay Sierra I promise." She said.

"Okay good. So, I told Sean today that I wasn't representing him anymore." I told her.

"What? And how did he take that?" She asked.

"He didn't say anything. I think it's something he wanted since we began to get close. The day I got shot I remembered him saying he can always find another lawyer but he could never find another me." I told her.

"That's some sweet shit. He really loves you Sierra. I watched the shit he went through when you left. He was depressed. He stayed on the balcony the business wasn't running right he wasn't able to think straight for months until Tech and Law gave him an intervention one day to get him to snap back in reality. That was the day he stopped calling. He was fucked up inside." She said.

"Well I'm here now and as long as he's honest with me from now on we'll be okay." I said to Mia.

"Did you tell him that?" She asked me.

"I did. And he finally told me the truth about everything." I said.

"Good. I'm happy for you both. Now this baby bump! I'm so excited." She said and I giggled.

"Yeah I'm excited too. I never knew it was possible to love something growing inside of you before it comes into the world. Every kick and every movement he makes, is something to cherish." I said ecstatically.

"You said he." She said.

"Yes it's a boy. I found out before I came back." I told her.

"Oh my God. I know Sean was happy to be having a junior." She said.

"Actually when I told him he just kissed me. He didn't say anything."

"He didn't need to. The kiss explained it all trust me." She said.

"So are you and Law doing good?" I asked her. Hoping he was treating my friend right.

"Better than ever. He treats me like a queen. But I realized something while I been here." She said.

"And what's that?" I asked.

"They love hard. They were never in anything serious until we came along. No woman ever got the treatment that we get from them. They worship the grounds we walk on and I see it. They don't give a fuck about no man or woman in the streets but they will give it all to the people that they love." She expressed to me.

"You love Law?" I asked her.

"Of course I do. We've been dating for a while now. And he loves me too. We didn't fall in love as quick as you and Sean but we are there now." She said and she giggled.

"Yeah it was fast with me and Sean but after I talked to him on the phone when Renee died, I couldn't help but think about another woman putting her hands all over my man. I cried at the thought of it. I refuse. I think I'll kill her." I said and Mia laughed.

"Wow I think he's rubbing off on you. Sean's crazy you know. I've heard some of his stories from some of the crew he really changed from the way he used to be. People are terrified of him in the streets. The only people bold enough to try him is Brian's Family. That's been a war since before he was even born." She informed me.

"I haven't heard the stories but I watched him kill Marc in front of me. It was like he blacked out." I told her.

"That's what he does. When he blacks out, they have to stop him. He blacked out that day you got shot and was in the hospital. They had to sedate him." Mia said.

"Really? I didn't know." I told her.

"Yeah, and sometimes he still has nightmares about it. He can't stop thinking about the way you fell into his arms when you got shot." Mia said.

"Damn. I guess I never considered how all of this affected him. I was only thinking about me. I admit that it was selfish." I admitted to her.

"Well your here now and that's all that matters. And I really hope the both of you can work it out because I'm not going anywhere. Law is everything I ever wanted and more." Mia told me.

"Aww that's sweet. Maybe the both of you should have a baby so we can raise our kids together." I said and she giggled.

"If it happens it happens. I wouldn't want anyone else to be the father of my kids." Mia said and I began to smile.

"Well I'm hungry I'm going to the kitchen to find me something to eat." I said and Mia laughed.

"I'll come with you lets go." She said and we both headed to the kitchen.

SEAN

As the boys and I were still talking I heard the girls laughing in the kitchen. I figured now would be a good time to bring my idea to Sierra.

"Sounds like our women are downstairs now. I need to run something by Sierra." I told them and they nodded and followed me to the kitchen.

"Well what's so funny in here?" I asked and they turned to look at me and they busted out in laughter.

"Well the fuck is so funny." I yelled out.

"Nothing babe. What's up?" Sierra said.

"I have a plan on how we can fix this shit." I said.

"How?" She asked.

"We're going to pin this shit on Lee." I said and they all reacted shock and surprised.

25 THE PLAN

SEAN

"Pin it on Lee? I need you to back up your motive." Law said.

"He's got a point. It could work." Sierra said and I smiled at her.

"Tell them baby." I said as I was glad, she took my side.

"If you can prove that Lee was there and that he left the crew a while ago that would give him motive as revenge. But how would you prove it? And do they know that Lee was even in your crew?" Sierra said.

"Well, when we saw the breaking news Lee was wearing the clothes that he had on that day at the courthouse. But hell no. Those motherfuckers couldn't point out a single person in my crew." I informed her.

"But there was only a clip from the video camera showing the back side of the outfit. So that would mean the police know that by now and they are going to try and use that against you." Sierra said.

"That's what I was thinking. But since we already believe Lee was a snake why not pin it on him. The dead can't speak for himself." I spoke out.

"Have you tried calling Louis?" Law asked.

"Who's Louis?" Sierra asked.

"Officer Louis, he's our inside of the police department." I told Sierra.

"Hold the fuck up. Officer Louis? He interrogated you that day I took you in." Sierra said.

"All part of the game baby." I told her and I winked at her.

"Wow he does a hell of a good job at hiding it. So, what about the gun he laid out on the table?" Sierra asked.

"He'll handle that. Why you think he wasn't asking that much questions.

He works for us. We pay him more than he could ever make in the police department." I told her.

"Has he called yet?" Tech asked.

"No he hasn't so I'm not worried about it right now. I know once there is something for us to know he will call." I said so all of them could hear me.

"Well you do have a point because he will always call." Tech said.

"Call him now Sean. I need him to confirm that they are going to try and pin it on you." Sierra demanded.

"Okay baby if that will make you happy." I said and I pulled out my phone to call Officer Louis.

"Sean, what's up?" Officer Louis said as he answered the phone.

"I see they found Lee." I said to him.

"Yeah they did. I'm trying to gather as much information as I can before I called you. But what I can tell you is that they know Lee was wearing the outfit from the courthouse shooting and the detective is believing this is her way of building a case against you." Officer Louis said.

"See I told you." Sierra whispered in my ear and my dick got hard immediately.

"So what should I do as of right now?" I asked him hoping he could at least give me something.

"Nothing. Once there is something important, I'll let you know. Right now, all she can say is what she thinks happened. She doesn't have any solid evidence." He informed me.

"So, what if we pinned this shit on Lee? Could that work?" I asked him curiously. I needed to get this shit off my back. I have a baby coming.

"It could. But I would need you to send me something solid so I can get her off your ass. She's willing to stop at nothing to see you behind bars. You're going to need to update Ms. Johnson on everything just in case." Officer Louis said.

"Yeah about that. She's no longer my attorney." I informed him.

"What the fuck Sean. You know that was the best lawyer you could get for this shit." Officer Louis said.

"She's not representing me any longer because she's having my baby." I said to him dramatically.

"Well, I'll be damned. You hit the jackpot my boy." Officer Louis said and the boys and I laughed.

"I'm literally right here." Sierra said.

"Oh shit. Hey Ms. Johnson. Now that you know my position in all of this, we could help each other out in a lot of cases." Officer Louis said.

"True. I'll take you up on that. Bring me the best you got." Sierra said.

"That's good to hear so who's going to represent Sean now? You were his best bet if this were to escalate." Officer Louis asked.

"Well I have someone in mind. But it's not going to be easy to convince him to take this case." Sierra said.

"Who?" I asked.

"I'll let you all know if I can get him to agree to it." Sierra said.

"That's a plan. On the bright side Sean, the only thing that's keeping this going in your favor as of right now is you being shot. That was the best part of the plan. They don't understand why you would have anything to do with it if you were shot along with everyone else. But I have to go. I don't want them coming out here looking for me." Officer Louis said.

"Alright Lou." I said and then disconnected the call.

"So I just have one question. That day I came here to take you to turn your ass in you already knew about it? And don't lie or I'll chop your ass with this frying pan." Sierra said and we all began to laugh.

"Yes I did. And why the fuck are you so violent now?" I asked her.

"I don't know these damn hormones have me all over the place." Sierra said.

"Law thinks you're a certified killer." I said and they laughed.

"Why would you think that Law?" Sierra asked him.

"Because. I just can't get over that headshot you gave a hitman. It was a clean shot. There was no way you never shot a gun before." Law said.

"Well to be honest it wasn't." Sierra said and I was shocked.

"Well I never heard this story." I said to her annoyed.

"It's not a big deal. Once I got out the foster system I didn't know where life was going to take me. So, I made it my business to know how to protect myself. I use to go to a gun range and taught myself how to **shoot**." Sierra said.

"Wow. Mia why the hell didn't you tell me?" Law said.

"Cause why is that any of your damn business?" Mia said and we laughed.

"Because I may be a man but babe, I love a good gossip." Law said and we all busted out in laughter.

"I know you do. And there are plenty of things no one knows about Sierra but it's not my story to tell." Mia said.

"It's okay Mia." Sierra said as she then filled Tech and Law in about her childhood and how she got to being the best lawyer. As I listened to her, something just doesn't add up. It has to be more to this story than she is saying. But as of right now, I'll let it go. We have bigger fish to fry.

"So is Harold who you're trying to get to represent Sean?" Law asked.

"Yes." Sierra said.

"Sierra you know he's not going to do it his wife will kill him first." Mia said.

"True but I'm still going to try and give it a shot." Sierra said.

"Well I hope you don't think your about to leave this house?" I informed her.

"And why would I want to do that your majesty?" Sierra said and Law, Tech and Mia laughed. She is such a damn smartass. But I loved her for it. I just rolled my eyes.

"By the way Mia, you and Emily's operations are shut down for the time being. I won't take any more chances on losing one of you." I said to her.

"Aww that's so sweet babe." Sierra said and she came up and kissed me.

"Girl I'm about to take you upstairs." I said as I slapped her on the ass and they all laughed.

"That's cool. Has anyone talked to Emily?" Mia asked.

"No she won't come out the room." Law said.

"Take it from me, the best thing you all can do for her right now is let her know that you are there for her even if it's just a text message and just give her space. None of us knows what's she's going through. She lost her best friend someone who she has years of memories with." Sierra said.

"That's a good point." Law said.

"Listen I know you all miss Sylvia but when the hell is someone coming to replace her?" Sierra said.

"We were just talking about that outside. Tech and Law will interview people." I informed her.

"No hell no. We can't take any chances on an outsider coming in here right now. We can't trust anyone. Promote a cleaner that's already in the house or something. Sylvia didn't have someone who helped her out when she was sick or anything?" Sierra began to say before she came to thought. "Matter a fact, she did. Chelsea. She kept Chelsea under her wing and trained her up. Promote Chelsea up. She knows Sylvia's work." She said to us.

"How the fuck do you know these people's names?" I asked her as I wondered. I never gave it the time of day. They worked for me. Why the fuck would I need to know these people.

"I mean, do y'all not want to know the people around you? You could have an assassin in this house and you all would never know it." She said.

"I swear Sierra you were made for this life no matter how much you tried to be a good girl." Law said.

"Isn't she?" Mia said.

"Well, I'm here now and we're family so we are all in this together." Sierra said and I smiled. I loved everything about her. To have her except this life, our life for what it is makes me happy. I'm going to marry her. She had to be my wife. We could take over the world together. I needed her extra brain. I needed her to be able to see what I couldn't. I needed **her**. I know it was early but I didn't give a fuck. I was going ring shopping. I pulled out my phone and called Sid.

"Hey pull around I need you to take me somewhere right quick." I told Sid.

"Where the fuck are you going?" Sierra asked.

"Shhhh, baby. I'll be back. Don't worry. I'll always come back to you." I said and I walked away headed to the front door to go ring shopping. I needed her to be my wife. I could never lose her again. She had to be mine when the time was right.

26 BLINDED BY LOVE

SIERRA

"The idea of pinning everything on Lee could definitely work. Law do you think you could reach back out to Louis and find out if Lee maybe had a phone on him at the time?" I asked.

"Sure, I'll shoot him a message and find out. " Law asked.

"And Tech how are you holding up today?" I asked him. I know he lost the love of his life and sometimes that is something no one can come back from.

"I'll just be taking it day by day Sierra. I know she wouldn't had wanted me to be drowning in sorrow. That's not who she was." Tech replied.

"Good to hear." I expressed to him.

"Louis said Lee had nothing on him." Law said.

"Shit. Okay so that means who ever killed him has his phone so they now have access to all of your numbers. Get everyone new numbers and phones asap to prevent them from hacking in your cellular service. With Lee being gone for so long there's no telling if they already have! Make sure to inform Louis to change his number as well. The whole organization needs new phones." I informed them.

"You got it. Anything else?" Law asked.

"We are going to have to dig deeper here. Whoever Lee is working for is smart. Because Lee has been gone for so long and hasn't been answering any of your calls there's no way to trace it." I said to them.

"What if we could trace the service from the last time any of us spoke to him." Tech said.

"That could work. If they haven't already hacked in and deleted anything that would trace to it. But it's worth a shot. Do y'all have anyone that's good in research and hacking?" I asked them.

"Tech get Gia on this one." Law said and Tech nodded as he went to give Gia a call.

"We all had our own locker down in the basement I'm going to break into Lees to see if I can find anything in there." Law said.

"Thank you, Law." I expressed to them.

"No problem. Don't tell Sean this but I like you better as our boss." Law said and we began to laugh.

"Your secret is safe with me." I told him and he left to go to the basement.

"You're really good at this." Mia said.

"I'm only good at this because I know how the law works **remember**." I hinted to her and she nodded.

"So, when are you going to call Harold?" Mia asked.

"Right now." I told her as I then pulled out my phone to call Mr. Harold.

"Hello." Harold said.

"Hey its Sierra." I responded.

"Sierra, it's good to hear from you. I haven't spoken to you in a while. Is everything okay? How's the company?" Harold said.

"There's so much that I have to tell you. Can you come over?" I asked of him.

"Sure, I can come for a few. Is it really that bad?" He asked.

"Yes." I expressed to him.

"Okay let me get ready and I'll be on the way." He said to me.

"I don't live in my old house anymore. I'll be sending you the address." I responded.

"Ok. I'll be there shortly." He said and I disconnected the call.

"What do you think he's going to say once he finds out this is Sean's house and you're having his baby?" Mia asked.

"I don't know but I know I failed him big time for even sleeping with my client and I won't be mad if he decides to take the company away from me. Maybe its best. With the way these men are in our lives there's no way things could ever be *just normal*." I said to Mia.

"Truth be told Sierra you don't have to go back. The company is yours. Harold was never there. He didn't need to be because he had you and other lawyers there to take cases." Mia said and she was a fucking genius.

"Mia your right! I don't have to be there. I can do whatever I want to do as long as I make sure the business side is handled. You're a damn genius." I said and Mia giggled.

"Do you think the old team is ready to come back in office? Maybe they like working from home." I said to her.

"While you were gone, I've spoken to a few of them and they asked when the company was opening back up." Mia said.

"Great I'll send out an email with an emergency meeting in a couple days and I'll let them know a promotion is on the line. Someone is going to have to take my place since I'm in charge now." I said to them.

"They are going to love that. Maybe have them study Sean's case. Whoever can come up with the best defense gets the promotion and your old job." Mia said.

"You know what that's even better. That way we won't have to get Harold involved in this at all. I could kiss you right now." I said and she laughed.

"Hey we are all in this together. As far as I'm concerned, we all should be thinking for each other." Mia said.

"Right. So as far as Harold is concerned. I'll just be catching him up on my life." I said to her.

"I think that's the best thing to do." She said and I nodded.

"I'll also post an ad that we are hiring. We are going to need one more lawyer and one more assistant. You think I could buy Greene out and have him come and work for me?" I asked her. Even though I was the best, Greene was good. And other lawyers out there had a hard time beating them.

"Greene? Sean didn't tell you?" Mia said.

"Tell me what?" I asked her curiously.

"Greene is dead." Mia said and I was shocked.

"How the fuck is he dead?" I asked her as my mind was blown.

"They killed him during the shooting at the courthouse and dumped his body." Mia said.

"How the fuck do you know all of this?" I asked her.

"Hey, I may be loyal to you but I'm loyal to my man too." Mia said and I giggled.

"Understandable." I expressed to her in agreeance.

"Listen don't go all batshit crazy on Sean. Maybe he forgot to mention Greene that's all." She expressed to me trying to take Sean's side. I can tell they really bonded over me being gone. I'm not sure if that's going to be a good thing or a bad thing. Mia always used to be on my side.

"How could he have forgotten when he was telling me about the courthouse shooting. How could he just forget to mention Greene as if Greene wasn't there?" I yelled out softly.

"Nobody knows." Mia began to say before the doorbell rang.

"It must be Harold. I'll go and get that." I told her as I headed to the door. I opened it and it was Harold.

"Sierra what's all this? Your pregnant?" Harold yelled out when he saw my stomach.

"Come in and I'll explain." I said as I opened the door fully and let him in.

"Congratulations. Where's Brian so I can congratulate him as well." Harold said.

"Please sit." I said as I then sat down and Harold did as well.

"I'm not pregnant by Brian. We are no longer together." I informed him hoping that he could begin to understand.

"Really? I'm sorry to hear that. You must have you a rich one now." Harold said as he laughed and I giggled. I was nervous. I had to tell him the truth and take his opinion as it is. But I won't let him disrespect Sean.

"I guess you could say that. How's the cancer coming along?" I asked him.

"Well, I'm just living everyday now as if it were my last. When the good Lord calls me, I'll be ready." Harold said.

"Amen to that." I said out loud.

"So, what's this about Sierra. You could have called me. I know you didn't bring me here just to see how I'm doing." Harold said.

"Well, I'm." I began to say before the front door opened. It was Sean.

"Baby who's this?" Sean asked.

"Baby?" Harold said as he then looked at me furiously.

"This is Mr. Harold. The one I always talk about." I told Sean.

"I'm having Sean's baby." I said and Harold got silent but you could see it all over his face that he was pissed.

"Are you going to say something?" I asked.

"What do you want me to say Sierra huh? That you are about to throw your life away for a criminal?" Harold said.

"Now wait a fucking minute. You're not about to bring your ass" Sean began to say before I cut him off.

"Can we have a minute please." I said and Sean nodded.

"I'll be in the kitchen." He said as he stared at Harold with a killer look as he walked by and went into the kitchen. I knew if I didn't get Sean out of there it would have ended badly and no matter the circumstance. I could not let him hurt Harold.

"Listen I know you're upset but that doesn't give you the right to disrespect him in his own house." I said to Harold.

"I wasn't trying to be rude I was speaking on exactly what it is. How do you go from working on his case to working on having his baby?" Harold said sarcastically.

"I deserve that. But I fell in love with him." I informed him. Again, hoping he would understand that sometimes things just happen that we have no control over. With the heart, being one of them.

"I'm not understanding. From the looks of your belly size, I would say that you are about five to six months along meaning that this was when you started taking his case when you got pregnant." Harold said.

"Your right. I am five months and I'm having a son." I informed him.

"Oh, Sierra. Didn't I teach you better than to let personal and pleasure get in the way. It never ends well. What about your career?" He asked of me.

"Harold, you gave me the company. I think my career was kind of done with from their since I have an entire building to run." I said to him.

"Yes but." Harold said and I then cut him off.

"No buts. I called you here because you were always the closest thing I ever had as a father. And I respect you enough as a father to tell you what's going on with my life. I'm aware of my mistakes and what I put at risk here. But that doesn't mean I can't have it all. Why can't I have a future with the man I love? Raise a family and still have my career?" I asked of him annoyed.

"Maybe that's because the man you love is a damn killer Sierra. Your blinded by love so you can't see that anymore. What happened to you? If I would have known you were going to run my damn company to the ground I would of never gave it to you!" Harold yelled. I was hurt. But most of all I was pissed.

"You know what you can go. You act like you aren't trying to make up for your mistakes? The only reason why your spending time with your wife is because you're dying. You were never at the office even before you got sick. Don't come in here judging me. Leave." I demanded him.

"Sierra look." Harold began to say.

"Leave!" I yelled and I went to the door and opened it for him. As he began to walk out the door he turned around and faced me.

"You we're always like a daughter to me too." He said and I then slammed the door in his face. Fuck that. He could have his company back. I had enough money to start my own even if I had to start small. No matter what anyone says about Sean he's my son's father and I love him no matter what they believe he is.

"I ran you a bubble bath." A voice said as I turned around and it was Sean.

"For what? So, I can drown you in it?" I yelled.

"What the fuck? What did I do now?" He yelled back out.

"Save it Sean." I said and I headed up to our room as he followed me. Once we reached our room, I tried to slam the door in his face but he caught it.

"What is wrong with you? Can you just tell me what I did?" Sean said.

"What didn't you do? We were supposed to be honest with each other and yet you lied again." I yelled at him.

"Baby I told you everything. What did I lie about?" He asked me.

"Greene. You sure left out that little detail." I informed him.

"That doesn't mean I lied! I wasn't thinking about his ass!" He yelled and I can't lie a part of me wanted to laugh on the inside. I knew he was trying to make me laugh by saying that but I refused to give in. So, I just stared at him until I was ready to respond.

"How? You killed him in the courthouse. How did you forget that part?" I asked him.

"I didn't fucking kill him Lee did!" He yelled out sarcastically. He was trying to be a fucking smartass.

"Under your order." I said to him.

"Look baby I didn't lie. I just didn't think about it okay." He said so gently as if he wanted to me to understand.

"Yeah whatever. I'm not doing this lying shit with you Sean." I said and he fell to his knees in front of me.

"Please don't leave me." He said to me.

"Sean what are you doing? Get up." I asked him. This was something that I never thought he would do.

"Don't leave me." He said as he rubbed my stomach and put his face in the front of my thighs. I could feel the air he breathes through my pants.

"I'm not going anywhere Sean I'm just going to get in the bath that you ran for me." I said and he bit my pants where my crease was. I got wet instantly.

"The water is going to get cold Sean." I sighed out as he then began to pull my pants down.

"Shhhh." He said as he laid me back on the bed.

"Just let me taste it for a minute." He said as he spread me open and began to put his face in it.

"Sean." I moaned out as I grabbed his head. He continued to suck and lick. He opened me up wider as he began to fuck me with his tongue. I cried out in ecstasy.

"Ooooh Sean. I'm coming already." I moaned out and he sped his tongue up faster. I then came all over him and he got up.

"You don't want more?" I asked.

"Nah, I just wanted to make you feel relaxed for a moment. Now let's go." He said as he then grabbed my hand to lead me to the bathtub.

"I could never get enough of making you feel good." He stated to me.

"Thanks babe. I love to make you feel good too." I told him.

"But on some real shit I didn't lie. I just didn't think about Greene." He said as he continued to wash my back.

"Okay Sean. I believe you." I voiced to him.

"It was part of the plan. Tee was supposed to ride with Emily in the ambulance to the courthouse but he never showed up." He revealed to me. And everything was now beginning to make sense.

"So that's why you killed Tee?" I asked him.

"That's right. Now you're getting it. I'll never hurt anyone if they don't cross me baby. I know I could be a monster sometimes but that's not who I want to be anymore. But anyways. Tech and Lee was supposed to dump Greene. But because Tee didn't show he rode with Emily and Lee went and dumped Tee's body." Sean said and then it dawned on me.

"That's it!" I yelled out.

"You okay baby?" He asked.

"Here me out. Lee is the one who shot Greene. Then he shot you. Then Lee was the only one who dumped Greene. That's it! Those things right there is key to help pinning it on Lee." I revealed to him.

"They won't find anything on him babe he had on gloves and besides residue only stays on stuff for 4-6 hours." He advised me.

"Your right but it may not be on him anymore but I can guarantee you that there's blood traces on his clothes. He didn't throw them away. If he was smart, he would have burned them like everyone else. You know where Greene's body is dumped right?" I asked him.

"Yeah." He stated.

"Tip it off to Louis and have him pin it on Lee." I told Sean and he just began to get quiet.

"Aren't you going to say something?" I asked.

"Will you marry me?" He said and I was breathless.

27 WHAT IS GOING ON

SEAN

I was nervous as hell as I waited for her answer. In all honesty I was only thinking it. I didn't mean to spit it out but since it's out there now and all I could do was wait on her to answer. Would she want to spend the rest of her life with me? My heart was racing. The cat was already out of the bag and the only thing that matters now is a yes or no.

"Are you serious?" She stated.

"Yes baby. My heart doesn't fully beat without you in it. You're my queen and I want to worship the ground you walk on until the end of time. I love you Sierra and I know you love me too." I expressed to her lovingly.

"I do love you, Sean." She informed me. My heart was dropping slowly. Was that all she could say?

"Okay so." I voiced.

"So, if I marry you, you know you'll have to deal with me forever, right?" She stated sarcastically.

"I wouldn't have it any other way baby. I want to give **you** the world, no one else. I can't spend my life with anyone but you. They say a man knows the moment he meets someone and baby you are it for me. So will you be my wife?" I asked of her again.

"And you promise to love me even on the days when I want to put a knife to your neck." She said and I laughed.

"Yes." I communicated.

"I just have one question?" She stated.

"And what's that?" I asked of her.

"Are you just marrying me because you really meant those things or because I couldn't testify against you?" She conveyed. I swear she knows how to kill a beautiful moment.

"Why do you always have to kill a beautiful moment? I want to marry you because I love you. I wasn't thinking about all that other shit!" I yelled out to her.

"Yes, I'll be your wife, Sean White." She said and a smile ran across my face. I was the happiest man alive right now. I kissed her slowly.

"Stay right here. I'll be right back." I told her as I walked out the bathroom to get her ring.

"Its beautiful Sean. When the hell did you have time to buy a ring?" She asked me.

"That's where I was today. I didn't have intentions on proposing today I wanted to do it at the right time. It just slipped out earlier. But the day you got shot I knew that moment I was in love with you. I even still have nightmares about the way you fell into my arms. I don't think I could ever forgive myself for not being able to protect you in that moment." I expressed to her.

"But it wasn't your fault. You didn't know nor expect for that to happen while we were on a date. And I'm sorry for not ever taking in consideration your feelings in all this. I was so caught up in mine I didn't think about yours. But all that's going to change now. Your stuck with me for life kid." She said and I laughed.

"I'm so happy baby I thought you were about to break my heart." I stated.

"Well, I have to go tell the girls now." She said and I laughed.

"Go ahead baby. I'll lay you some comfortable clothes out." I told her and she nodded. Once I laid her clothes out and headed downstairs. The house was quiet. Where the fuck was everyone at?

SIERRA

I couldn't believe I was getting married. It was all so soon but I didn't care. I was going to be marrying the man I love and the father of my child. After everything I been through, I could never see myself giving another man a piece of me. So why not just spend it with the man I know who loves me and only me and would do anything for me. I got out the tub and got dressed and headed downstairs.

"Why the fuck isn't my phone working. What the fuck is going on? Where the fuck is everybody?" Sean was yelling out.

"Calm down babe. I can explain." I informed him.

"I'm listening." He stated.

"I sent the boys on a job." I told him.

"You sent my men on a job." He said and he began to laugh.

"Why is that so funny?" I asked curiously.

"Because I can't imagine hearing you giving orders. Care to update me?" He asked of me.

"Well, we were all talking and I asked Law to find out from Louis if Lee had a cellphone on him. Louis said he didn't have nothing on him so that meant." I began to say before he cut me off. I hated when he does that shit.

"That whoever he was working for could have potentially been hacking our phones. Shit." Sean said.

"Let me finish asshole." I said and he laughed.

"I told Law to inform everyone that they will be getting new phones and new phone numbers. After he was done with that, he's going to check Lee's locker to find out if Lee could have left something in there. As for Tech, he's getting a hold a someone name Gia to do some research and hacking on the service location of Lees cellphone from the last time he spoke to anyone of you. That way it could possibly give you a hint on who he was working for. Emily is still in her room and Mia is somewhere around here." I informed him.

"Wait a minute? You got the guys to do all that and they didn't give you no lip?" Sean said.

"No, they didn't." I stated.

"Interesting." Sean said.

"Why?" I asked him.

"Because that means they like and respect you. If they didn't, they wouldn't have listened to shit you had to say because you aren't their boss. They don't care if you are my woman. They don't listen to no one but me. And if I know Law the way I think I do, I'm sure his smartass said something as if he likes you better as his boss than me." Sean said and I laughed.

"Damn you know him well." I said as I continued to laugh.

"Better than he knows himself." Sean said and Law walked through the front door.

"What the fuck are you looking at Sean?" Law said and we laughed.

"So, your taking order from someone besides me now?" Sean said.

"Yeah, because I like her more than I like you." He told Sean and sticked his tongue out and we all began to laugh.

"So, Sierra there was nothing in Lee's locker." Law said.

"Don't tell her motherfucker tell me. I'm your fucking boss." Sean said and Law and I laughed.

"Awe babe your jealous. That's not how we want to start off a marriage is it?" I expressed to him.

"Marriage?" Law asked.

"Yeah man we're getting married." Sean said.

"Well, I'll be damned. Congratulations. And when the fuck did you have time to buy a ring?" Law asked.

"That's the same thing I said!" I said to Law and we began to chat.

"Okay okay, I don't want to interrupt your bonding moment but that's where Sid took me earlier." Sean said.

"So, when's the wedding?" Law asked.

"Who's getting married?" Mia asked as she walked in the living room towards us.

"We are." I told Mia and she screamed in excitement.

"I'm so happy. Wait, when did you buy a ring?" Mia asked.

"Shit do I need to post the answer to this question on the fucking wall or something?" Sean said and we all busted out in laughter.

"Sid took me earlier." Sean said.

"So, are you going to have a wedding?" Mia asked.

"I just want us to do something small with just everyone in this house. That's it." I said to all of them.

"Whatever you want baby. The world is yours." Sean said and I smiled.

"Awww. I think I'm going to cry." Mia said.

"For what?" Law yelled out.

"Dammit Law you better have my fucking phone you asshole." Tech said as he walked in the living room.

"What the fuck is your problem?" Law asked.

"Nothing. I just wanted to say that since we split up earlier." Tech said and everyone began to laugh and we all turned to Mia as she was crying.

"What the fuck is wrong with you? You need to take a pregnancy test." Law said.

"That's what I was doing when everyone split up earlier. It was positive." Mia said and Laws mouth dropped.

"Well, you spoke that up into existence." Sean said and him and Tech laughed.

"Yeah Mr. maybe I should get Mia pregnant." Tech said and him and Sean laughed again.

"Fuck the both of you. What made you take a test love?" Law asked Mia.

"Well after everything that was going on I assumed that the reason why I was late was because of stress. So, I just took one just in case to rule it out. But I guess stress wasn't the reason why." Mia said.

"I'm so shocked I don't know what to say." Law said.

"So, you don't want me to keep the baby?" Mia said as she then ran off crying upstairs.

"Wait that's not what I was saying." Law said and we could hear Mia slam the door.

"Great, Sierra's hormones made her a killer and I got a cry baby." Law said and we laughed.

"I'll talk to her." I informed Law.

"No not yet. I got it for right now. I made this mess now I have to clean it up." Law said as he then walked upstairs to their room. As Law was walking upstairs a small piece of paper with a phone number fell out. Sean went over to pick it up.

"Doctor Pierce? Wait isn't that the doctor from the hospital?" Sean asked.

"Yeah, he's the one who did my surgery." I informed him.

"What the fuck is Law doing with his phone number? You don't think?" Sean began to say.

"Naw man. I can guarantee it's something else. Law could never cross us. The only question I want to know now is, is my brother sick?" Tech said.

"Good question?" Sean said and the whole room began to get quiet. You can feel the sadness building up in the room. What the fuck is really going on?

28 NEEDING ANSWERS

SEAN

It's been two months and still there wasn't a single word. I've never gone this long without getting answers on a problem. My son will be here within the next two months. I still don't know why Law had the doctor's number. And I still don't know who the fuck killed Lee. I'm beginning to feel overwhelmed. I was beginning to get pissed. Sierra's birthday is tomorrow and so is our wedding. It felt like my fucking world was spinning. I needed some answers and I needed them to fucking day starting with Law. I hopped out the bed and kissed my girl on the forehead, washed my ass and headed to Laws room. I didn't give a fuck if he was sleep. I knocked on his fucking door.

"Who is it?" Law said.

"Get the fuck up we need to talk" I demanded.

"Can't it wait?" Law said.

"Hell no. You got five minutes. I'll be in the garden. And brush your fucking teeth." I yelled to him.

"Fuck you. I'll be there in a minute." Law said and I headed to the garden to wait for him.

"What the fuck is this all about Sean?" Law said as he got to the garden.

"Why the fuck do you have Doctor Pierce's number?" I asked him bluntly.

"Man, you woke me up for that shit?" Law said.

"Don't bullshit me man. My son will be here soon. I can't get no answers from the fucking streets. I still don't know who the fuck Lee was working for. I've been stressing the fuck out for the last two months because I don't know whether you're sick or not!" I yelled at him.

"Wait a minute. I'm not sick Sean. The way Doctor Pierce saved Sierra's life I thought it would have been a good idea to put him on the payroll. I hired him to be our backyard doctor." He informed me.

"Okay. So that brings my stress level down a little. But what I'm not understanding is why is his number just dropping out of your pocket when we haven't seen Pierce or been to that hospital in months. Do not lie to me Law." I said to him furiously.

"What do you want me to say Sean? I fucked up okay. And I don't know if Tech and Emily will ever forgive me." Law said.

"Forgive you for what?" I asked him.

"About Renee." He stated.

"What about Renee. Law what the fuck did you do?" I asked him. Renee was dead. Could he have saved her and didn't? Wait the fuck was this motherfucker going to tell me next.

"Renee is with Pierce okay. She's alive." Law yelled out. And I was stunned. I didn't know what the fuck to feel. I didn't know whether I wanted to kill him, fuck him up or thank him. But the one thing I was sure of, is that I was pissed.

"What the fuck Law. You put everyone through these emotions thinking that she was dead." I yelled.

"I know and I'm sorry but I had to do what I had to do for the time being because I needed to protect her and the baby." Law said.

"What baby?" I asked. What the fuck is going on? Everyone was pregnant around this fucking house.

"She told me she was pregnant when everyone left out of the room. I had to save her Sean. I had too. She was losing so much blood it was beyond what I know how to do. So, while everyone left out the room, I called Pierce and surprisingly he lived right around the corner so that's where Renee is. She's still in an induced coma. I didn't tell anyone because I didn't know if she was going to make it. Honestly, I still don't know if she is going to make it. Last I spoke to him she was still in an induced coma. Believe me Sean. I needed the attackers to believe that she was dead. So, I made sure the casket was closed and no one was able to view the body because there is no one in there." He revealed to me.

"You are a fucking idiot you know that. How the fuck are you going to tell Tech that Renee is not dead?" I asked him furiously.

"Renee's not dead?" a voice said and we turned around and it was Tech. Shit. We shouldn't have had our backs turned from the fucking door.

"Tech let me explain." Law said.

"You're my blood brother and you lied to me. My heart was broken and you couldn't just tell me?" Tech said.

"Tech I know your mad but I think you need to hear him out." I expressed to him.

"Fine. Talk." Tech said angrily.

"I'm not sick. Renee is with Pierce. I hired him to be our backyard doctor when shit goes down. This was back when Sierra got shot. When everyone left Renee and I in the living room I called Pierce because I couldn't save her and Pierce stays right around the corner. Renee was pregnant Tech. I had to try and save her and the baby. I had to make everyone believed that she was dead so the attackers would think that she was dead as well.

When I got her with Pierce, she barely had a pulse. I thought she died in my arms Tech. I had to fix this. She was like my sister I couldn't just let her go without trying something first. I just talked to Pierce and she was still in an induced coma and she was going to be ready to come out of it soon. I was going to bring her here and surprise everyone and tell y'all then. I wasn't doing this to try and hurt anyone. I didn't know if she was going to make it or not at the time so I did what I had to do in that moment." Law said to Tech and Tech had tears falling down his eyes.

"I'm going to be a father?" Tech said sadly.

"I'm going to be an uncle." Law said as he pulled Tech into a hug.

"I love you Tech I would never do anything intentional to hurt you. You're my brother." Law said.

"I just want to know how the fuck do you plan on explaining this to Emily." I yelled at him. I didn't give a fuck about his intentions. This was one loss that had affected everyone in their own way.

"Shit I didn't even think about that. She may kill me." Law said.

"She's been in her room depressed ever since Renee died. I think she deserves to know. Hell, we all deserved to know. We're safer together than we are apart." Tech informed Law.

"Your right. Gather the girls and I'll tell everyone." Law said to us.

"Wait why can't we just move her here?" Tech said.

"Because we don't have the tools and shit here to take care of her." Law said.

"Motherfucker we're rich" I yelled and they laughed.

"Hiring Pierce was a good fucking move. You bought Pierce all the tools and shit to keep at his place when you hired him right?" Tech said.

"Yeah, I did." Law said.

"Okay well he can do his operations for us here because once we go to war, we don't know what's going to happen we're going to need him here. There's still that big empty room in the basement move the shit and Renee home. Pierce can work from here. Anything he needs we got him. Does he have a family?" I asked Law. The world could say whatever they wanted to say about me, but I always took care of my people. The money that I have didn't just began with me taking over the business at a young age. The wealth in this family went on for generations.

"A wife. No kids. She knows what he does for us on the backend and she helps him with Renee." Law said.

"Call him and find out if we can move her home for now and he can do house visits to check on here. We'll install security." I said to him.

"No, I want her in my room." Tech said.

"Tech." I stated.

"Sean don't Tech me. You of all people should understand. You wouldn't leave that hospital when it was Sierra. Don't fucking tell me I can't do the same thing for the woman I love." Tech yelled.

"Okay Tech. I understand. Do you want to move to a bigger room so there would be enough room?" I asked him because he was right, I do understand.

"Yeah, that'll work." Tech said.

"Can y'all believe that we all have babies on the way." I yelled out.

"I never thought I would have seen the day." Law said.

"These are going to be some bad ass fucking kids." Tech said and we laughed.

"Good morning, everyone." Sierra said.

"Good morning." Tech and Law said.

"Good morning baby." I told her as I walked up to her and gave her a kiss. I then kissed her belly.

"How did you sleep?" I asked my queen.

"Great it would have been better if I could of woke up with some sex this morning." She said and we laughed.

"Shhh baby. Daddy will make it up too you I promise. Can we go do that now?" I asked and they laughed.

"Later on, now babe my back is hurting." She expressed to me in pain.

"Are you still having contractions?" I asked her.

"Yes, but these aren't the real thing these are Braxton hicks. They are minor contractions. But baby I know you want to keep me safe but I need a doctor to do my checkups. I need to make sure the baby is okay." She informed me. What is it with this woman? Her ass was always on time with some shit.

"Done. Law call Pierce right now." I told him and he pulled out his phone to call Pierce.

"Wait we know why he has Pierce number now? Is everything okay? He's not sick, is he?" She asked and I knew if I didn't stop her now, she was going to go on and on and on with them damn questions.

"No, he's not everything is okay." I informed her.

"Pierce said he's on the way. He's also going to bring Renee." Law said.

"Renee? Wait. What the fuck is going on?" Sierra asked.

"I honestly don't want to have to explain this all over again. Can we gather the rest of the girls and when she gets here, I'll explain to you all?" Law said and Sierra nodded.

"Can you just tell them I have a surprise and that I wanted you all to meet in the living room." Law asked Sierra.

"Sure." Sierra said as she walked off to go and get the girls.

SIERRA

I was confused as hell on what was really going on. What the fuck does he mean bring Renee? But I'll keep my word and tell everyone it's a surprise. I'll start with Mia.

"Knock Knock." I said as I entered her room door.

"Hey girl. How are you feeling?" Mia asked.

"I'm good. I'm excited for tomorrow. I'm having some pain today but it's nothing I can't bare right now." I informed her.

"Junior is almost ready huh?" Mia asked.

"Yeah, he is. I can't wait to hold him. Anyways the boys want us downstairs. They have a surprise they say." I told her and she nodded.

"First let's grab Emily and we can all head down their together." I said and we left to go to Emily's room. Once we got to Emily's room I knocked.

"Who is it?" She asked.

"It's Sierra and Mia. May we come in?" I asked.

"Sure." She said and we entered her room.

"How are you feeling?" I asked her.

"Honestly, I'm getting better. I still can't believe she's gone you know." Emily said.

"I understand. And truth be told you may always be affected by this. But we will be here for you whenever you need us ok." I expressed to her and she smiled a little.

"Thank you, Sierra. And I'm sorry if I have been distant, I'm going to do better I promise." Emily said.

"One step at a time. We love you girl." Mia said and she pulled us in for a hug.

"I can't believe everyone is having a baby. I think what really hurts the most is the fact that I knew Renee was pregnant." Emily said and we were shocked.

"Pregnant? We didn't know." I said as I was shocked.

"Yeah no one knew except for me. Before she died, she was going to tell everyone and her and Tech planned to tell everyone about their relationship. He was going to find out that day about the baby. I'm sure if he ever found out that would have killed him but that was the part was killing me. I didn't know how to look Tech in the face and tell him." Emily said.

"We get that. And I'm sure they would understand that. I'm not sure what they have in store for us right now but I know they want all of us to meet in the living room. They said they had a surprise." I told her.

"Sure, let's go." Emily said as we then headed down stairs to the living. Once we got to the living room, I couldn't believe my fucking eyes.

"Renee?" Emily yelled.

"Hey Em." Renee said. My stomach began to hurt.

29 LOST IN HIS KISS

SIERRA

Was I dreaming right now? I couldn't believe what the fuck I was seeing right now. Renee alive and sitting in a fucking wheelchair? What the fuck is going on?

"Your alive? What the fuck Renee? I was fucking depressed over you. I thought I lost my best friend. Knowing that you lied to me hurts even more." Emily said.

"Wait, don't blame her it's all my fault." Law said.

"What do you mean?" Emily said.

"I hired Pierce to take care of Renee. Her wounds were too deep and I couldn't fix it because I didn't have the proper tools I needed. So, Pierce came and took her in. I thought she died in my arms Em. I swear I didn't do this to hurt anybody. I did this to protect her and the baby. She told me about the baby before she passed out. That's when I thought she died. I made everyone think she was dead because I wasn't sure if she was going to make it and I needed the attackers to believe that she was dead. I'm sorry Em." Law said.

"I should kill you right now you bastard." Emily said as she cried into Laws arms as she was hitting his chest.

"I'm sorry Em for real. I wanted to surprise everyone if she made it through." Law said.

"You could have told us you asshole." Emily said as she continued to cry with joy.

"So how long has she been out of the coma doc?" Sean asked.

"For a few days now. But I needed to make sure she was going to be in good shape before I brought her back. She's healthy. The baby is healthy.

But I see bellies everywhere in this house." Doctor Pierce said and we all laughed.

"Yeah, we have been getting busy a lot around here. Speaking of which you think you can start doing house calls for the girls. A lot is going on right now and we are trying to do whatever we can to protect them before things get bad." Sean said.

"Sure. Sierra good to see you again." Doctor Pierce said.

"You as well Doctor." I said to him with gratitude. He was a great Doctor and had the training to do everything. For him, I'd forever be grateful for saving my life.

"How far along are you now. About 7 months, right?" Doctor Pierce asked me.

"I am 7 months. How do you remember?" I am asked.

"I don't forget about any of my miracle patients." Doctor Pierce said and we laughed.

"And do you know the sex of the baby or are you keeping it a surprise?" He asked.

"No sir. I know. It's a boy." I informed him.

"Well congratulations. And you, young lady I remember your face but I can't remember your name." He said as he was referring to Mia.

"Mia." She said to him.

"And how far along are you?" Doctor Pierce asked.

"I'm three months now." Mia said.

"Great so you're getting ready to enter in your second trimester. Are you having any morning sickness?" He asked her.

"Terribly Doctor. I can barely keep anything down." Mia said.

"Well apart of that problem could be you aren't getting the vitamins you need because you haven't been seeing a doctor. I'll be checking your iron today, getting you started on prenatal vitamins and we'll do an ultrasound so you can hear the baby's heartbeat and we can make sure everything is okay." Doctor Pierce said.

"Can I be in there for that doc?" Law asked.

"Of course. And Sierra, you still had prenatal vitamins, right?" He asked.

"I was but I ended up giving them to Mia because she needed them more in the first trimester than I did towards the end." I told the doc.

"Your right. And now I know she has been receiving some kind of care so that's good. So, we have Sierra at 7 months. Mia at 3 months and Renee at 5 months. I checked Renee before we came and the baby is doing great. She didn't want to know the sex of the baby yet because she said she wanted to make sure the father was there do so. So, for now, I'll make sure everything is good with Mia and Sierra. I brought what I am going to need here right now. But if you want me to have my own stuff downstairs, I'll need help moving those over." Doctor Pierce said.

"I'll tell you what Pierce, you can keep all that stuff to work at your house. We'll buy you everything new here that way you can have what you need there and here. How's that sound?" Sean said.

"Well, if that works for you. I didn't want you to have to waste your money." Pierce said.

"Money could never be wasted when it comes down to family. Your apart of our family now Pierce. Anything you and your wife need we got you. Only thing we ask for in return is your loyalty." Sean said.

"You got it Sean. Thank you. I'll go grab the things and we can get started." Doctor Pierce said and Sean nodded.

"Babe." Renee said and Tech kissed her immediately.

"How are you feeling?" Tech asked.

"I'm just exhausted babe. Can we go in the room so I can lay down?" She asked.

"Sure babe." He said and she sat up out the wheelchair and Tech picked her up in his arms.

"I'll carry you." He said and she smiled.

"I'll see everyone in a bit okay." She said and they went up to their room.

"This is fucking crazy. I can't believe she is alive." Emily yelled and she began to cry again.

"Em all of the girls' operations are cancelled for the time being. Anything y'all need just let one of us know." Sean said.

"Thank you, sir. I'll be more than happy to spend your money and not mine." Emily said and we laughed and Pierce walked back in with some equipment.

"Sierra are you ready?" He asked and I nodded. Sean and I then took the elevator up to our floor with Pierce so I could get a checkup. Once we got to the room I put on the gown and laid out on the bed. He put the cold gel on my stomach and the baby's heart began to beat.

"This was always my favorite part." I told Sean.

"I can see why all I can do is smile." Sean said.

"So, I'm looking here and you said you were having a boy, right?" Pierce asked me as if something was wrong.

"Yeah, that's what the last Doctor told me. Is everything okay? You sound as if some bad news is going to come next." I said to him.

"Well, no bad news. She just missed one." He said as he then turned the screen our way.

"It looks as if his sister finally wants to show herself." He said to us and our minds were blown.

"Sister?" Sean and I both yelled out.

"What the fuck?" Sean said and Pierce laughed.

"Yes, your having twins." He informed us.

"Doc, how's this possible?" Sean asked.

"Well, it's more common than people think. Some twins develop in their own sac and some share just one. So, when they share one it increases the chance of one twin hiding behind the other making it impossible for a doctor to catch it. But now because your babies barely have any room left to share, it makes it impossible for her to hide any more. But don't worry. As far as I can see she is completely healthy. But the only thing about this now is that with twin pregnancy they always come early. So, I can guarantee you that you will be delivering within the next month." Pierce said.

"Shit now we are going to have to redo the entire damn baby room." Sean said and I laughed.

"So, how's everything else. Well, I'm getting ready to check your cervix to see if you began dilating." Pierce said.

"Watch it doc." Sean said and we all laughed.

"Now you're going to feel some pressure just breathe for me." Pierce said and I did exactly as he asked.

"Great. You did good. So, you are already 1cm dilated. Have you been having pains?" Pierce asked.

"Yes, my back was hurting pretty bad earlier." I told him.

"Well, that's because you're dilating. You are beginning to have contractions now. It's no longer Braxton Hicks. I'll need to start seeing you every week starting today. Now is the time for you to start timing them. If your contractions begin to be 5 minutes apart lasting for 1 minute for an hour or longer, I need to be called right away. That means the babies are definitely coming. Keep in mind because you are 1cm now, that can change as soon as I walk out these doors. Babies come when they are ready. Not when we are ready. So, starting right now I want you to be on bedrest. We want the babies to stay in as long as they can." Pierce said.

"You hear that baby. **BED REST**." Sean said.

"Shut the hell up Sean. Am I able to still move around the house?" I asked him.

"Of course. But I need you to be resting more than moving. Understand." He insisted.

"I got it." I informed him.

"Okay. So, I'll clean up here, then I'll go and check on Mia." Pierce said and we nodded. He then packed up his things and went to Mia and Lawrence room.

"Baby, we're having twins. How the fuck is this possible?" Sean said.

"Well first you have sex and then you," I began to say as he busted out in laughter.

"Trust me I know how to do all of that. I'm just shocked you know. We are having twins." He said again.

"Yes, we are." I told him as he leaned forward and I got lost in his kiss and his phone began to ring.

"What you got for me?" He said as he answered.

"Bring him to the basement." He said and he disconnected the call.

"Who was that?" I asked him curiously.

"One of my men spotted someone in Brian's crew. Shit is about to get bloody." Sean said and all I could feel was the war beginning. Not only was shit going to be bloody, shit was about to get ugly.

30 IN ON IT

SIERRA

"So, is it time?" I asked him.

"Time for what?" Sean asked.

"Time for the war?" I asked and he kissed my forehead.

"Not yet baby. But I am about to make an example out of this motherfucker." He said so demandingly.

"You know I love you right." I said to him.

"Don't start that shit." Sean said.

"Start what exactly?" I asked him.

"That you know I love you shit because you're worried about me. I'll always come back to you. And besides he's bringing him here to me. It's him who should be worried." Sean said.

"Well in that case don't you think you should let the boys know." I informed him.

"I will as soon as I finish this." He said as he slid his hands up my gown and began to twirl his fingers inside of me.

"Can I feel you just a little bit baby." He asked.

"Of course." I moaned out. I don't think I could ever get enough of his touch. This pregnancy made me crave sex more and more. I had to have him always. He sped his fingers up as he moved his head closer and licked up all my juices.

"I need you now daddy." I moaned out as I then turned to my side. He got up and took his pants off. He laid next to me and entered me slowly. I gasped softly. He squeezed my waist as he continued to move in perfect rhythm.

"Fuck. Can u arch in a little deeper baby or your stomach is too big now? " He whispered. I arched in a little more and he began to thrust me a little harder. I screamed out his name. He thrust even harder and he began moaning loudly.

"You love me?" He asked.

"Yessss." I moaned softly.

"Louder." He demanded.

"Yesssssss." I screamed out.

"Who gone take care my baby like me?" He moaned.

"Nobody." I yelled in pleasure.

"Fuck. I'm cumin." He said as he thrust harder as he let go inside of me. He then turned me over to face him and kissed me.

"**If only you knew** the things I would do to a man if they ever tried to take you from me." He stated to me demandingly.

"Your all I ever want." I explained to him.

"Good because I'll kill his ass." He said and I laughed.

"Maybe you should go and get the boys now. I'm tired again so I'm going to take a nap." I told him and he then kissed my forehead, got dressed and headed to get the boys.

SEAN

Once I finished making love to my girl, I knew it was time to get down to business. I washed my dick and got ready. I had to put on the right gear because things were going to get messy. My first stop was Law. I knocked on the door.

"Come in." He said and I entered the room.

"How'd everything go with Pierce?" I asked him and Mia.

"Good, the baby is healthy. We got to hear the heartbeat and see the little hands and toes." Mia said.

"This shit is amazing man. I love this kid already and it's not even here. Why didn't our parents give a fuck about us man?" Law asked.

"Fuck them. Here's our chance to do things differently. So, not only am I having a son but I'm having a daughter as well.”? I informed them.

"Wait. What the fuck?" Law said.

"Wait. Twins?" Mia yelled out loud.

"That’s right." I stated.

"Oh, fuck that." Law said and Mia and I laughed.

"But listen that's not the reason I came in here. Jay spotted one of Brian's men. He's about to bring him here and I'm taking his ass too the torture room." I explained to Law.

"Shit yeah. I'm coming. I'll be back shortly love." Law told Mia and she nodded.

"Should we get Tech?" I asked him.

"I don't know. Maybe just give him the option to come. If he, doesn't it's understandable. He did think Renee was dead for months." Law said.

"Ok well let's go tell him what's going on." I said as we then headed to Techs room.

"Yo asshole, were coming in." Law said as he then opened the door.

"Don't you know how to fucking knock?" Tech said.

"Kiss my ass. How you feeling Renee." Law said and she laughed.

"I'm good is everything okay?" She asked.

"Jay found someone in Brian's crew and is on his way with him now. We're going to the torture room and just wanted to let everyone know and find out if you wanted to come. If not, we understand." I explained to Tech.

"I'll miss this one. I'm going to stay with Renee for the rest of the day." Tech said.

"The hell you are." She said to him.

"Listen I just got you back. I can't leave you alone again." Tech told her.

"Tech I'm right here. I'm not going anywhere. I don't want you to lose focus because there's still a job to do. Go kill those assholes. I'll be here when you get back and besides, I'm going to spend some time with Emily and the girls." She told him.

"Are you sure?" He asked.

"Yes, now go." She demanded him and he nodded. We then headed to the basement to the torture room. Once we walked in Jay already had him tied up to the chair with a bag still over his head. This was one of my favorite parts. The fear in their eyes when I take the bags off their head and they realize it's me who kidnapped them. They are terrified of me and they should be.

"Where am I?" The guy said in a drowsy voice. I then lifted the rag from over his face.

"Surprise motherfucker." I said and he attempted to try and escape from the chair until he realized he was tie down to the chair.

"Oh hell no. Please don't kill me. I don't have nothing to do with any of this shit." He said to me as I then pulled out my saw.

"And what shit is that exactly. You got so defensive you obviously know something Cam." I said to him.

"I don't know nothing Sean. I told them I didn't want nothing to do with this shit." Cam said.

"Law nail his hands in the chair." I demanded and Cam began to plead.

"My pleasure." Law said and he began to laugh.

"You see Cam here's the thing. I'm not buying shit you're saying. First you said you didn't have anything to do with this shit. I want to know what shit is that exactly." I stated.

"I don't know what you're talking about Sean. I don't have shit to do with nothing. I get my shit sell it and that's it. I don't get involve with anything besides my money." Cam said.

"Hammer it." I demanded Law and Cam screamed out in pain as Law hammered the nail into his bone.

"So, who did you tell that you didn't want to be involved?" I asked Cam.

"I can't tell you that man. I'm still loyal to my crew." Cam cried.

"Hammer his other hand to the chair Law." I said and Cam then screamed out again in pain.

"Now next, I'm going to take my saw and I'm going to cut your fucking legs off if you don't give me some fucking answers. But first." I said as I then nodded to Tech and he came over and started beating Cam in the face.

"Man, I missed this shit." Law said to me and we both laughed.

"I'm going to kill him either way. And send his ass back to Brian in a fucking body bag." I informed Law.

"Full body or in pieces." Law asked.

"You know I wouldn't be me if I didn't send his ass in parts." I said and we laughed.

"So that means." Law began to say before I finished his sentence.

"I'm going to behead his ass. Yes." I said to Law.

"Whewww shit I'm excited." Law said and we laughed.

"You always have to make a joke out of every fucking thing." I said to him.

"The life we live is hard man. What better way than to laugh about it. Hell laughing makes it easier for me to live." Law said and he was right. The life we lived was hard and that's no one's fault but ours because that's how we choose to live it. But we might as well laugh to make things easier. So, I continued to watch Tech beat the fuck out Cam's ass.

"Alright enough." I said and once Tech stepped aside you couldn't recognize Cam at all. His entire face was swollen.

"So, Cam here's the thing. You're going to tell me what I need to know or I'm going to have my man's here finish whopping your ass and if that still doesn't work, I'm going to start chopping your ass up into little pieces are we clear?" I explained to him.

"What do you want to know?" He said as blood dripped all over his face.

"Did Brian have something to do with all this shit going on?" I asked him.

"Yeah man him and Lee set up the whole thing." Cam said.

"Wait Lee was in on all this shit?" I asked furiously.

"Yeah, your whole operation, your entire movement everything. How you think the hitman knew how to get around your security? It was all Lee.

Lee is Brian's half-brother. Brian's dad had an affair on his mom and Lee was an outside child." Cam said and I was shocked.

"So, which one of them motherfuckers shot Renee?" I asked furiously.

"It was Lee. Brian ordered him to take out some chick name Mia. He said it was so Sierra can hopefully get depressed and lose the baby. Lee missed the shot and it hit the other girl. She wasn't a target. So, Brian killed Lee for fucking up the operation. They put the outfit on Lee so everything can get traced back to you." Cam said. I then began to see black. I was tired of this shit. It was one thing for these motherfuckers to be coming for me but I'll be damned if they come for the women in my life and that's where they got me fucked up at. I kicked the fucking stool and rushed behind him a pulled his head back. I put the knife to his fucking throat. I then grabbed his face.

"So, tell me motherfucker. What role did you play in all this?" I said angrily. He better had hoped he said the right thing next.

"I'm the one who gave the drop on you and Sierra when hitman shot her." He said and I sliced his neck. I continued to cut until his head fell over. I kicked the head a crossed the room.

"Motherfucker the reason why my girl almost died. Law, Tech finish chopping his ass up and box that motherfucker up. Once you finish ship his ass to their fucking door step." I said and then once I turned around Sierra was standing right there. Shit. I hope she didn't see none of this shit.

31 THE GIRLS

SIERRA

As Sean turned around to see I was standing right there it was obvious that he didn't expect me to be there. I watched him behead a man and I honestly didn't know how to feel. Would it be cruel to say that I didn't feel anything? I can only assume this is the monster in him that they are talking about. The monster in him that he doesn't want me to see.

"Baby look." He said to me.

"Is that the monster I wasn't supposed to see?" I asked.

"Some of it. This isn't shit compared to what other things I have done to motherfuckers. But I swear I didn't know you was right there." He tried to explain to me.

"Okay." I said to him.

"Just, okay?" He asked me.

"What else am I supposed to say? If I'm going to love you, I have to accept you flaws and all right." I expressed to him.

"That would be nice." He said as he then leaned in for a kiss.

"Hold it right their bucko. You need to clean this blood off of you. I do not want that shit on me." I said and he laughed.

"How are your contractions right now?" He asked.

"Still the same. My lower back is still in pain." I told him.

"I can massage it." He said as he winked.

"Yeah, well how long will the massage last before we move to other things." I said and then giggled.

"Well." He started to say as he got closer to move his hands between my legs. My legs began to quiver.

"There's a way I can still massage it. I can turn you over and stroke you from the back while massaging your back in the process." He said as he then licked the side of my ear.

"Can we go now." I said and he laughed.

"Later baby. I got shit I need to handle down here. After the shit I just found out we are going to have to change up every fucking thing. Our operation the way we move our products everything. I'm even going to fire the security team." He revealed to me.

"Damn babe. What happened?" I asked him being nosey.

"He said Brian is behind this whole shit and that Brian was Lee's half-brother." He explained and I was shocked.

"What!" I yelled out.

"You didn't know?" He asked.

"Hell no. He told me before that his father had an affair on his mother but he never mentioned an outside child." I informed Sean.

"Yeah, well that motherfucker Lee is his brother and was telling Brian everything. It explains how hitman was able to get through security to kidnap you and enter the house to kill Sylvia. I'm going to have to hire new security because I'm going to kill every last single one of them motherfuckers outside. Fuck firing." He said to me in an angry tone.

"Wait babe. Don't kill all of them because you don't want to kill any innocent ones. Tell me do your security have to log in for every shift?" I asked him.

"Yeah, they do." He informed me.

"Find out who was on shift the day they kidnapped me and killed Sylvia. The common name is the problem." I explained to him

"Nah, fuck all that. I think I'd rather just kill all their ass. Plus, it was Lee who shot Renee. Brian gave Lee the order to kill Mia thinking it would have stressed you out so you could lose the baby. But Lee missed Mia and hit Renee so that's why Brian killed him. I can't wait until the day I see him one on one. I'm going to do his ass the worse." He said demandingly.

"That son of bitch. I can't believe him. So, what now?" I asked him.

"Well now I have to put together a whole new operation. Now that I know who is behind this I'm going to start planning accordingly. I want to plan to get this done before the babies arrive." He explained to me.

"Listen babe. I know you want to make sure there isn't a threat to me or the twins but don't rush the plan. Shit can go wrong. Let's just take it one day at a time." I expressed to him.

"Okay baby. It's going to be a long fucking day. I'm going to kill those fucking security motherfuckers I don't care what you say. I then have to hire new ones and hopefully get them started today and fix my operation." He explained to me again. He's trying to tell me something and instead of him just saying it, he'd rather beat around the fucking bush.

"Okay Sean. So that means I probably won't see you until tonight? That's what you're trying to tell me without just saying it." I said to him annoyed.

"Probably not. But Renee said she was going to get together with all of you anyways. I guess y'all can have a girl's night or whatever the fuck it is that y'all do." He said to me.

"Great. Girls' night and I can't have 1 fucking drink." I said and he laughed.

"Well hopefully you won't get pregnant so soon after the twins are born." He voiced to me.

"Right. Because you can't keep your hands to yourself." I stated to him.

"Stop it. Every chance you get you want to grab my dick." He said and I busted out in laughter.

"I love you; you know." I expressed to him lovingly.

"I know baby. I love you too." He said and I smiled.

"Well, I'm going to head upstairs to the girls. But don't forget Sean or I'm going to be pissed." I said to him irritated.

"Be pissed about what? I know tomorrows your birthday and I know we're getting married tomorrow." He said reassuring me.

"Wait how did you know that's what I was talking about?" I asked him. He completely through me off already knowing what I was talking about.

"Baby I even know when you breathe different." He said and I smiled.

"Ok. Try not to behead anyone else you here." I said and he laughed.

"See you later baby." He said as he kissed my cheek and I then walked away to head back up to see what the girls were up too.

Once I got to the entertainment room, I seen the girls wrapped up in blankets laughing having a good time while a movie was playing on the television. All I ever had was Mia and now I'm really seeing what it was like to have a sisterhood.

"Hey Sierra. Get in here." Emily said as I then sat next to her and put some of the blanket over my legs.

"You know I'm sorry I didn't get to experience all of this with you guys longer before I left." I expressed to them.

"Don't sweat it girl. We have nothing but time now. And besides, we are women so we understand." Renee said.

"True. When you left, I told Sean everyday how much of a stupid motherfucker he was." Emily said and we laughed.

"He had me so pissed girl I could have killed him. I really didn't think I was going to fall for him so fast." I told them.

"Well, you know not everyone has the chance to get to know the real Sean. He's a psycho son of a bitch." Renee said and we laughed again.

"Tell me about it. I just watched him behead a man." I gossiped to them.

"Whatttt. Damn I wish I would have seen it." Emily said.

"Right. He hasn't done that in so long I know they are having a ball in the torture room." Renee said.

"Wait so you two have seen all this before?" I asked them.

"Hell yeah, plenty of times. They use to keep people in the torture room a while back." Renee said.

"Remember when we use to be pissed off and they would let us go down there to release some anger." Emily said.

"Man, I miss that shit." Renee said.

"What did you do down there exactly?" I asked them as I was curious.

"Well, I butchered someone." Emily said.

"And I got to use the saw." Renee said and we laughed.

"And it really made you feel that good?" I asked again curious. As crazy as it may seem but watching him, looked as if it felt good.

"Hell yeah. But I don't mind killing someone. Killing someone has to make you feel good in order to enjoy it. And that doesn't mean just kill anyone because we only harm the ones who want to harm us or fuck up our operation." Emily said.

"Yes. Please don't ever try and fuck up my money." Renee said and we laughed.

"You know when I shot and killed the hitman, I felt nothing." I told them.

"At all?" Emily asked.

"Nothing." I stated.

"Mmm Mm." Renee said.

"Girl." Emily said.

"What?" I asked.

"Seems like you are more alike with Sean than you think." Renee said.

"How's that?" I asked.

"Because when Sean kills people, he doesn't feel anything. There's no emotion whatsoever. Once he gets in his mind that he's going to kill you just go head a prepare your own damn funeral." Emily said.

"True. Remember that time when he had that man and his wife here and he had her cut his dick off and made her suck it before he killed both of them." Renee said.

"Yeah, he was an evil son of a bitch back then." Emily said and we laughed.

"Well, he was pissed when he cut the man head off just now." I advised them.

"Did the guy say something about you?" Emily asked.

"Yeah, he did." I enlightened them.

"That's why. Can't no one say anything to him about you without pissing him off. Hell, he would have killed the Doctors in the hospital that day you were shot just because they didn't have information to give him yet. He'll kill anyone behind you girl." Mia said.

"Well truth be told I think they'll kill anyone behind all of us." I said and they giggled.

"True. You don't fuck with the women in their lives. The four of us are their families. They'll burn the fucking world down behind us." Renee said.

"I still can't believe you got shot." Emily said.

"Shit you telling me. I thought I was dead." Renee said.

"Speaking of which. It was Lee who shot you." I informed them and they all began to gasp air.

"No way." Emily said.

"Girl a lot of shit was going down. We knew you were stressed about Renee so we didn't bother you. Apparently, Lee was Brian's half-brother and Mia was the target. Lee missed the shot and hit you Renee on accident. So that's why Brian killed Lee." I explained to them.

"Lees dead!" Emily and Renee yelled at the same time.

"Yes, it was breaking news a couple months ago. They found him in an alleyway with the clothes on from the courthouse shooting." I advised them.

"That snake son of a bitch." Emily said.

"Wow I can't believe it." Renee said.

"But why would Brian make me a target?" Mia asked.

"Well, he assumed if he killed you, I would be depressed and lose the baby." I said to them.

"Oh, I can't imagine what Sean is going to do to him when he finally gets a hold of his ass." Renee said.

"I can't even imagine because now he's on a killing spree." I said out loud.

"What do you mean?" Emily asked.

"He's killing the entire security team and hiring new ones." I said and they laughed.

"Why are y'all laughing." I asked the girls.

"Because that sounds like him. He doesn't want to take the time to figure out who was the snake in the security team so they all have to suffer for it." Emily said.

"You know the thing about all this is when I was watching him behead that guy down there it was one of the sexiest things, I've ever seen him do." I said and the girls began to look at each other.

"What?" I asked.

"Girl, you are a psycho path just like him." Mia said and they laughed.

"I'm serious. The look he had on his face while doing it just turned me on." I said as I then tightened my legs.

"You two might as well have blood pouring at the wedding tomorrow." Emily said.

"Wait who's getting married?" Renee asked.

"Sean and I." I said and Renee screamed.

"Damn you Lee. You bastard made me miss all the good shit." Renee said and we all laughed.

"You guys haven't even heard the most shocking part." I said to the girls.

"What?" Renee said.

"Not only are we having a son. But we are having a daughter as well. Fucking twins." I said and Renee and Emily's mouth dropped.

"Wait you aren't surprise Mia. Why not?" I asked her.

"Sean told Law and I earlier." She informed me.

"That asshole." I said and they laughed.

"You know what the three of you can have all the babies you want. I'm just going to be the cool auntie." Emily said.

"You don't want any kids?" I asked Emily.

"Hell no. I love what I do too much and I don't want anything getting in the way of that. I'll love all of your children as if they were my own. I just don't want to have my own." Emily said.

"So, you don't want to get married or anything?" I asked her interested in her answer.

"Nope. I don't need a near motherfucker trying to tie me down. I love my peace. And most importantly I love my space." Emily said and we giggled.

"You know I really love this. Just being here with you girls makes me feel like I have sisters." I expressed.

"Well, we are sisters. The guys have their relationship and bond and we have ours." Renee said.

"True. I'm so happy. Mia, you have been quiet what's going on?" I asked waiting for her to spill the tea about something.

"Well while you bitches were bonding, I've been trying to watch the damn movie." Mia said and we laughed.

"We're sorry crybaby. What is it?" I asked as the girls and I laughed.

"Hey, these hormones are kicking my ass. And just so you know I'm watching Saw V." Mia said.

"Fine. I'll pop us some popcorn and we can watch the movie with you." I said and I got up to fix the popcorn. It felt so good to be able to just sit down and laugh and talk with the girls. It felt good to finally feel at home with everyone you love there. Once I finish popping the popcorn I went back in there and got back in the blanket. I watched the movie until I began to doze off.

As I began to wake up from dozing off on the movie, the girls were laying there still sleep as well. That movie was fucking boring as hell. They don't make the saw movies like they use to. Shit. What fucking time was it? I then looked down at my phone and it was almost 9pm. I was hungry as hell. I really hope Chelsea was still up because baby could throw down. Sylvia trained her well. I then walked to the kitchen and Chelsea was just beginning to wipe everything down.

"Oh, thank God you're still in here Chelsea." I said and she giggled.

"Yes ma'am. You're hungry, aren't you?" She asked and I swear I almost died.

"Starving. Now I know why I was always so damn hungry. I'm feeding for two." I said to Chelsea.

"Congratulations, Sierra. You must be excited." She stated to me.

"I am but I'm also nervous you know. I'm about to be a first-time mom of not one but two damn kids!" I yelled out and Chelsea began to laugh.

"I wish I could tell you how to feel or what to do but unfortunately I don't have any kids," she informed me.

"Is it that you don't want any or is that by choice?" I asked of her.

"Well maybe both to be honest. With me being here most of the time I really don't have time for it. And I love my job and the money that it pays. Don't worry, Sylvia trained me really well. I'm even trained on what to do for when the babies come. Even though I'm the head of the kitchen, I'm the head of the front of the house." She explained to me.

"That's awesome Chelsea for real. I really don't want to cut our conversation short but I swear my stomach is touch my back." I told her and she giggled.

"Three turkey ham and bacon sandwiches add cheese?" She asked me. I swore I loved her.

"And a glass of orange juice. Oh, God yes." I said and she continued to chuckle.

"Would you like for me to bring it up to your room?" Chelsea asked.

"Would you please?" I asked her as she nodded and I took the elevator up to my room as I then waited for her to bring up the food. Once she brought up the sandwiches, I ate and then I fell asleep thinking about my wedding day.

32 THE WEDDING

SIERRA

Today was the day that I was going to marry the love of my life. I was nervous yet excited at the same time. But was I ready to really enter the world of Sean White? Was I ready to be the wife of a man that everyone was afraid of? Was I ready to be the wife of a man who made a living off drugs and missions? Was I ready to be the wife of a man who would go to the end of the world for the people he loved? Was I ready to be the wife of the man who was the father of my children? Was I ready to be the wife of a man who was madly in love with me? Die for me? Was I ready to risk it all for him? I can't lie, being with him gives me a sense of power and I feel unstoppable.

But one thing that I know is that power can also be dangerous. And the high that I feel while I'm in it, I refuse to give it away. So yes, I was ready to marry him. I loved him so much that I would kill for him. I can't live without his kisses, the way his touch makes my body shiver. Shit where the fuck was, he? I hope everything was okay. I haven't seen or talked to him since I saw him in the torture room yesterday. I wanted to feel him one more time before we became husband and wife. As I thought about him, I wanted him more and more. I guided my hand down in between my thighs and started to circle around my clit. I tilted my head back in ecstasy as I went in and out of myself thinking of him.

knock knock knock

Shit. Why the fuck would someone pick now to knock on my door? "Who is it?" I yelled out annoyed.

"It's Mia. May I come in?" She asked. Dammit Mia.

"One second." I said as I then went to the bathroom to wash my hands. Once I was done, I opened the door to let her in.

"Hey what's up?" I asked her.

"Happy Birthday Mrs. White are you ready for today?" She asked.

"Thank you and technically I'm not Mrs. White yet." I advised her.

"Girl please don't let him hear you say that." She said and I giggled.

"Sierra White. It does have a good ring too it doesn't it?" I asked and we both laughed.

"You damn right." Mia said and I smiled.

"I just love him so much Mia I don't think I can breathe without him." I expressed to her.

"I know you do. And trust me you may feel as though you can't breathe without him but he can't live without you. He doesn't even think straight when you're not around." Mia said.

"I know. But do you think I'm ready for this?" I asked her. I needed Mia to tell me that everything was going to be okay. I needed her to tell me that this was going to be the right move.

"I know you are. We both fit in their worlds so quickly as if we always belonged. I've never seen you glow with Brian the way that you do with Sean. And you can't say you aren't ready because he kills people because you have **bodies** on your hands too." Mia said and I laughed.

"No, no, it's not that. I don't care about what he does or how he does it. What I mean is, am I ready for my life to change? I'm going to be married to one of the most powerful men in the country." I informed her as I began to breathe out slowly.

"And you know what that makes you?" Mia asked.

"What?" I responded to her.

"One of the most respectable and powerful women in the world. The world fearing you because of your husband. Everyone listening to your command. Giving orders without anyone second guessing. Its power Sierra. The question now is, what are you going to do with it?" Mia asked and she was right. What was I going to do with it? Harold still hasn't sent the papers back over for my consent to release the company back to him so I don't know if I still own it. Do I just continue to run a firm while being the one of the most feared women? If so, would they still come after my husband knowing I'm still the best damn attorney in New York City? It would be tricky. Not only could I never testify against him because we are married, they would know they would have to bring everything they got before they think they could ever touch my husband. And that gives me more power. The power to protect my husband.

"I want it all Mia. I want to become the female version of him. The one who they should really fear. And I still want to run a firm. But my life here they would never know. I would be who they least expect. If I keep the firm going, I can protect my husband and everyone else in our family by all means. My husband wants business all over the world and I want to help him get it there." I said and Mia clapped.

"Yessss. Sean brings back out the bad in you and I love everything about it." Mia said and I laughed as someone knocked on the door again.

"Come in." I said and Renee and Emily walked in.

"Oh my gosh girl you aren't dressed yet?" Renee said.

"Girl do you see how big this damn stomach is?" I asked and they laughed.

"Are you in any pain?" Emily asked.

"Yes, but they aren't coming back-to-back just yet. But they are worse than yesterday but its bearable" I explained to them.

"Maybe you should rest. Sean would understand." Emily said.

"Oh no ma'am. I'm marrying my man today." I said and they laughed.

"So, where's the dress?" Mia asked.

"What dress? I asked.

"You see I'm glad we were able to get this at the last minute." Renee said.

"Get what?" I asked and they reached behind the door and grabbed a dress.

"Happy Birthday!" Renee and Emily yelled and a tear fell from my eye.

"Bitch are you crying?" Mia asked and we laughed.

"That dress is so beautiful. I was not expecting this at all. I hate you bitches." I said and they laughed.

"Well, here I got you something too." Mia said as she then handed me a box. When I opened it there was a diamond necklace to match the sparkling diamonds in the wedding dress. I began to cry some more.

"This is the best birthday ever. I love you guys so much." I said as I pulled them in for a group hug.

"Just make sure to name your daughter Emily." Emily said and we all busted into laughter.

"I'm going to need help putting this dress on." I stated to them.

"We already know. That's why we are all here." Mia said.

"Now what exactly were the two of you going to do. You both have bellies." Emily said to Renee and Mia and they laughed.

"Hey, grade us 100% for effort okay." Renee said and we laughed. Emily then helped me into my dress. I looked in the mirror and this was one of the most beautiful dresses I have ever seen. I sat down and Mia slid some matching slides on my foot so I could be comfortable. I then sat in the chair while Renee put my hair in an updo style.

"You really are beautiful." Renee said.

"We all are." I said and they all smiled.

"Yeah, well today is about you." Renee said.

"Ouch!" I yelled.

"What's wrong?" Emily yelled and the rest of the girls looked concern.

"Nothing. One of twins kicked me on my side with the heel of their foot." I said and they laughed.

"That shit hurt doesn't it." Renee said.

"Yes, it does. But I wouldn't trade them for the world." I said and they smiled.

"Alright enough mushy stuff. Are you ready to do this Mrs. White?" Mia asked.

"I'm ready." I expressed to them.

"Okay now remember just because your life is about to change and more power will be in your hands doesn't mean we will ever stop being here for you." Mia said.

"Sisters till the end." I said as I looked at them.

"For life." They said and they all hugged me and we began walking out the door. As I slowly walked down the hallway my heart was racing. I even thought I began to sweat at one point. Once we got downstairs and headed to the garden, the girls opened the door and Sean was nowhere in sight. Where the fuck was, he? All I see is Law Tech and the officiant. My phone then began to ring and my heart began to ache.

"Who is this?" I asked when I picked up the phone.

"Is this Ms. Johnson?" the person on the other line asked.

"Yes, it is. Who is this?" I responded.

"This is Doctor Krane from the Memorial Hospital. We have 2 unidentified bodies here and one has you as a secondary primary contact. Can you please come and identify?" The guy said and my heart began to drop. I fell to the ground in tears. Everyone ran over to me.

"What the fuck? Sierra what's going on?" Law yelled out. But I was stunned. I was in shock. I felt like I couldn't breathe. I couldn't talk. All I could do was cry. The only person not here right now was Sean. I can't think about him being dead. On our wedding day? On my birthday? My heart was broken. I felt like dying.

33 MY VOW TO YOU

SIERRA

"Sierra look at me. What the fuck is going on?" Law said. My vision was beginning to get blurry.

"Seaaa. Sean." I kept trying to say and Law started screaming out Sean's name. My world was beginning to turn. He just can't be dead. We were supposed to be spending the rest of our lives together. Next thing you know I smelt a familiar scent.

"Baby, baby, are you okay?" What the fuck happened." He asked as he was about to panic.

"Seaa. Sean. You're not dead?" I asked in a faint tone of voice.

"Dead? Why the fuck would I be dead?" He yelled and I began to cry a little harder.

"Listen baby just breathe." He said to me and I began to go out of it a little more.

"Shit." I heard him say as he picked me up and carried me into the living and placed me on the couch.

"Everyone get the fuck out. Once I find out what's going on I will let everyone know." He commanded them and they all left. I began to breathe heavier. He ran to the kitchen and came back.

"Here baby drink some water." He said as he lifted my head to help me drink some of the water. I began to breathe rapidly.

"Breathe baby. Calm down. Tell me what's wrong. Are you having second thoughts? We can push it back whatever you need." He expressed to me while I began to breathe slowly like he asked.

"That's it. Take one big breath for me." He demanded. I did what I was told.

"Now tell me. What's going on?" He asked.

"I thought you were dead." I explained to him.

"And why would you think that?" He asked.

"Well, when the girls opened the doors to the garden, I didn't see you there. Next thing you know I get a phone call from the Memorial Hospital asking me to come and identify 2 bodies. One of them had me down as the emergency contact. I can't lose you Sean." I said and I began to cry again and he grabbed me close and began to hold me tight.

"Shhhh baby. I'm right here. I'm not going anywhere." He enlightened me and then all of a sudden it hit me. I slapped his ass.

"What the hell did I do?" He yelled.

"Where the fuck was you? You weren't there when I was coming through the door." I yelled and he laughed.

"Baby I was trying to do one last security check before you came out. I wouldn't miss seeing you in this beautiful dress for the world." He advised me.

"Don't try and butter me up Sean White. I should kill you!" I yelled out to him. I honestly thing these hormones are getting the best of me today.

"For what? He said as he laughed. I went in to slap him again and he grabbed my hand and pulled me in for a kiss.

"Happy Birthday Baby." He said seductively.

"Thank you. But listen what two people is there for me to identify at the hospital?" I asked him.

"What hospital did they say come to?" He asked.

"Memorial Hospital." I replied to him.

"Okay which one?" He asked.

"They didn't say. They just said come to the Memorial Hospital." I said and he began to get angry.

"Law!" He yelled out and he came running inside.

"What's up?" Law said.

"Do you want me to kill your ass now or later?" He said threatening Law.

"Is never an option?" Law said and I busted out in laughter and Sean gave Law a stare.

"I need you to get Sierra another phone later on today with a new number." Sean said demandingly.

"Ok. Everything good?" Law asked.

"Well, when I didn't see Sean out there when I was coming out, I began to panic. Then I received a phone call telling me to come to the Memorial Hospital to identify 2 bodies." I explained to Law.

"They didn't say which hospital?" Law asked.

"No, they didn't Sherlock. Just get the damn phone like I said." Sean yelled.

"Will you stop yelling. Today is about happiness. Today is all about love." Law said sarcastically and I giggled. He knew exactly how to get under Sean's skin.

"Law, I have already been slapped on my wedding day. Please don't make me have to place a bullet in your ass!" Sean yelled and Law and I laughed. Sean then turned to face me.

"Would you still like to be my wife?" Sean asked and I smiled.

"I wouldn't have it any other way." I said as he then took my hand and Law guided us outside. When they saw us coming, they all began to clap. We walked directly in front of the officiant.

"Thank you to the friends and family that are here today to celebrate the union of Sean White and Sierra Johnson. This occasion not only marks the beginning of their marriage commitment together, but it is a commemoration of the love nurtured and shared between these two. Together, they embark today on a new life together, built on the foundations of trust, compassion, and mutual respect. Who gives the bride away today?" The officiant asked.

"I do." Mia said and I looked at her and smiled.

"Marriage is an ancient human tradition. The personal and social merits that accompany the bonds of marriage have led to its continued endurance and have paved the way for us to be standing here before God celebrating the union between these two people today. As we celebrate this bond of unity today under the eyes of God, it is important that we keep in mind that, while this is certainly an occasion of tremendous joy, the promises we witness here today are serious and life-altering commitments. As Jesus said: "Have you not read that He who made them at the beginning 'made them male and female," he also taught that, "For this reason a man shall leave his father and mother and be joined to his wife, and the two shall become one flesh'? So then, they are no longer two but one flesh. Therefore, what God has joined together, let not man separate. It is with simultaneous feelings of elation and expressions of respect that we proceed. At this time, before proceeding with the bonding ceremony, I would invite the couple to share their vows. Sean, would you please deliver yours first?" The officiant asked and Sean nodded.

"Sierra, my beautiful bride and the love of my life. The day I first laid eyes on you I knew that if I pursed this any further nothing was going to go as planned. I knew you were going to come in and change my life for the better. But I didn't know it was going to be for a lifetime. Every morning I wake up, I want to love you even more than I did yesterday. From this day forward I promise my life to you and our children. I promise to worship the ground you walk on. Protect you and our family always. This is it baby. I, take you and only you Sierra Johnson, for my lawfully wedded Wife, to have and to hold, from this day forward, for better or worse, for richer or poorer. I promise to be true to you in good times and in bad, in sickness and in health. I will love you and honor you all the days of my life, until death do us part. This is my solemn vow." Sean said and tears ran down my eyes. There's no way I could love anyone else ever.

"Sierra, you may now make your promise." The officiant said.

"Sean, my king and lover. I've been dreaming about you since I first laid eyes on you on television. Even after meeting you face to face for the first time my heart sank. I thought I was still in a dream when really, we were in a bar. It was my reality and I couldn't breathe. You took the air right out of me and even then, my dreams never stopped until the day I finally became yours. I know this was fast and not the way many people would expect it but I love you and I want nothing more than to be your wife. Do you remember our first kiss?" I asked him.

"I'll never forget it." He responded to me.

"It wasn't long enough. The first date. All of our conversations. They were never long enough. There is no better man for me than you. I know you want the world and with me by your side I promise we'll get it together. I crave you and only you every night and day. I crave your presence, your love your touch. Seeing you is a reflection of myself. I can't let this go. I'll never give up on you and I hope you'll never give up on me. I know you'll be a great husband but most important a great father. I never want to lose the one thing that holds me together and that's you. Your one of the only things that make sense in my love. I'll do whatever it takes to keep you in my life. I love you Sean and I promise to take you to have and to hold, from this day forward, for better or worse, for richer or poorer. I promise to be true to you in good times and in bad, in sickness and in health. I will love you and honor you all the days of my life, until death do us part. This is my vow to you." I said and he smiled.

"Sean and Sierra please face one another and join hands. Under the eyes of God, Sean, do you take Sierra to be your lawfully wedded Wife? By making this commitment, you are joining in the sacred covenant of marriage. Do you Sean promise to honor her in love, to be sensitive to her needs, to comfort her in difficulty, and to put your full and complete trust in her, so long as you both shall live?" The officiant asked Sean.

"I do." He said to the officiant.

"Under the eyes of God, Sierra, do you take Sean to be your lawfully wedded Husband? By making this commitment, you are joining in the covenant of marriage. Do you promise to honor him in love, to be sensitive to his needs, to comfort him in difficulty, and to put your full and complete trust in him, so long as you both shall live?" The officiant asked me.

"I do." I responded.

"To commemorate this union, you may now exchange rings. The circle formed by each ring symbolizes your eternal love and commitment to one another. Let these rings remind you always of that love, and of the promises you have made here on this day. You may now exchange rings." He said and Sean put a ring on my finger and I did the same.

"By the power vested in me, by the state of New York, I pronounce you, Sean and Sierra as Husband and Wife. Sean you may now kiss your bride." The officiant said and Sean pulled me in and kissed me so deep and passionately.

"Okay y'all save it for the bedroom." Law said and we all laughed.

"Ladies and gentlemen, it is my pleasure to present to you Mr. and White!" The officiant said and everyone began to clap. Sean then grabbed my hand and led me back into the house. I then sat down on the couch. This day was everything that I ever wanted. I know its not the "dream" weddings all the girls normally think about. But it was just right for me. I had the love of my life and the people we loved surrounding us. But the most important thing about this day was we still had each other.

"Here Mrs. White I have something for you. Happy Birthday." He said as I took the box from him.

"What is it?" I asked him.

"Open and you will see." He said and I opened the box there was a note and a key.

Because you love me for who I am, I could never ask you to not love who you are. Not only do you have the key to my heart but here a key to the city. There's nothing I would never do for you. The world is yours. Your dreams are whatever you decide to make it. Happy Birthday Mrs. White.

Your Husband.

"Sean what is this?" I asked him as I began to get teary eyed.

"Your first key to the city baby. A building bought by me for you to start your own firm." He said and tears ran down my eyes.

"Are you serious. You know I had the money to do that." I explained to him.

"Baby I don't ever want to hear you say anything to me about money ever again. You're my wife. What's mine is ours. I love you Sierra and I never want you to stop being who you are because you love me. I still want you to love yourself and what you worked so hard for." Sean said and I continued to wipe tears from my eyes.

"Were you eavesdropping on Mia and I earlier?" I asked him out of curiosity.

"Why the fuck would I do that?" He said dramatically.

"Mia came in before all this to make sure I wasn't getting cold feet. And I told her that I wanted it all. I wanted to become the female version of you. The one everyone would least expect. If I continued to run the firm, I can protect you and everyone in our family by all means. I'd have the power to protect my husband always. You want the whole world baby and I want to help you get it." I said and he smiled.

"Are you sure that's what you want baby? To be a female version of me?" He asked.

"Yes. I'm your wife now. And we both share the power. And besides. Two heads are better than one." I explained to him.

"Which head you talking about?" He said and I laughed.

"You know what I mean. Shit! Chelsea!" I yelled out and she came running from the kitchen.

"Yes mam." She said to me.

"Please tell me the food is ready." I said and she giggled.

"Yes mam. We're setting up a table now so you all can eat together. Give us 10 minutes." Chelsea said and I nodded.

"Congratulations to the both of you. It's a celebration of love. I even have your favorite cake cooking." Chelsea said.

"Oh my gosh Chelsea, I love you!" I said and she laughed.

"No problem mam." She said and she headed back into the kitchen.

"Did you have anything to do with this my darling husband?" I asked him

"Well, I may have given her the word about the cake." He said and I giggled.

"You working for these panties today huh." I informed him sarcastically.

"Oh, I was going to get that either way." He said and I laughed. He then grabbed my feet and began massaging them.

"Are you in pain today?" He asked.

"They are a little stronger from yesterday but they aren't coming back-to-back yet." I explained.

"I can have them bring the food to you upstairs if you need rest." He said to me.

"No love it's okay. I want to eat dinner with everyone. Speaking of which where the fuck is everyone?" I stated loudly.

"Good question. Tech!" He yelled out and Tech came running in from outside.

"What man?" Tech said and Sean and I laughed.

"Why the hell is everyone still outside.?" Sean asked.

"Shit we didn't know what the two of you were doing in here. None of us wanted to hear that shit." Tech said and Sean and I busted into laughter.

"We'll wait until tonight asshole. Tell everyone to come inside. Dinner is almost ready." Sean said and Tech nodded. A few minutes later he came back in with Renee Emily and Mia.

"Where's Law?" Mia asked.

"He went to get Sierra a new phone. He should be on the way back." Sean said and she nodded.

"Excuse me sir and ma'am. Dinner is ready." Chelsea said and Sean nodded.

"Let's hurry up and eat. I'm ready to take my wife's panties off." Sean said and we all laughed.

"Wait call Law." I told him and he rolled his eyes and picked up his phone to call Law.

"Where the fuck are you, asshole?" Sean said.

"Right here dumbass." Law said as he was opening the door at the same time.

"About damn time." Sean said.

"I was only gone for 20 minutes asshole." Law said.

"Well thank you. Come on let's go eat dinner." Sean said and we all headed to the dining area to eat dinner. We laughed and we talked.

"This is really nice. We should do this every day." I advised everyone.

"Oh, hell no!" Sean said and we laughed.

"Shut the hell up Sean. Family Dinners are important. We are family we have 4 kids coming really soon and giving them some sort of tradition can help ease our mind off of everything else that goes on outside this house. We owe this to our children. For them to see a strong family no matter what the world throws at us." I said and the girls smiled.

"I do not want to be at dinner with those two assholes every day." Sean said and we laughed again.

"We love you too brother." Law and Tech said at the same time and Sean rolled his eyes. The girls and I giggled.

"All jokes aside. I love and appreciate everyone at this table. I want to thank you all for risking your lives not only for me or my wife but for us as a family. I love every last single one of you and I'll kill any motherfucker over all of you." Sean said to them.

"Was that a toast?" Emily asked.

"Fuck you all." Sean said and we all began to laugh. Next thing you know my old phone began to ring.

"Hello." I said once I answered.

"Sierra, its Ann. Harold's wife." She responded.

"Of course, I know who this is, how are you?" I asked her.

"Not good baby. Harold died a couple hours ago." She said and my heart began to sink.

"No. This can't be happening." I said and my eyes began to water.

"I know this isn't something you want to hear on your birthday and I'm sorry baby. But I'll keep you posted on service details." She said and I ended the call-in tears.

"Baby what's wrong." Sean asked.

"Harold died." I said and I began to cry. Sean then carried me upstairs to the room and laid me down on the bed. He undressed me and put me in some comfy clothes. My heart was broken. It was a good day. It was one of the best days of my life. And my only father figure left me. I didn't get to say goodbye. I didn't get to apologize about our fight. I just need one more chance to tell him that I love him. Sean got in the bed and held me until I cried myself to sleep.

34 LETTING GO

SIERRA

It was a new day and not only was I waking up married next to the love of my life but I was also sad about losing Harold. I knew he didn't have much time left but I didn't think it would of came not to long after our fight. I was hurt. I just needed one more conversation to make this right. I just needed one more conversation just to say that I was sorry. I needed one more conversation just to say I love you. I removed Sean's hands from around my waist and I headed to the bathroom and relaxed in the hot bath. I pulled out my phone to give Harold's wife a call to see if she needed my help with anything.

"Hello?" She answered.

"Hey Ann. It's Sierra." I responded.

"Hey baby. How are you?" Ann said.

"I should be asking you that." I expressed to her.

"Oh baby, I'm okay. Because I've had time to prepare myself for this moment, I'm stronger than I was before. I held his hand down to his last breath. Things started to take a turn for the worse these past couple of weeks and we knew it was time. How are you holding up?" Ann said.

"It's hard you know? The both of you were the closest thing I had to parents. I wish I could bring him back for just one more minute so I can hug him and tell him I'm sorry." I explained to her.

"Sorry for what? The fight you had?" Ann asked.

"He told you about that?" I asked her.

"Of course, he did. Harold came in here so mad after he left." Ann said.

"I know. We never had a fight like that before. But I love him. I knew there was a chance I could have been taking with my career if I pursued this but my heart just wouldn't let me walk away even though my mind knew the consequences." I informed her.

"Oh, baby you don't have to explain to me. And truth be told Harold was more upset about the fact that you didn't tell him you were pregnant. Granted he was upset about that young man as well but he knew that he loved you." She explained to me.

"Really? I couldn't tell." I told her.

"He said even though he doesn't agree with the lifestyle he could have seen it in his eyes that he was madly in love with you. That gave him some sort of peace that if he were to leave this world, he knew you would have been taken care of." Ann said.

"We are actually married now." I stated.

"Congratulations my baby girl. I'm happy for you. I'll also be able to see my grand baby, won't I?" Ann asked.

"Grandbabies." I told her.

"What?" Ann screamed out and I laughed.

"Yes mam. Twins. A boy and a girl." I informed her.

"Wow if the cancer didn't kill Harold, then that would have." Ann joked and we both laughed.

"I'm going to miss him so much I just wish he knew I was sorry." I said to her as I then began to get sad all over again.

"He knows baby trust me. He left something for you but he wanted me to give it too you after the service." Ann said.

"When's the service? And do you need anything?" I asked her.

"Oh no baby I'm fine. The service is in the next couple of days. Harold didn't want anyone going days grieving him. He had everything planned out the moment the doctors gave him his time frame. The service and burial planning was done long ago." She explained to me.

"Ok. What are your plans now?" I asked her.

"What do you mean?" Ann asked.

"Are you going to keep staying in that big house alone?" I asked.

"I sure am. Harold and I were all we had besides you even though you were already grown when he found you. I'll be okay baby. You don't have to worry about me." She enlightened me.

"If that's what you want, I won't argue with that. So, the service is which day exactly?" I asked her so I can know how to prepare.

"At the city memorial grave site Wednesday. He wanted a short service at the burial site at 2:00." She explained to me.

"May I say a few words please?" I asked her.

"Sure, you can." She said to me.

"Thank you. Well, I'll let you go and I'll see you then." I stated.

"Okay baby." She responded to me.

"Okay I love you." I expressed to her.

"I love you too." She said and we both then disconnected the call. I wondered what Harold left for me? I had two days to prepare for the service and I knew it wasn't going to be easy because I really did love him like a dad. I began to breathe in and out because my contractions were a little stronger today. They have been coming closer and closer but I had so much going on, I haven't been keeping track with the time. I'm sure it's okay as I was only still 1cm dilated. I then slouched down in the tub some more so I could relax in the warm water.

SEAN

As I began to open my eyes, I turned to see my wife was gone. I jumped out of the bed quickly. Where the fuck was, she?

"Baby." I said and there was no response. Shit. I threw on my robe and I wanted to be sure before I panic and killed a motherfucker. I ran into the bathroom and there she was sleeping in the bathtub. Was she fucking crazy?

"Sierra!" I yelled and she jumped up.

"What the fuck Sean?" She yelled out.

"Don't what the fuck me. Why would you fall asleep in the bathtub? What if you would have slipped down and drowned?" I yelled frustrated.

"I'm sorry babe. I didn't think of any of that. Forgive me? I didn't mean to scare you." She said softly but I didn't care. I was about to let her ass have it.

"Don't do that shit again Sierra. I can't see my life without you. When I woke up to see you were gone, I immediately panicked. You know there's a lot of shit going on right now. Even if you just going to take a nap I need to know until we get all this shit under control. Nothing is guaranteed right now baby. I may have hired new security but that doesn't mean any of them motherfuckers earned my trust yet. This shit isn't just a job anymore. You are my wife and we have children coming and I have to make sure my family is safe at all times. Do you understand that I'll burn this whole fucking city down if it meant protecting y'all?" I told her in a demanding voice.

"Okay Sean, I get it. I'm sorry. It won't happen again. I didn't do any of this intentionally. I was on the phone with Harold's wife about the funeral service and I took a bath. The contractions were coming a little stronger so I ended up dozing off trying to zone out the pain." She said and my heart began to get a little softer for her.

"How's the pain now?" I asked her.

"It's coming and going but I think they may be coming closer." She replied.

"Have you been tracking them? And when is the funeral service?" I asked her.

"Wednesday at 2:00 at the city memorial site and no I haven't been tracking them." Sierra said.

"Why the fuck have you not been tracking them Sierra. I'm about to call Pierce. And who has a funeral in two days. What the fuck?" I said to her.

"Sean please. You dump someone the same day you kill them." She said and I laughed even though I know she was trying to avoid the fact that she has not been tracking the contractions.

"Well, you do have a point there." I said to her.

"Anyways. It's what Harold wanted. He had everything planned out already and didn't want to drag things along. I'll be speaking at the funeral." She said to me. I started look at her as if she was crazy.

"Sierraaaaa." I said out loud.

"Don't Sierra me. I'm going Sean. You have to understand that." She tried to explain to me.

"I do baby. But if it was in a church, it would be different. Having you outside makes you an easier target. You fell into my arms Sierra." I said as I placed my forehead into my hand.

"Can't we just double up on security? It's not even going to be that long. He didn't want it that way. Plus, she said Harold left something for me." She informed me.

"What do you think it could be?" I asked her.

"I'm not sure honestly." She said to me.

"Sit up baby because I know you didn't get your back good enough." I said and she giggled.

"You know your wife well. This stomach is so huge I had a hard time getting in the tub and I may need help getting out." She informed me.

"Oh, trust me once I finish washing your back, I'm helping you out and how about take showers for now on. I can't have you falling for trying to do something you already know you're not supposed to be doing." I told her annoyed and she nodded. I continued to wash her back and then rinsed her off. I then helped her out of the shower and she was right. Her stomach was way bigger than it was yesterday.

"Damn. It's amazing how your stomach grew that big overnight." I said to her amazed. This whole shit was mind blowing. Being able to experience and watch her body grow with my seeds inside of her was just incredible.

"Isn't it. This whole experience has been amazing. I fall in love all over again with every kick," she said and I smiled. Man, I loved this woman and I was glad that I made her my wife. I helped her get cozy in some clothes and we laid back in the bed.

"So, what's your plans for today?" She asked.

"Well, I have to finish up trying to get the new operation put together. I have to push some product out because I don't want to miss another dollar." I explained to her.

"Sean, we have plenty of money on top of yours and mine." She stated.

"As great as that sounds baby but I honestly don't care. I'm a business man. Every penny counts." I said as I winked and she rolled her eyes.

"So, what's the move? Besides, I thought Tech handles the operations." She said to me.

"Well, I have a ton of laundry mats that I clean money through but I think I'm about to expand a little. And yeah, he does handle the operations, doesn't mean he's the one that creates the plan on how they move." I explained to her.

"Wait you own laundry mats?" She asked.

"Yes, my love and if you really want to do this with me, I need to teach you everything there is too it." I explained to her.

"Okay." She responded.

"So, drug money is good and all of that but you need to have a way to clean it to prevent dirty money to get traced back to you. And what I mean by cleaning it, is putting the money towards something to invest in. So, the laundry mats have been doing good so far but baby we are rich and I think it's time we add some more investments. I have a business venture with a guy from Italy coming real soon. If that goes as plan then we'll be expanding. But right now, here in the city I'm thinking we open a hotel and build up some housing. Instead of selling the houses we will rent them out to keep a constant cash flow along with cleaning our money through it." I explained to her.

"You have any buildings you looking at so far?" She asked.

"Well, there's one in Manhattan that I was looking at buying. I want that to be a top-notch luxury hotel. Valet parking. Chef's kitchen while every mean is cook to order. I'm thinking of having a restaurant inside the hotel as well along with casinos. Give the people a taste of Vegas in New York City. Each hotel room will be a penthouse of either 1 to 3 bedrooms with a city view." I informed her.

"That's actually a great idea babe. The hotel will have cash flow coming from everywhere. And as for the housing let's do apartment complexes and maybe an area with some duplexes." She suggested.

"Why those?" I asked her as I was curious.

"Because you know everything in New York is so close together if you're going to do houses you would need to go further out in the country. But right here in the city majority of people can afford apartments or duplexes with no problem and it makes the construction plan so much easier with every other building in the city that's damn near side by side." She said and I smiled.

"You're the best wife a man could ever ask for." I said and she smiled.

"Mr. White are you trying to get into my panties?" She said and I laughed.

"As much as I would love to get all up in that. I think we should wait until after the twins is born." I explained.

"Really? You can wait six weeks after the twins is born?" She asked.

"Six weeks? Oh hell no." I yelled and she laughed.

"Yes. The doctor says after you have babies its best to wait six weeks to give my body time to heal and plus those are the most fertile times a woman has is during those six weeks. So, it would be easy for me to get pregnant again." She explained.

"Well, I'm here to tell you baby girl that's not happening. The moment you stop bleeding I'm in there." I said and she busted out in laughter.

"I'm serious baby. I don't care about how many kids we have or none of that. I just want you to be happy and if you don't want any more kids or you want to wait a while then I'm fine with whatever you want to do. I'll do my best to pull out." I said and she laughed.

"Oh, don't test you luck Mr. White. You and I both know damn well you will not pull out on time. And besides I was looking at some birth control options for the time being. And it's not that I wouldn't want more kids with you but I just want to be able to kick start my career at some point in my life." She said to me.

"Whatever you want baby its yours. And your right. I'm not pulling out a damn thing." I said and she giggled.

"Trust me I know my husband." She said as she smiled.

"I know you do. Which you should know now that I need to get ready so I can get shit together." I stated.

"I know baby." She said as she got up and walked over to my side of the bed and kissed me. Damn I didn't want to let her go.

"I'm going to head to the kitchen and talk to Chelsea for a bit. I'll see you later and stay safe okay. Remember." She began to say.

"I'll check in Sierra I promise." I said and she nodded.

"I love you." I voiced to her.

"I love you too." She said and as she turned around, I slapped her ass. I then got up to shower and got ready to strategize these plans. It was going to be another long fucking day.

****** THE DAY OF THE FUNERAL ******

SIERRA

Today was the day we were getting ready to lay Harold to rest. As much as it hurts, I know there was nothing I could do about it. I was just grateful that I was going to be able to speak at the service. I was just about ready to head out.

"Baby its almost time. Are you ready?" Sean asked.

"Yes. I'm just having a little trouble putting these damn shoes on." I informed him.

"Why didn't you just say something?" He asked as he then came in to help put the shoes on my feet.

"Now are you ready wifey?" He asked and I smiled.

"Yes I am." I said as he then helped me up and led me to the car. It was going to be a 30-minute drive so I decided to take a nap until we got there.

"Baby wake up. We're here." Sean said as he kissed my forehead. I then got out of the car. I was sad. I was nervous. It was as if you could feel the sorrow around you. Sean then led us to the seats next to Ann. I could hear the murmurs around us but I didn't care. He was my husband and I was never letting him go no matter what anyone has to say.

We gather here today to honor the life of Harold Johnson, as we transfer his spirit to God's keeping. We give thanks for his life and ask God to bless him now that their time in this world has come to an end. For Harold Johnson, the journey is now beginning. But for us, there is loss, grief and pain. Every one of us here has been affected - perhaps in small ways, or perhaps in transformative ones by Harold Johnson. His life mattered to us all. It is important for us to collectively acknowledge and accept that the world has fundamentally changed with his passing. We are all grieving. Life will not be the same - nor should it be. Together, let us open our hearts and commemorate the impact Harold Johnson had on us. Today we will only have one guest speaker. His daughter Sierra Johnson. Sierra will you come up here to say a few words. " The preacher said as I then went and stood in front of the casket.

"I never thought this is somewhere I would be so soon. Losing someone you love is one of the hardest things you can face in life. They say if you really love someone you let it go, but is it really possible with the ones you have so many memories with? I say this from the bottom of my heart. Always remember, tell your loved ones you love them while they're here. Because once they are gone, you'll want them to know. My heart is broken. To know Harold was to love him. I'll forever be grateful to him for the life he granted me with. He prepared me to be the successful lawyer that I am today and I'll forever live on his legacy. I love you Dad." I said as I then walked back to my seat.

"Please stand." The Preacher said and everyone who attended then stood up including myself and Sean.

"Harold Johnson is now safe. He is already on their way to heaven to enjoy all which awaits there. Let us say this final farewell as we commit Harold Johnson's spirit to its natural end. Harold Johnson, we bless you and thank you for being a part of our lives. We honor your life on Earth and we pray for your peace ever-after. We will not forget you. Go well into the kingdom of heaven. We have been remembering with love and gratitude a life that touched us all. I encourage you to help, support and love those who grieve most. Allow them to cry; to hurt; to smile and to remember. Grief works through our systems in its own time. Remember to bless each day and to live it to the full in honor of life itself - and of Harold Johnson. We often take life for granted and yet it is the greatest gift God gave us. It is now time to say your final farewells." The preacher said and everyone then came to shake Ann and my hand along with Sean's, rubbed the casket and then left. Once everyone was gone it was just Ann and us left.

"Here you go baby. Harold left an envelope for you. Don't hesitate to ever call me you here." She said and I gave her a long hug.

"I won't I love you." I said to her as she then kissed my cheek and left. I walked up to the casket to let out my final goodbyes.

"Everyone is gone now and the tears just won't stop. How is my life going to be the same without you in it?" I began to say as I felt a sharp pain shoot through my stomach and a trickle of water started to run down my leg. Shit.

"My water just broke." I cried out and Sean ran over too me.

"Fuck. Let's get you to the car. I need to call Pierce." Sean said as he then rushed me to the car. The moment my water broke I could feel the pressure. The pain was beginning to come back-to-back.

"Hello?" Pierce said as Sean had the phone on speaker.

"Pierce, Sierra's water just broke." Sean said.

"Shit. Okay you're going to have to bring her to the hospital. I'm on duty right now and can't leave. And now that her water has broken the babies can come within the next few minutes to a couple hours. I need you to get her here as soon as possible." Pierce said.

"Fuck. Ok. We have to do what's best for her right now. We are on the way." Sean said and I began to yell in pain. The contractions were started to come stronger than they ever were before.

"Sierra, deep breaths. I just need you to take deep breaths for me it will help zone out the pain. Can you do that for me?" Pierce asked.

"Yes." I said loudly and I started to take deep breaths.

"That's it. Nice deep breaths. Sean have her work on her breathing all the way up until she gets here. And do not let her push." Pierce said.

"We'll be there in 15." Sean said and then he disconnected the call. I then cried out in pain again.

"Sean it really hurts." I yelled.

"I know baby. Just breathe for daddy." He said as he then grabbed my hands and helped guide my breathing.

"I love you!" I cried out to him.

"I love you too. Watching you go through this, you're the strongest woman I know. I couldn't have chosen a better baby mama." Sean said and I slapped him and he laughed.

"Too early for jokes?" He said as he laughed.

"Yes, you asshole." I said as I continued to breathe heavily.

"Well, the pain sure didn't stop that slap from coming." Sean said as he chuckled.

"Now is not the time Sean. I could kill you right now." I yelled as the contraction came a little harder. I kept breathing and we finally arrived to the hospital. Sid came to the car with a wheelchair. Sean then helped me in the chair and the front desk then paged Doctor Pierce. Once Doctor Pierce came, he led us to a room as Sean helped get me in a gown to get comfortable.

"Okay Sierra I need you to take a deep breath for me. I'm getting ready to check your cervix to see how far you have dilated. So, take a deep breath for me." Pierce said and I did as I was told.

"Jesus Sierra, I felt the baby's head almost instantly. Your 9 and half cm dilated. You have the urge to push don't you." Pierce asked.

"Yes." I yelled out.

"Great. On the next contraction I want you to push really hard for me okay." Pierce demanded and I nodded as I broke out in sweat and continued to breathe.

"You got this baby. Pull me. Scratch me. Bite me. Whatever it is that you need you got it." Sean said as he then kissed my forehead. I felt a contraction coming and I began to push with the go of Doctor Pierce.

"That's good. But I need you to push just a little harder for me okay." Pierce said and I nodded. Seconds later, another contractions came and I pushed as hard as I could.

"Perfect. Now breathe in for me. I'm going to check you to see where we're at." Pierce said as he then checked my cervix again.

"Good now you're at 10. So, depending on how hard you push on the next contraction we can either get the baby out with one push or plenty more. Are you ready?" Pierce asked.

"I don't know how much more I got left in me Pierce." I said as I was completely out of breath.

"Come on baby you got this. Squeeze my hand as hard as you can love." Sean said and I nodded. Once the contraction came, I pushed as hard as I could and I felt relieved. There was then a little cry.

"Congratulations. Baby number 1 is a boy." Pierce said and I looked at Sean and he smiled.

"Would you like to cut the cord?" Pierce asked Sean.

"You damn right I would." Sean said as he then took the scissors and cut the cord. They immediately placed him in my arms. I fell in love instantly. All of a sudden, the pain began to hit me again. The nurses grabbed the baby to check his vitals.

"Okay Sierra. Same thing. I need you to breathe in so I can see how far along she is." Pierce said and I breathed in.

"Shit she's breach. I need an anesthesiologist stat." Pierce yelled and I then began to panic.

35 WHAT DID YOU JUST SAY

SIERRA

"Listen don't panic." Pierce said.

"What the fuck you mean don't panic. What the fuck does all this mean?" Sean yelled.

"Your daughter is wanting to come out feet first. Which can be dangerous to both mom and baby. So, I'm going to do an emergency c-section as soon as possible. Turning her around now will be too dangerous. I wouldn't know if the umbilical cord is wrapped around her neck or not. It's the safest option." Pierce said and Sean nodded.

"Do what you have to do Pierce. Just please don't let me die before I can see both of my babies." I explained to him.

"You're not going to die Sierra. I won't let that happen trust me." Pierce said and then another doctor came rushing in and began to ask me a bunch of medical questions.

"Okay so I need you to sit up for me. I'm going to put this needle in your back and it's going to numb your body so you won't feel anything for the surgery you got it. Whatever you do don't jump you risk your chances of being paralyzed." He said and I agreed. He then places the needle in my spine and they helped me lay back down on my back.

"Let me know the moment you can't feel anything." Pierce said. And the moment I felt nothing I let him know. He then took his tools and slice my stomach open to begin the procedure to get baby girl out. About 30 to 45 minutes later I started to hear a little cry and my heart began to melt again. They laid her in my arms and she was definitely an angel. I began to cry. I looked over to Sean and he began to smile.

"I'm so proud of you baby, you're the strongest woman I know. I love you." Sean said.

"I love you too." I told him as the nurses then came to grab her so they can check her vitals and make sure everything was ok.

"Sierra, I'm going to stitch you back up now the recovery for a c-section can be up to a week depending on how quickly your body heals. Don't worry the way I made the cut won't require you to have a c-section for future births. These stitches will dissolve on its own." Pierce said.

"Thank you, Pierce." I replied.

"Do you both have any more questions for me?" Pierce asked.

"Yeah, so when can I get back up in it, Pierce?" Sean said and Pierce and I both busted into laughter.

"Well, she's still going to be bleeding from the vaginal birth and that part depends on her body and healing time but after the bleeding is over and you're not rough I don't see why not. But just remember the first 6 weeks is when she'll be her most fertile and chances of pregnancy are high." Doctor Pierce informed Sean.

"Oh, don't worry I don't plan on being rough I just need to feel my wife." Sean said and all I could do was shake my head.

"I totally understand." Pierce said. And Sean began to look at me.

"What?" I asked him.

"You're glowing. Your just so beautiful you know. There are no words to describe the way I feel right now. My wife is the strongest woman I know who just gave birth to two of the most beautiful children in the world." He said and a tear came down my eye.

"I appreciate you and everything you do babe and this is just the beginning there's so much more to do. Speaking of the children I'm sure you want our son to be a jr." I said to him.

"You fucking right I do. Did you not see that boy when you held him? He's my fucking twin!" Sean yelled and I giggled. "And baby girl is going to take my heart away. She looks like you." He said to me.

"You think so?" I asked him.

"Hell yeah. You decided a name for her?" Sean asked.

"I was actually thinking about Amirah." I informed him.

"Why Amirah?" He asked.

"Because Amirah means queen ruler." I said and he smiled.

"Woman I can give you another baby right now." Sean said and everyone in the room just laughed.

"And done." Pierce said. "The nurse will take you to the recovery room. I know the situation so I'll try to get you discharged today for at home care." Pierce informed us.

"You're the man Pierce." Sean said and Pierce laughed and walked out. Sean then followed us as the nurses took me to another room. As they continued to roll me down the hallway through one of the doors, I seen a shadow of someone that seemed vaguely familiar but it couldn't be. He was dead. I had to be just seeing things. But to be on the safe side I needed to have my babies checked on.

"Baby if you don't mind, please go to the nursery and check on the kids." I asked Sean.

"Of course. I'll be back." He said as he then turned off to head to the nursery. The nurses then got me comfortable in the room and I waited for Sean to come back. I was also glad some of my feeling in my body was coming back. I began to get frustrated. What the fuck was taking so long? Next thing you know I heard the room door open. And it was him coming from around the corner. I quickly grabbed the call button.

"Do not push the buttons or the babies will die." He said to me.

"What the fuck Lee. Your supposed to be dead." I yelled. I was shocked about the man standing before me.

"Listen I don't have much time but I need you to get Sean not to kill me." He pleaded to me.

"And why the fuck would I do that? You blew up the entire operation and you fucking tried to kill Renee." I yelled out.

"Wait so she made it? Thank God." He said in relief.

"Listen I can explain all this shit from my end I just need you to prevent him from killing me once I do." Lee said.

"Listen Lee you and I both know that once he has his mind made up about something there's nothing no one can do about it. and besides he thinks you're dead so you need to keep it that way if you want any chance of survival. Aren't you working for Brian? Why the fuck would I want to help you?" I yelled out to him.

"Because I fuckin hate Brian I never wanted any of this shit. I never spoke to Brian a day in my life since I found out we were half-brothers. But he always knew. I didn't find out until I got the call about my mother being sick. Once I got there to my mom's place it was a setup. My so-called father and half-brother had my mother tied to a chair promising to kill her if I didn't give them intel on Sean. But I swear I never gave them anything legit. I love Sean and the crew I couldn't do that too them. Brian made it seem as if I'm the one who took the shot and missed but it was him. So, I faked my death I found a look alike and added some DNA so it could seem as if it was me who was dead." Lee tried to explain.

"Yeah, but you put the clothes of the operation on the body you were supposed to get rid of that! " I yelled. "You want me to save my husband from killing you but threatened my children's if I called to have you escorted out of here. Do you really think he wouldn't kill you for threatening his kids?"

"No, did he not think I wouldn't blow his motherfucking brains out right here right now in this hospital is the question." A voice yelled and we turned around to find Sean with the gun pointed at Lee's head.

"Sean listen, let me explain. " Lee pleaded. Next thing you know Sean struck him in the front of his head with the gun and blood splattered onto the wall. He then stood over Lee.

"You see the problem with you motherfuckers is you think you can cross me and I'll let that shit slide. I'm the realest motherfucker any of you stupid bitches ever met in your life and despite the monster I am, I showed you genuine love." Sean yelled as he then struck Lee in the face and blood splashed again.

"Sean please just listen before you kill me. I can explain." Lee cried barely in conscious and Sean raised his hand up again.

"Wait!" I yelled out and Sean looked over too me.

"Let's take him to the torture room and deal with it there. I am curious about the rest of his story." I said to him.

"Baby listen maybe this isn't for you. This job doesn't require a soft heart." He said to me.

"Sean White what the fuck did I just say? Don't tell me what the fuck I can't handle." I yelled and he instantly rolled his eyes and began to hit Lee three more times in the face.

"Sean!" I yelled and he dropped Lee and picked up the phone.

"Sid come pick this motherfucker up out Sierra's room. Have him thrown and chained into the torture room." Sean demanded and then disconnected the call. Pierce then walked in and scanned the room.

"Ok so no need for me to ask what happened here just tell me you have a crew to come clean this shit up. This is still a hospital Sean, no one needs to know what you do outside of us" Pierce said.

"Thank you. Maybe that jackass will listen to you because I tried to get him to stop." I said trying to explain. But you could tell his mind was elsewhere. He then picked up the phone.

"Get a clean-up crew to the hospital. Ride with Sid. He's about to leave. Stat." he said as he then disconnected the call.

"Okay, well I have you discharged right here. After your husband gets this cleaned up. You'll be free to go. I'll come by tomorrow to check on you." Pierce said and I nodded and he walked out the room. I sat in the room which felt like forever but in reality, it was only 30 minutes before the guys came in. My husband and I sat in pure silence. I was pissed about what he said and he was feeling however he was feeling. The men followed orders and cleaned everything up quickly. Sean paged transportation and they escorted my babies and I too the car and we headed home. And still there was complete silence.

As soon as we arrived to the house, Sid opened the house door and we entered. The girls began to scream.

"What the fuck Sierra we didn't know shit about this!" Mia yelled.

"I went in labor at the service. So much shit happened." I tried informing them.

"Yeah, well save that let me hold the babies!" Mia yelled as she grabbed Junior and Emily grabbed Amirah.

"Oh, my God. They are so beautiful. Did you name them?" Emily asked me.

"Yeah, he's a junior and her name is Amirah." I replied.

"So why aren't you over the moon excited?" Emily asked.

"Because Sean and I are having a fight. And Lee's alive. " I said and Emily jumped up.

"Hey be careful with the baby." I yelled.

"I'm sorry, but what the fuck did you just say?" Emily demanded.

"Lee's alive and Sean tried to kill him inside the hospital room and I stopped him. I wanted to hear Lee's side of things but Sean isn't hearing that." I said trying to explain.

"Girl you can't stop Sean in act that's why he's pissed. And he has every right to be. He tried to kill my best friend and as far as I'm concerned you just helped him." Emily said as she then handed me the baby and stormed off. That bitch had some nerves just now. See they don't know the old Sierra that I tried to put away. I would buss Emily in her shit. But don't worry, her little comment will be addressed in due time.

"Whoa. That was a little extreme. What happened to Renee was not your fault." Mia said.

"I know and I'm definitely going to check her about that when I see her and if she wants to fight to let off steam, we can do that too." I said and Mia laughed.

"There's a lot of things about Sierra that they are going to find out." Mia said and she giggled.

"Yes, the quiet Sierra is long gone in the past. But listen Mia it was some of the things Lee was saying before Sean came in that had me thinking that maybe he might be telling some truth. Think about it. The operation didn't get changed because of Lee. They switched operations because of the fucking security team. So, if Lee was giving them anything on the operations shit would have been fucked up. He also said it wasn't him who took the hit at y'all it was Brian and Brian was the one who missed. He was happy to hear Renee made it out alive. I'm telling you Mia. Something in my gut is tell me we should hold off on killing Lee." I explained to Mia.

"So, what are you telling me for. You need to tell your husband." Mia said.

"Right, my husband." I said as I then rolled my eyes.

"It's fine Sierra, it's not y'all first fight and it's not your last. Go find your husband and talk to him." Mia said. I then grabbed the babies and took them to their rooms to sleep. I headed to the torture room to see if Sean was there. I started to hear a machine crank up. Once I got around the corner, I seen Sean holding the saw towards Lee's neck. I screamed. **"STOP!!!!!! PUT THE FUKING SAW DOWN NOW!"** I yelled out to Sean.

PREVIEW OF IF ONLY YOU KNEW 2

SIERRA

I yelled so loud in that moment I thought I blew my own eardrums out. I couldn't believe he tried to go behind my back and do this. I specifically told him to wait. So now I'm going to make him choose.

"Sean, I specifically asked you to wait. But instead, you turned your back on what I said instead of us thinking through this together. So, here's how it's going to go. If you kill him. I will leave you and I will not think twice about coming back!" I yelled and he immediately dropped the saw. I stormed out of there; I was pissed I could have killed him. Next thing I knew I felt someone grab my wrist and pushed me up against the wall roughly.

"Listen you can't think you can just come and throw our fucking marriage on the line just because shit isn't going to go your way all the fucking time. I won't have that shit Sierra. I love you to death but I won't let you use the love I have for you as a way to control me. I said it once and I'm going to say it again I'm a business man at the end of the day and if you can't deal with that shit then maybe us getting married was a big mistake." Sean yelled.

"You act on emotion Sean and you don't think shit through. You want to kill a man before you can see what you can get out of him. I'm not sure which part you walked in the room in but Lee was giving me some good information." I tried to explain to him.

"Yeah, because they think getting to you is the way they can get to me and I won't have that shit Sierra." Sean yelled. I was beginning to get frustrated.

"Wait a minute did you fucking forget that you're the blame for a lot of this shit too? You had me walking around here thinking I had a brain tumor and I was shot the whole time! If it wasn't for me your ass would be stuck in a lot of situations right now. So yeah, fuck you, Sean. I'm out of here!" I yelled and he punched the wall next to my face.

"We're you just going to hit me?" I yelled.

"No why the fuck would I do that. I would never put my hands you but I want you to understand something if you walk away from me right now, you're turning your back on us and this marriage. And I won't chase you anymore." Sean said. My heart began to beat a little quicker. He was really angry. This is a side that I've never seen. But everyone did try not to unleash the beast inside of him.

"Listen all I'm saying is let me talk to him. If you want to kill him after that then so be it. I just want you to hear what he told me and think instead of acting out." I said to Sean.

"Fine Sierra." He yelled and he led me down to Lee.

"Sierra." Lee cried out.

"Yeah. So, listen you're going to have to tell them everything that you started to tell me. That's the only way things will begin to make sense out of this whole thing. Help me help you." I said to Lee.

"I can do that. I've been wanting to do that but they wouldn't let me explain." Lee said.

"Man, what the fuck is this!? Law yelled.

"I don't want to hear shit this bitch ass motherfucker has to say. He tried to kill my girlfriend." Tech yelled.

"I'm just as angry about this as you both are but Sierra seems to think that he could be useful to us. So, let's see what he has to say." Sean said and the guys nodded.

"Talk Lee." Sean demanded. And even though he is allowing Lee to talk, I know Sean. I just had a feeling that he was still going to kill him. And the way that he had that saw in his hand, Lee was definitely going to be cut into pieces.

ABOUT THE AUTHOR

Currently a native from Goose Creek, South Carolina, Michelle is a mother of two beautiful children. Since she was a child, she always loved reading books. As she got older her love for reading never once died. She spent so much money on paying to read other stories she came up with the idea to write a book on her own. She loves to read romance drama books. So, her dedication to read these books eventually became her passion to write them. She is currently studying in book publishing and is starting her dream to open up her own book publishing company. She believes everyone's success starts with a form of reading.

Made in the USA
Columbia, SC
15 July 2023

20110939R00129